With Best Wishes!
Gloria V Phillips
Christmas 2010

A Pilgrim's Daughter

Gloria V. Phillips

Printed and bound in Canada

Library and Archives Canada Cataloguing in Publication

Phillips, Gloria, 1956-
        A pilgrim's daughter / Gloria V. Phillips.

ISBN 978-0-9783356-2-5

        I. Title.

PS8631.H553P53 2010   C813'.6   C2010-907725-3

To my mother Alice,
who has freely shared her memories with me
that I might write this story,
and has given me the liberty to turn the facts
of her life into a work of fiction.

Author's Note

Prior to writing *A Pilgrim's Daughter* I spent many hours talking with my mother about her early life. As a child born into the prosperity of the post-war era, I wanted to know what it had been like for my mother to grow up during the Great Depression and to live through the Second World War. I listened as Mom told me of her childhood and the years leading up to her marriage, and I scribbled down page after page of notes.

After interviewing my mother, I met with other seniors and heard their stories of life in Canada during the 'Dirty 30s' and the war years. I browsed through old newspapers and historical documents to get a true feel for the time period.

Taking what I had learned from these sources, I wove together a story of a little girl growing up – as my mother did – in Toronto during the depression and the war.

It is impossible to tell my mother's story, or any part of it, without speaking of the Christian faith that has been the foundation for her life. The Bible says that the evidence of God's spirit at work in a person is love, joy, peace, patience, kindness, goodness, faithfulness, gentleness and self-control.

Those who know my mother know that these nine words sum up who she is better than any story I could ever tell. For those who have not had the privilege of meeting my mother, it is my hope that *A Pilgrim's Daughter* will tell her story, just as *A Pilgrim Passing Through* told the story of her parents.

Gloria V. Phillips

2010

The grey haired lady sat on the bed in her new quarters and looked around. A tear formed in her eye as she surveyed her surroundings. The room she had been given was almost as small as the bedroom she'd had in her childhood home.

It was just as efficiently laid out, too. The nursing staff saw to that.

She smiled as she thought of the nurses. Her mother should have been a nurse. Mama's kind, caring ways and her soothing touch had always brought comfort to those in need. Even when she had grown old and her health had failed, Mama's gentle nature had done more for her caregivers than their physical ministrations had done for her.

Mama would be pleased if she could see this room, the woman thought. *For the first time in my life, I am clutter free.*

She had always taken pride in being like her mother, but in this area she fell short. In all her life she'd never met anyone as organized as her mother had been.

'A place for everything, and everything in its place,' had been Mama's motto.

No one could ever accuse me of being too organized, the woman thought. She chuckled. *I'm not even neat and tidy, never mind organized.*

The chuckle turned into a sigh.

I've tried to be, but somehow I've never been able to keep things the way my mother did.

It's not that I live in chaos, she reminded herself. *I know where everything is. It just takes time to find it.*

She shook her head. That statement was no longer true. Her lifetime of belongings had been divided between her children and grandchildren. What they could not use had been given away. A few things – things she simply could not bear to part with – were stored in one of her daughter's basements. She knew it was unlikely she would ever see those items again, but it gave her comfort to know they were being kept for her.

What is it about the things we collect that make them so important to us?

She pondered the thought for a moment, wondering if women were more attached to things than men. Her late husband had never been bound by material things, and he'd never understood the attraction they held for her.

'We can't take it with us,' had been one of her husband's favourite sayings. Whether it was his time, his money, or his material possessions, he'd seen them all as a gift that was meant to be shared.

Maybe it is because we had so little when I was a child that I find comfort in my things, the woman mused. *My pictures, for instance.*

Her eyes lifted to the portraits covering her walls. Her daughters had teased her when she'd told them she planned to take all her photos with her to her new home.

"You won't have room, Mom," one of them had exclaimed. "You're going into a nursing home, not another apartment."

When the woman said nothing in reply, her daughter had continued. "I'll leave them out to take, Mom, but I'll only have to pack them all up and bring them back home again. There won't be space for them."

"We'll see," she had replied.

She did not argue with her daughter. It was not in her nature to argue. It never had been. And in the end, she'd had her way. Her daughters had found room for the pictures on her walls, and she was surrounded by the faces of those she loved.

With effort, Alicia rose. Clutching her walker, she moved to a spot where she could better observe the hanging pictures.

There was a photo of her four daughters, grown women now, taken the last Christmas they were all together. She studied their faces. Sometimes when she looked at them she saw similarities, but at other times she thought their faces were as different as their personalities.

She eased the walker forward a few steps, moving on to her grandchildren. There were eight of them, all good looking young people. It was hard to believe that some of them now had children of their own.

Her gaze turned to the smiling faces of her great-grandchildren. She smiled back at them, unaware that she was doing so. What pleasure these little ones brought! She looked at the label her daughter had put on the photo and read it.

'Alicia's great-grandchildren.'

My great-grandchildren, she thought. *How can it be? Where have the years gone? It seems that only yesterday Sarah and I were that age ourselves.*

She turned to look at the pictures that lined the top of her dresser. Easing herself onto the seat of her walker, she studied them. There was one of her with Sarah, taken when she was six years old. Large eyes set in solemn faces stared back at her from that photo. Beside it was a shot of her alone, taken on the occasion of her graduation from high school. She picked it up, then lifted her eyes and gazed at the image reflected in the mirror above the dresser.

It's strange, she thought. *My body tells me I'm an octogenarian, and the mirror certainly attests to the fact, but inside...*

Her eyes dropped to the photo in her hand.

Inside, I still feel like the young girl in this picture.

She looked again from the image in her hand to the one in the mirror. So much had happened in the years between.

I should have kept a diary, she thought, *but I was too busy living my life to worry about recording it.*

Now I wish I had.

There was so much about her early years that her family didn't know. So much they would never know.

With shaking hands and tearful eyes, Alicia set the picture back on the dresser, and made her way slowly to her bed. The day had been tiring, both physically and emotionally. Perhaps she would feel better after a rest.

She lay down and closed her eyes, longing to escape into the world of dreams, but in spite of her weariness sleep eluded her. In its place were memories of yesteryear.

It was 1930.

***

1930 - 1938
The Great Depression

Toronto, Canada

Six-year-old Alicia burrowed deeper into her hiding place under the back porch, wishing she never had to leave. It was one of her favourite spots; her very own private place. This was where she came to play alone or to think, and no one bothered her, not even her sister Sarah.

Alicia grinned, thinking that even if she had been willing to share her special place with Sarah, she couldn't have. Sarah was three years older, and three years bigger. She would never have been able to squeeze through the entrance.

"I wish we didn't have to move, Peggy," she whispered to the doll she clutched in her arms. "I wish we could stay here forever."

She wondered if her new home would have a spot like this that she could call her very own. She furrowed her brow, trying to remember what Mama had told her about the new house. Mentally, she recited the things her mother had said.

The new house is closer to my school, but farther away from Grandpa and Grandma Mitchell's home. There is a store two doors from it, where Sarah and I can go to buy things when Mama needs them. The house has a nice back yard where Daddy is going to plant a vegetable garden.

Alicia frowned, wondering if there were any trees at the new house. Her mother hadn't mentioned trees, but she hoped there would be some. The house they were moving from had a big tree outside the dining room window. Daddy had built a double swing from ropes and a board and fastened it to a branch of the tree. On Sundays after dinner Alicia and her sister liked to sit together on the swing and watch their parents through the dining room window.

"Alicia!"

The sound of her mother's voice interrupted her musings. Alicia sat quietly, hoping that by ignoring the call she could buy herself a little more time. She listened for the echo of receding footsteps, but heard none.

"Alicia!"

The call came again.

"Alicia Abighail Miller!"

The voice was louder now, and Alicia knew better than to ignore it.

"I'm coming, Mama." She crawled out through the hole behind the steps, brushing her clothes off as she stood.

Mama looked at her. "It's time to leave, Alicia. You and Sarah can walk to the new house while Daddy and I accompany the men with the furniture."

"Can I keep Broken-Headed Peggy with me?" Alicia was reluctant to entrust her cherished doll to the hands of a moving man.

"I think that would be an excellent idea," Mama responded. "You can push Peggy in her pram. Daddy was concerned that it might fall off along the way."

Mama took her hand, and together they walked to the road.

Alicia stood back while her mother whispered something in Daddy's ear. He nodded, then moved forward and retrieved the doll buggy from its perch atop the furnishings on the wagon. When the carriage was set safely on the sidewalk, Alicia placed Broken-Headed Peggy in it.

"You'll be safer walking with me," she whispered to her doll as she tucked a blanket around her. "It wouldn't do to have you fall and hit your head again."

She frowned as she looked at the crack that ran across Peggy's forehead. Sarah told her that the doll had not always looked this way, but Alicia could not remember a time when the doll's beautiful porcelain face had been unmarked.

"She was just called Peggy back then, and she was as pretty as a princess," Alicia's sister had informed her. "Then one day you dropped her down the stairs and broke her head."

Sarah had paused and eyed the doll.

"She doesn't look like a princess now," she'd sniffed. "Now she's just poor Broken-Headed Peggy."

"I'm sorry I dropped you," Alicia whispered to Peggy as she remembered Sarah's words. "You're still beautiful to me."

She wheeled the carriage over to where her mother stood.

"Peggy and I are ready, Mama." She looked around. "Where's Sarah?"

"Sarah has gone next door to say goodbye to Bessie," Mama answered. "You can leave as soon as she returns."

"It's all right, Peg," Alicia rocked the pram gently. "We're just waiting for Sarah."

The front door of the adjoining house opened as she spoke, and her sister skipped out.

"I'm ready, Mama," Sarah informed her mother when she arrived. "I've said my goodbyes, so 'Licia and I can go now."

Mama placed a hand on each girl's shoulder and turned them to face her.

"Take your time," she instructed them. "Walk slowly. You'll likely arrive before Daddy and I do. When you get to the house, wait for us outside. We'll be along soon."

"We will, Mama," Alicia and Sarah answered in unison.

Mama looked at Alicia. "Remember your sister is in charge when I'm not with you. You must do as Sarah tells you."

Alicia nodded. She looked over to see Sarah smirking at her.

I always have to do what Sarah tells me, she thought. Sometimes she wondered what life would be like if she were the oldest.

Mama bid Alicia and Sarah goodbye and the two started walking. They turned and looked back when they reached the corner. Their mother was on the front porch, supervising the loading of their goods. She saw them looking and waved, and the girls waved back.

"Do you know where the new house is?" Alicia asked as her sister led her down an unfamiliar street.

"Of course I do," Sarah responded.

"Have you seen it?" Alicia questioned.

"No," Sarah admitted.

Alicia frowned.

"Then how do you know where it is?"

"Mama told me the address," Sarah replied airily.

"What is the address?" Alicia wondered why her mother had not entrusted her with this information.

"I'm not telling," Sarah answered with a grin. "You'll just have to trust me."

"Mama said I had to obey you, not trust you," Alicia told her sister.

"They're the same thing," Sarah informed her with a laugh.

Alicia frowned again, wondering if the words *trust* and *obey* really did have the same meaning. Sometimes she had difficulty knowing whether Sarah was serious or teasing when she said such things.

I'll ask Mama some time, she decided, knowing it would do no good to try to get further information from Sarah.

They reached a crossroads where they waited for a vehicle to pass before venturing across the street.

"I didn't think the new house would be so far away," Alicia commented as they zigzagged through a multitude of streets.

"It's not so far, really," Sarah told her. "It just seems like a long way."

They came at last to a corner with a store, and Sarah turned. The street she turned on to was only one block long. At the end of the street was a school – their school. Alicia turned and looked at Sarah.

"We took the long way," Sarah said, laughing at the look on her sister's face. "Mama told us to take our time."

"We still got here before Mama and Daddy," Alicia answered, surveying the empty street before her.

"Let's go explore the new house." Sarah ran toward the address she had been given, but Alicia hung back.

"C'mon, 'Licia, let's go look around."

"Mama told us to wait outside," Alicia reminded her sister.

"We'll only explore the outside. We won't go inside," Sarah assured Alicia. "Look, the gate to the back yard is open."

The words were scarcely out of Sarah's mouth before she disappeared through the opening. Alicia hesitated only a moment before following. Trespassing before her parents arrived was more desirable than being left to wait on the street alone.

As Sarah had said, Alicia found that the gate was open. *I don't think it can close,* she thought when she saw it. The lock was broken and the fixture hung by one hinge. It was badly in need of a coat of paint. Going through the opening, she found herself in a yard overgrown with weeds and long grass. She looked around for Sarah, but her sister was nowhere in sight. Alicia was about to retrace her steps when a voice from above called out playfully.

"You're it! Catch me if you can."

Alicia looked up to see Sarah grinning at her from the back porch of the house. She ran up the steps to tag her sister, but before she could touch her Sarah jumped onto the railing of the porch. She balanced there while Alicia begged her to get down.

"I can't come down." Sarah laughed. "If I do you'll catch me."

"No, I won't." Alicia moved to the back of the porch. "I'll wait till you're in the yard."

Sarah hopped from the railing, raced past her younger sister and down the steps. Alicia followed and they chased each other around the yard, each taking turns at being *it.*

"Hey! You there!"

Alicia and Sarah looked up to see a pudgy boy of ten or twelve standing by the fence. His mop of curly red hair was only partially covered by his hat and a scowl creased his round, freckled face. Frightened by his presence, Alicia took refuge behind Sarah as the lad moved toward them.

"What are you doing here? You don't belong here!"

Alicia trembled at the harsh tone, but Sarah stood her ground. If she was frightened, she gave no indication of it. "How do you know we don't belong here?" she asked boldly.

"I know!" the lad stated emphatically. When his intimidation appeared to have no effect on Sarah, he added, "I know 'cause I'm looking after the place for the new folks."

He paused, waiting to see what the reaction to his words would be. When he got none, he continued. "The new people are moving in today, so you better scat. They won't take kindly to finding you two here when they arrive."

"I think the new people might be rather pleased to find us here," Sarah told him sweetly.

"That's hardly likely! Now get out of here before I get Detective Hawthorne. He lives right next door and he'll make you leave in a hurry."

He scowled at them, but when the girls showed no sign of leaving, the lad turned and walked away.

"Do you think there's really a detective next door, Sarah?" Alicia asked when they were alone. She had no idea what a detective was, but there was something about the word that frightened her.

"I don't know," Sarah answered slowly.

"Maybe we better go," Alicia whispered. "I don't feel like playing anymore."

"There's nothing to worry about," Sarah told her bravely. "That boy is all bluff and blunder. He's all talk and no action. He's just trying to frighten us."

"It worked," Alicia answered, making a weak attempt at a smile. "I'm frightened."

"You don't need to be. No one is going to hurt you." Sarah put her arm around her sister's shoulders, looked down at Alicia and smiled. "Let's go wait for Daddy and Mama on the front porch, all right?"

Alicia nodded, and allowed her sister to lead her to the front of the house. They climbed the stairs together and sat on the top step to wait.

***

The New House

Alicia and Sarah sat to one side of the porch, patiently waiting for the family's belongings to be unloaded. They watched the pile of boxes and household furnishings on the wagon grow smaller as their father and the moving men trudged back and forth between the house and the wagon parked at the roadside.

"We're almost finished," Daddy told the girls as he left the house and walked past them. "Just one or two more trips and everything will be unloaded."

"Does that mean we can go inside now?" Sarah asked eagerly.

"Not yet," her father informed her. "Mama and I will take you inside in a few minutes and show you all through our new house."

The girls settled back to wait.

When the wagon was emptied of all their belongings, Daddy walked out to the roadway with the moving men. He thanked them for their assistance, then took out his pocketbook and withdrew the amount they had agreed upon for their services. He then shook hands with both men and bid them farewell.

Alicia and Sarah watched as their father turned and walked back to the house, whistling cheerfully. He was about to mount the steps when a voice hailed him from the street.

"Good day, Mr. Miller."

Their father turned and retraced his steps to the end of the walkway, where a middle-aged man had stopped.

"Detective Hawthorne, how nice to see you again." Mr. Miller extended his hand as he spoke.

Alicia and Sarah looked at each other when they heard the man's name, then moved together to the edge of the veranda. From this vantage point they could not only see their new neighbour, but hoped they might also be able to hear the men's conversation.

"Are you settled in?" Detective Hawthorne asked.

"Our possessions have been moved," the girls' father answered. "I expect it will be some time before we are really settled."

Both men laughed.

"I understand that the house needs a bit of work," the detective commented.

"It is in rather poor condition," Mr. Miller admitted. "It is nothing, however, that a little paint and paper won't fix."

"A little paint and paper and a lot of hard work," their neighbour responded.

"I have plenty of time to devote to the task at present," Mr. Miller answered. "It will be good to have something to keep my hands occupied again."

"This is a difficult time for everyone," the detective answered, acknowledging his neighbour's reference to his lack of employment. "The stock market crash has affected all of us."

"Even those who had no investments are feeling the effects," the girls' father agreed. "I'm hopeful things will get back to normal again soon."

"I'm not so certain they will," Mr. Hawthorne replied. "I've heard predictions that it will take months, maybe even years, for the economy to recover from such a blow."

"I suppose that is possible," Mr. Miller answered.

He turned and surveyed his family's new dwelling. It was obvious to any passer-by that the residence they had chosen was the shabbiest looking property on the street.

"In the meantime I am grateful for the home that has been provided for us and I look forward to restoring it."

"I wouldn't be in too much of a rush to do that if I were you," their neighbour warned. "Your new landlord is known for buying derelict properties and luring tenants with the promise of cheap rent in return for free labour. He'll wait till you have the place in tip-top shape, then he'll put it on the market again."

Mr. Miller listened to the warning, and thought for a moment before speaking.

"Perhaps," he replied slowly, "by that time we will be in a position to buy the place."

"This is the day we move into our new rooms," Alicia reminded Sarah as the girls walked home from school together a few weeks after the move.

"I can hardly wait," Sarah answered.

"Neither can I," Alicia told her.

The prospect of having a room all to herself was exciting. She had never had her very own room.

She and Sarah had been sleeping together in the living room for the past weeks while their father worked on the house. Alicia remembered the disappointment she had felt when Daddy and Mama had finally taken them into the house on moving day. Detective Hawthorne had been right – the house was a mess! Bare bits of wood showed through where the paint had chipped off on the moulding around the doorways. The wallpaper in the hall was peeling, the banister on the stairway leading upstairs wobbled, and the pocket doors between the living room and the dining room seemed to be permanently jammed into the wall.

"Our old house was better than this," Alicia whispered to Sarah as their parents led the way to the upper floor.

"Hush!"

"Well it was!" Alicia insisted. She would have said more, but a glare from Sarah silenced her.

"I'll explain later," was all Sarah had time to say before they joined their parents upstairs.

"Daddy and Mama didn't *want* to move," Sarah told Alicia later when they were alone. "They *had* to!"

"Why?"

"They had to move because they couldn't afford to stay where they were with Daddy not working." Sarah looked at Alicia. "Mama and Daddy didn't tell me this. I only know because I overheard them talking one night.

"I was thirsty, so I went to get a drink of water," she explained. "I was on my way downstairs when I heard them discussing things."

"What kind of things?" Alicia asked.

"They were discussing adult things," Sarah told her. "Things they didn't think we should know about."

She paused.

"I don't really understand it all," she admitted, "but something happened a few months ago at a place called the Stock Exchange.

"I don't know what the Stock Exchange is," she told Alicia, "but whatever it is, it must be big."

Sarah frowned.

"Maybe it was where a lot of people worked or something. I don't know. Anyway, whatever happened there affected an awful lot of people. Daddy said he hasn't had this much trouble finding work since the war, and he told Mama lots of other people have the same problem."

"I still don't see why we had to move," Alicia told her.

"We had to move because it cost too much money to stay where we were," Sarah explained. "Every month Daddy has to give the man who owns the house money for us to live in it. The owner of this house wants less money for us to live here than the owner of our old house wanted."

"That's because this house isn't as good as the old house," Alicia countered.

"It will be," Sarah informed her. "Our father is one of the best carpenters in the whole city. He'll have this place looking even better than our old house before you know it!"

Sarah had been right, Alicia thought as she surveyed her new room later that evening. The space was tiny, but it was hers, all hers. Fresh wallpaper adorned with tiny blue flowers covered the walls, while the door and trim boasted a new coat of crisp, white paint. Sarah's room had been decorated in much the same manner.

Her father had been busy in the weeks since their move. He had fixed the wobbly banister, added a railing to the stairs leading to the cellar, and dislodged the pocket doors from their hiding place. New paint and paper had been applied throughout the house. The bedrooms had been the last of the indoor work. Now that he was finished inside, Daddy planned to turn his attention to the outside work.

This is nice, Alicia thought as she lay in her bed. She had expected to feel lonely without Sarah snuggled beside her, but found that she was quite content to have the bed, and the room, all to herself. For the first time the new house felt like home.

***

The Wolf at the Door

The first year passed in their new home, and still Alicia's father had not been able to obtain regular employment. He had long since stopped looking for a job in his trade. Instead he gratefully accepted any bit of work he was able to acquire, even if it was only a few hours labour here and there. Anything that would bring a bit of money into their cash-strapped household was welcome. The family's finances were never discussed in the presence of Alicia or Sarah, but even the children noticed that the portions of food on the table had become less plentiful.

"It isn't carpentry work, but at least it will help keep the wolf away from the door."

These were the words Alicia heard her father speaking as she entered the house after school one day. Clutching her school books, she stole up the stairs and went to her room. She sat down at the desk her father had built and spread her homework out on it. Her intentions of doing it were good, but she found it difficult to concentrate after the words she had heard downstairs.

Alicia rose and opened her bedroom door. She wanted to be certain that she saw her sister when she arrived home. She needed to talk to Sarah about what she had heard.

"I didn't know we had any wolves near our house," Alicia confided to Sarah when she came upstairs a short time later.

"We don't," Sarah told her.

"Then why did Daddy say we do?" Alicia asked.

"Tell me exactly what Daddy said," Sarah said patiently. "I think maybe you misunderstood him."

Alicia repeated her father's words as best she could remember them.

"It sounds like Daddy might have a new job," Sarah said thoughtfully when her sister was finished.

Alicia frowned.

"What does a new job have to do with wolves?" she asked, envisioning a dreadful creature like the one that had eaten Little Red Riding Hood now stalking little girls in her own neighbourhood.

Sarah laughed.

"It's a silly expression that adults use," she explained. "They talk about keeping the wolf from the door, but they don't mean a real wolf."

"What do they mean then?"

"I think when they talk about a wolf at the door they just mean that times are difficult and that there isn't enough work or enough money," Sarah explained.

"Oh." Alicia wondered why anyone would talk about a wolf outside their door if what they really meant was that there wasn't enough work or enough money. Why wouldn't they just say that there wasn't enough work or money?

When I grow up, she resolved, I*'m going to say things that make sense, not talk in codes.*

"Sarah! Alicia!"

Their conversation was interrupted by their father's call.

The girls went downstairs, where they found their parents seated in the dining room. A leather case filled with an assortment of goods sat on the floor, while one end of the table was covered with literature.

"Your father has a new job," Mama informed them proudly.

The girls waited, curious to learn what kind of job would involve the materials they saw spread before them.

"I have obtained a position as a representative with the Rawleigh Company," Daddy explained. "They are a supplier of common household items and medicinal remedies. I will be taking orders for their products and delivering them to customers." He looked at the girls. "It is possible that I may require your help on occasion."

Sarah nodded.

Seeing her sister nod, Alicia nodded her head too. She had no idea how she might be able to help her father with this new venture, but she was willing to do whatever he asked if it would keep that wolf away from their door.

The following morning Daddy came downstairs dressed in his Sunday best before the girls left for school. He left the house at the same time they did, carrying his sample kit with him.

He was not home when Alicia and Sarah returned from school, and still had not returned at supper time. Mama kept the meal warm as long as she could, but in the end she made up a plate of food and set it aside for Daddy then sat down to a meal with the girls alone.

Alicia and Sarah were upstairs preparing for bed when the front door opened and their father entered, weary from his long day. The hour was late, so in spite of the girls' eagerness to see their father, Mama insisted that they remain upstairs.

"You'll hear all about your father's first day at his new job tomorrow," she assured them as she went downstairs to greet her husband and reheat his meal.

Alicia climbed into bed after her mother left. She was almost asleep when a soft rap sounded at her door and Sarah peeked in.

"What are you doing here?" Alicia whispered. "Mama told us to go to bed."

"Shh," Sarah cautioned as she moved closer. "Mama told us to stay upstairs. She didn't actually tell us to go to bed, did she?"

"No," Alicia agreed. Sarah was right. Mama hadn't told them to go to bed, but she had certainly implied that they should.

"So if Mama didn't tell us to go to bed, then aren't disobeying as long as we stay upstairs. Isn't that right?"

"I suppose so," Alicia agreed reluctantly. "But it is bedtime."

"Don't you want to hear about Daddy's first day?" Sarah asked. She beckoned with her finger, and Alicia rose to follow her. When they reached the register in the hallway, Sarah looked at Alicia and held her finger to her lips, then sat down on the floor beside the vent and pressed her ear against it.

Alicia mimicked Sarah's action, though she wasn't sure why. To her surprise, she found that with her ear pressed against the register she could hear most of the conversation taking place in the room below. Sarah moved away from the vent and motioned her sister to do the same. She bent her head close to Alicia's and whispered in her ear.

"They must be sitting beside the register downstairs," she informed her. "That's why we can hear them. Remember, if we can hear them, then they'll be able to hear us too if we make any noise."

Alicia nodded and the two girls slid back into position.

"You wouldn't believe it, Gladys," their father was saying. "I walked miles today! I canvassed our entire neighbourhood without success, then went further afield. All that walking and I only made one sale."

The girls strained to hear their mother's response, but were unable to.

"These are desperate times," their father went on. "The streets are filled with men whose wives think they are out looking for work but who have given up searching. They leave home early each morning and wander the streets till dark.

"I stopped at a park today for my noon meal and talked with some chaps. Some of them spend their days there.

"I shared the meal you had provided," he told her. "I didn't think you would mind."

"Of course not," Mama replied. "What kind of a man would tell his wife he is out looking for work and instead spend his day in the park, Paul? I'm sure you would never do such a thing."

"I wouldn't, Gladys, but I can understand how a man could. I talked to a man today who has seven children."

Alicia and Sarah's eyes widened at the thought of such a large family.

"His family lives in a two-bedroom flat. Imagine – nine people and only two rooms for them all to sleep in.

"The poor man has been looking for work for months and has just given up. He leaves home each day and lets his wife believe he is out seeking employment."

There was silence for a moment.

"He told me," Daddy went on, "that he leaves because he cannot bear to stay at home and watch his wife scrubbing clothes for the wealthy while he is unable to provide for his own family."

"There are many families worse off than we are," Mama commented.

"There certainly are," Daddy agreed. "It makes me thankful for what we have."

"We really do have much to be thankful for," Mama reminded him.

"Including the sale I made today." Daddy laughed. "Just think, Gladys, ten hours of walking and I made one twenty-five cent sale!"

"Perhaps tomorrow will be better, Paul," Mama encouraged.

"I expect it will," he replied. "After today, I shall consider every day that I am not forced to spend sitting in a park while my wife thinks I am out searching for work a good one."

A brief silence followed this comment, then he spoke again.

"I think I'll go upstairs and check on our little ones."

The sound of chairs scraping on the floor below alerted Alicia and Sarah to their need to move quickly. By the time their father reached the bottom of the stairs, both girls were nestled snugly in their beds.

In the days that followed, Alicia's father finished canvassing the part of the city closest to the Miller home, then began to expand his territory. Using his bicycle for transportation, he began going further and further from home.

The door to door sales was difficult work, but over time he was able to build a reasonable business with repeat customers from various parts of the city. Regular shipments arrived from the Rawleigh company and Alicia and Sarah took great delight in helping their father sort the products for delivery. On occasion

Daddy would permit the girls to accompany him on his deliveries, instructing them ahead of time that they were to speak only if spoken to.

While Alicia found pleasure in walking hand in hand with her father on the deliveries close to their home, Sarah enjoyed accompanying him to some of the homes further away.

"You should see some of the houses Daddy goes to," she told Alicia one Saturday when she and her father returned from a delivery. "They're really quite grand!"

She went on to describe in detail one of the residences she'd visited with their father.

"At this home," she told Alicia, "we weren't allowed near the front of the house. It was a huge place, with a hedge all around it and iron gates at the entrance. I'd never seen anything like it.

"When we got there, we walked right past the main gate and entered at a small gate at the side. Then we went to the back of the house where Daddy gave the order to a lady he called Cook.

"When we left I asked Daddy why he had called the lady by her last name, but didn't say Mrs. or Miss first. He smiled and told me that he didn't even know the woman's name. Everyone just calls her Cook."

"That's a funny name," Alicia said, interrupting her sister.

"She's called Cook because she does all the cooking in that house!" Sarah exclaimed.

"Isn't there a mother there?" Alicia asked, trying to understand why any household would need someone to prepare meals if there was a mother in the house.

Sarah looked thoughtful.

"I don't know," she said, "but if there is, she doesn't cook or clean! Daddy said that in addition to the cook there are maids to keep the house clean, and there's a man who looks after the gardens outside."

Alicia stared at her sister. The home she was describing sounded like something out of a fairy tale.

"Are you making this up?" she asked finally.

"It's the truth, honest!" Sarah told her.

Alicia shook her head. She thought of their father, walking or biking miles each day to keep the wolf from their door. She thought of the man Daddy had told Mama about, who had seven children and no work.

"What's wrong?" Sarah asked her. "Don't you believe me?"

"I believe you," Alicia answered slowly. "I'm just trying to figure out how any one person could have so much. I thought houses like that were only real in books."

"I know what you mean," Sarah answered. "It just doesn't seem right that some people have so much while others don't have enough food to eat." She paused, debating whether to tell Alicia about the other experience she'd had that day.

"If I tell you about something that happened today, will you promise not to tell Daddy and Mama that I told you?" she asked.

"I promise."

Sarah took a deep breath.

"Most of the time when we go out with Daddy he's just making deliveries, right?"

Alicia nodded.

"Well, today he decided to go to a house he didn't have an order from," Sarah told her. "It was a big place, near the one I just told you about."

She paused, remembering.

"It wasn't as big as the other one, but it was still pretty impressive. Daddy told me that he had been there before, but no one was there, so he decided to try again today when he was in the neighbourhood."

"Was anyone home today?" Alicia asked.

"They sure were," Sarah answered. "A lady came to the door almost as soon as Daddy rang the bell. Before Daddy could say a word she told him to go to the back door and she would see him there."

"Maybe she had just washed the floor and it was still wet," Alicia commented, thinking of the times she and Sarah had been

32

told to use the back door at home. When Sarah said nothing in response, Alicia asked, "Did you go to the back door?"

"We did," Sarah answered. "We walked around to the back of the house and we waited and waited but no one came. Daddy rapped on the door but still no one came. We were about to leave when the door finally opened. The lady we had seen at the front was there."

Sarah paused.

"And she invited you in. She'd sent you to the back because the floor was wet in the front hallway," Alicia said. She smiled, pleased to think that she had interpreted the woman's actions correctly.

"No, she didn't," Sarah told her. She looked at Alicia. "She sent us to the back door because she felt sorry for us."

"Why would she feel sorry for you?" Alicia asked.

"The lady thought we were begging," Sarah whispered, a flush spreading over her face as she said the words. "When she opened the door she offered us each a sandwich and a glass of milk, and she tried to give Daddy a nickel!"

"Oh, no!" Alicia gasped. She stared at her sister as the reality of what Sarah had experienced sunk in.

"Are we poor, Sarah?" she asked.

Sarah thought about her sister's question for a moment before answering.

"I think we may be a little bit poor," she answered slowly, "but we certainly are not that poor!"

***

Digging

Alicia pulled the covers up snugly under her chin, leaving nothing but her face exposed to the chill night air. She checked the doll beside her, ensuring that her face was not covered by the blankets. When Mama came in to bid her good night, two tiny heads were all that could be seen protruding from the piles of hand-made quilts.

"I see you have a friend sharing your bed tonight," Mama said with a smile.

Alicia smiled as she looked at the doll nestled beside her. She did not often receive gifts like this one!

Aunt Elizabeth had visited them earlier in the day, accompanied by her sister-in-law Sadie. Though no direct relation to the family, the lady had been introduced to Alicia and Sarah as Aunt Sadie, and as such they had addressed her.

Aunt Sadie had recently returned from the country of China, where she worked as a missionary. She had endeared herself to Alicia and Sarah by involving them in the adult conversation, and had presented each of them with a gift before she left. For Alicia there had been a porcelain doll, dressed in traditional Chinese clothing, while Sarah had received a book filled with colourful pictures and Chinese writing.

Before she left, Aunt Sadie had promised to return another day to tell them more of her life in China. She had even promised Sarah that she would teach her to read some of the simpler Chinese characters written in her book.

"Have you given your new doll a name yet?" Mama's voice interrupted Alicia's thoughts.

"Not yet," she told her mother. "I might call her Chinee, but I haven't decided for sure."

The name had seemed perfect to Alicia, but when she'd shared the idea with Sarah her sister had broken out in song. Sarah's teasing words echoed in Alicia's mind.

Chi-nee, Chi-nee,
She's all the way from Chi-nee.
Treat her right,
She'll stay for life,
Throw her down,

Alicia had cringed at her sister's reference to Broken-Headed Peggy's fall.

She'll turn around,
And go back home,
To Chi-nee.

The name Alicia had chosen had lost some of its charm after Sarah's impromptu singsong, but she had been unable to come up with any other name for the doll.

"I think Chinee is a good name," Mama told Alicia as she observed the doll. "I think it suits her."

Alicia angled her head so she could have a better view of the doll. She nodded soberly.

"I think it suits her too," she said, echoing her mother's words. "I guess her name is Chinee."

Several weeks passed before Aunt Sadie had opportunity to visit them again. When she returned she took time, as she had promised, to tell Alicia and Sarah more about the people and the customs of the country she worked in.

"How far away is China?" Alicia asked, trying to picture the foreign country in her mind.

"China is very far away," Aunt Sadie told her. She was about to explain where China was located when Sarah interrupted.

"I know where China is," she burst in. "I learned about it at school. Let me get a piece of paper and I'll show you."

Sarah ran from the room, but returned a moment later with a piece of paper and a pencil in her hand. Boldly she drew a circle in the center of the page.

"This," she explained, indicating her drawing, "is the world."

Alicia stared at the drawing. It didn't look like the world to her. It looked like a lopsided ball. Sarah marked a spot midway down on the left side of the drawing.

"This is where we live," she informed Alicia.

Alicia nodded.

"This," Sarah said as she drew a mark mid-way down the circle on the right side, "is China.

"If you started here," she placed her pencil on the mark that represented their home, "and dug a hole all the way through the earth," Sarah drew a line across the circle from left to right, joining the two marks, "you would end up in China!"

"Isn't that right, Aunt Sadie?" Sarah asked, looking at the older lady for approval.

"I couldn't have explained it better myself." Sarah beamed at Aunt Sadie's praise.

"Do you have time to teach me some Chinese?" she asked.

Aunt Sadie nodded.

"If you would like, I can teach you some words from your book," she told Sarah.

Sarah brought her book and the two were soon engrossed in their language lesson. They invited Alicia to join them, but she chose to play with her doll instead. As she played, she contemplated the geography lesson Sarah had given her.

"If I wanted to go to China," she thought, "all I would have to do is dig a hole. If I dug long enough and far enough, I would end up in China."

It was an option worth considering, Alicia decided, as she sat her doll aside and went to set the table for Mama. Perhaps someday she would dig her way to China.

The girls saw Aunt Sadie one more time before she returned to China.

"Will you write to us, Aunt Sadie?" Sarah asked.

"I will," Aunt Sadie promised. "I hope you'll write to me too."

"We will," Alicia and Sarah agreed eagerly.

As Aunt Sadie prepared to depart, Alicia slipped her hand in her adopted aunt's. The older woman looked down and smiled. Alicia tugged slightly, and she bent low to hear Alicia's words.

"I'll not only write, Aunt Sadie," Alicia whispered. "I might even come to see you sometime."

A smile lifted the corners of Aunt Sadie's mouth.

"I should like that very much, Alicia," Aunt Sadie whispered back, "and will look forward to your visit."

Alicia thought of Aunt Sadie and China often in the weeks that followed. She'd been intrigued with the notion of digging her way to China ever since she had seen where it was located on Sarah's hand-drawn map. The fact that China was far away did not trouble her in the least. After all, Uncle Adolph lived far away, but her family had made the trip to visit him before.

I expect it will take me a long time to dig all the way through the earth, Alicia thought, *but I am certain I can do it.*

Having made the decision, she waited impatiently for the snow to melt and spring to arrive. She waited until Daddy had his garden planted and the seedlings had begun to sprout before she started. At last, on a bright sunny Saturday in June, she began.

The weekly chores were finished and Mama had given the girls permission to go outside until supper time. When Sarah was occupied playing hopscotch with a friend, Alicia made her way to the back yard.

Standing on her tiptoes, she reached up and opened the door to the shed. Inside the building, she pulled a stool over and stood on it. Stretching up to reach the tools on the shelf, she removed her father's hand spade. Gripping it firmly, she exited the building and closed the door securely behind her. She checked to be certain no one was watching, then made her way to the spot she had chosen behind the shed and began digging.

The ground was harder than she had anticipated and progress was slow. With aching arms, Alicia wondered where her father had found the strength to dig the large patch of soil for his garden. She managed to create only a small hole before Mama summoned her for supper.

I'll work faster next week, Alicia resolved as she straightened up and shook the dirt and grass from her dress. She returned the spade to its rightful spot on the shelf in the shed, and hurried to join the family indoors.

When she returned to her project the next Saturday, Alicia was dismayed to see that the hole she had dug had been filled back in. The ground was packed down firmly and there was no evidence of her labour a week earlier.

She began digging again, refusing to allow the setback to deter her from her efforts to dig her way to China. When the call came for supper, Alicia sat back and surveyed her work. She felt a sense of satisfaction as she saw that the hole this week was considerably deeper than it had been when she finished the previous week.

It rained the following Saturday, preventing Alicia from working on her project.

I'll be glad when school lets out for the summer, she thought. *Then I can work at digging every day. If I work hard, I expect that by the end of the summer I can make it to China.*

What a story she would have to tell when she returned to school in the fall, she thought. What fun it would be to visit China!

She wondered what the people on the other side of the earth would think when she finally made it all the way through. Alicia laughed as she envisioned the look on the faces of the people there when she broke through the ground and her head popped out of the hole like a groundhog.

On the last Saturday in June, Alicia returned to her project with renewed energy. Sarah was occupied helping Aunt Elizabeth with some cleaning, so Alicia made no attempt to disguise where she was going. She got her tools and rounded the corner of the shed. A frown creased her forehead when she saw that once more the hole she'd dug had been filled in.

Disappointment flooded over her and she wondered if she would be able to complete her mission before school started again in the fall. She sat down on the ground, debating what to do. Should she abandon her goal of reaching China by the end of the summer, or should she persevere? There was hardly any point if someone or something insisted on filling in every hole she dug.

I'll give it one more try, she decided finally. Having made the decision, she set herself to the task and was happy with the results at the end of the day. As she put her tools away, Alicia was thankful that summer vacation had finally started. When Monday came she would be able to start working on her project every day.

Sunday passed in the usual way. Though she would have enjoyed doing more digging that day, Alicia knew such an activity would be forbidden. Sunday was the Lord's Day. The family walked together to church service in the morning, then Daddy escorted Alicia and Sarah to Sunday School in the afternoon.

Monday finally arrived and Alicia woke early, eager to get back to her digging. She picked at her food at the breakfast table, and squirmed impatiently, longing to be excused. When the meal was over, Alicia helped her mother clear the table.

Daddy remained in his place at the head of the table, sipping his morning coffee and searching the paper for opportunities of employment. He had built a reasonable clientele for his Rawleigh business, but with the depression going into its third year, even his well-to-do customers were purchasing less.

Understanding his situation, one of his clients had passed Daddy a copy of the newspaper when he'd delivered her order on Saturday afternoon. He was looking at it now, hopeful that he might find an advertisement for work that he could apply for.

Daddy set the paper aside as Alicia began washing the dishes and spoke to Mama.

"I think we may have a mole in the back yard."

"That's unusual in the city, isn't it?" Mama replied.

"It is, but something has been digging a hole behind the shed," Daddy answered. "I've filled the hole in three times now. If it continues, I'll have to set a trap."

Alicia's hands trembled. So it was her father who kept filling in the hole! She dried the dishes, then went upstairs and made her bed without being reminded to do so.

What do I do now?

She decided to venture outside and survey the situation. When she arrived at the place where she'd been digging, she found that nothing had been touched since Saturday.

She peeked around the shed. The coast was clear. The urge to visit China outweighed the logic that her father would continue filling in the holes she dug. She retrieved the spade from the shed and began digging. She worked feverishly, determined to achieve as much as possible in as little time as possible.

Intent on her project, Alicia did not realize she had an audience until a dark shadow fell across the hole, causing her to look up. Her parents stood watching her.

"So you are the mole," Daddy said dryly. "Are you digging for buried treasure?"

"No," Alicia answered quietly. "I'm digging my way to China." She searched her father's face, uncertain whether or not she was in trouble.

"Now what ever gave you the idea you could dig your way to China?" Daddy asked, struggling to keep from smiling.

"Sarah and Aunt Sadie said that if you dug a hole all the way through the earth, you would end up in China," Alicia answered. "So I'm doing it."

"It's impossible to actually dig through the earth," Daddy told Alicia, crouching down beside her. "They were just trying to explain where China is and how far it is from here."

"But I want to go there!" Alicia told him.

Her father smiled.

"Perhaps someday you will go to China," he told her. "But, if you do, it will likely be by boat, not by digging a hole through the earth."

He looked at the hole.

"Do you want me to fill it back in?" Alicia asked contritely.

"I think that would be a good idea," Daddy told her. "Then I'm certain Mama can find some work for you to do in the house for the rest of the day."

Alicia nodded. Her father was being fair, she decided. He realized that she had not been trying to do anything wrong, but that she had simply taken what she had been told literally.

She worked quickly, pleased to find that filling the hole was far easier than digging it had been. Later, alone in the house with her mother, Alicia brought up the subject of China again.

"I really wanted to go there, Mama," she said. A tear formed in her eye as she spoke.

"Why did you want to go to China, Alicia?" Mama asked. "Is it because Aunt Sadie is there?"

Alicia nodded.

"You'll see Aunt Sadie again next time she is in Canada," Mama reminded her.

"I know," Alicia answered. "But I wanted to see her now. I wanted to see her in China, not in Canada.

"When I grow up," Alicia stated resolutely, "I'm going to go to China and help Aunt Sadie. I'm going to be a missionary!"

***

Pussy Willows for Mama

"It's hard to believe we've lived in this house almost three years, isn't it?" Sarah asked Alicia as the girls did their chores together one Saturday morning.

Alicia looked at her sister in surprise. Had it been only three years? To her it felt like this house had always been her home. She could hardly remember a time when she had lived anywhere else.

"Just think," Sarah went on, "when we moved here, I was nine and you were six. Now you are nine and I am twelve."

"I'm almost ten," Alicia reminded her.

Sarah nodded. "And I am almost thirteen. Next year I will be a teenager."

She stretched in an attempt to look taller than her height of four feet, eight inches.

"I wonder if Mama and Daddy would let us go on a hike today," Sarah said, changing the subject abruptly.

Alicia smiled. If her sister didn't stop talking, they would not be going anywhere. It would take them all day to get their work finished.

"What do you think?" Sarah prompted.

"Where would you like to go?"

"I don't have anywhere special in mind," Sarah told her. "It's just such a nice day that I'd like to be outside. Maybe if we get our chores finished early, Daddy and Mama will let us go somewhere."

With the goal of an afternoon outdoors motivating them, the girls returned to their cleaning. They worked quickly but diligently, and finished their chores by the time Mama called them for the noon meal.

"Would it be all right if Alicia and I went for a hike this afternoon?" Sarah asked when dinner was almost finished.

"It's rather early in the year for a hike," Daddy responded. "The snow has scarcely melted away."

42

He looked at the girls' mother, who nodded slightly, giving her silent consent.

"Where did you plan to go?" Daddy asked.

"We're not really sure," Sarah replied. "We'd just like to go for a long walk somewhere. Right, 'Licia?"

"That's right," Alicia answered, even though the idea of walking all afternoon appealed less to her than it did to Sarah.

"Perhaps we could all go," Daddy suggested. "What do you think, Mama?"

"The three of you are welcome to go," Mama responded. "I have already made plans to visit my parents this afternoon."

"Did you want the girls and me to go with you?"

"I think it would be better if I went alone this time," Mama told him. She looked at her daughters and smiled. "I am pleased to think that the three of you will be occupied while I am out."

Half an hour later the family left the house. Alicia, Sarah and their father accompanied Mama to Grandpa and Grandma's house, then continued on their way. They walked briskly until they reached a river that ran through a wooded area. There they wandered through the grass and trees, carefully avoiding the mud near the water's edge. It felt good to be out in the cool spring air.

"I wish there were some flowers," Alicia commented. "It would be nice to take a bouquet home to Mama."

"It's still too early for flowers," Daddy said, "but I think we may be able to find something your mother will enjoy just as much."

They continued walking until they found what Daddy had been looking for; a tree with pussy willows in bloom. Carefully they climbed down the slope to reach the tree, and Alicia and Sarah each selected some branches. Their father took his pocket knife out and cut the chosen limbs from the tree.

"Won't that hurt the tree?" Alicia asked.

"Not at all," Daddy told her. "It is very much like cutting your hair. It doesn't harm the tree, and if it is done properly it encourages new branches to grow."

43

Content with their find and tired from the outing, Alicia and Sarah began the long walk home with their father, each clutching their pussy willow branches.

"Why does it seem farther going back home than it did coming out?" Alicia asked.

Daddy laughed.

"It's always that way," he told her. "A poet would say that it was the excitement and sense of adventure that made the trip out seem shorter, but I think the return trip seems longer because our bodies are tired."

"I'm not only tired," Sarah told them. "I'm hungry. I'll sure be ready for supper when I get home."

"Your mother may not be back from your grandparents' yet," Daddy reminded them. "Supper may be late tonight."

They were pleased when they arrived home to find that Mama was already there and had the evening meal waiting for them.

"I'm glad you have supper ready, Mama," Sarah told her. "I'm so hungry I could eat a horse!"

A look of shock crossed Mama's face at Sarah's comment, then she burst out laughing.

"Horse meat is not on the menu tonight, dear," she told Sarah. They all laughed as they sat down to the meal Mama had prepared. It was not until the meal was finished and they were clearing the table that the girls remembered their pussy willows.

"We have something for you, Mama," Alicia said, nudging Sarah as she spoke. Sarah went to the hall to retrieve the forgotten pussy willows.

"We picked these for you, Mama," Sarah offered as they presented their mother with the bouquet.

"We wanted to bring you flowers, but we couldn't find any, so we brought these instead," Alicia told her mother. Her disappointment at not finding flowers was obvious.

Mama took the pussy willows and put them in a vase, then turned to hug each of her girls.

"Perhaps you didn't know this," she told them, "but I prefer pussy willows to flowers."

"Really, Mama?" Alicia asked. "Why?"

"Pussy willows," Mama informed her, "grow only in the spring – very early in the spring. Flowers grow from spring to fall. Pussy willows will last a long time in a vase and don't require water. Flowers last only a short time after they are cut. And pussy willows are soft and grey, like a kitten.

"That is why I prefer a bouquet of pussy willows to a bouquet of flowers," she told them with a smile.

***

A Special Birthday

Alicia stirred and opened her eyes. She looked at the Baby Ben clock on her bedside table. She closed her eyes again. There was no need for her to get up so early on a Saturday. This was the day that she got to stay in bed an extra half hour.

She was in the habit of waking at her usual time on Saturdays, then burrowing back under the covers and dozing for another thirty minutes. This morning, however, she was wide awake and found herself unable to fall back into a state of slumber.

Alicia rolled over, wondering why she was finding it so difficult to go back to sleep. What was it about today that filled her with such a sense of excitement and prevented her from resting?

Her eyes popped open wide as she remembered and she bounded from her bed, eager to start the new day. This was her birthday! It was not just any birthday either, she reminded herself. Today she was ten years old.

She had been waiting for this day ever since Sarah turned ten three years ago. *Now Sarah won't be able to tease me about being the baby anymore,* she thought. At ten years old one could hardly be accused of being a baby! She washed and dressed, then went downstairs, where she found her mother in the kitchen, cooking pancakes for breakfast.

"Good morning, Mama." Alicia went over to where her mother stood by the stove and gave her a kiss.

"Good morning, Alicia," Mama answered. She turned and wrapped her arms around her daughter in a warm embrace. "Happy birthday, Little One."

"Happy birthday, Little One." Sarah echoed her mother's words as she entered the room. She ruffled her sister's hair.

Alicia glared at her.

"I'm ten now," she stated emphatically. "I'm not little!"

"You're still the baby, 'Licia," Sarah teased.

"I'm not a baby," Alicia protested.

"Sure you are," Sarah informed her. "You're the youngest in the family, so you are the baby."

"You are both correct," Mama intervened. "You are not a baby, Alicia. Why, at ten years old, you are almost a young lady."

Alicia beamed at her mother's words.

"Sarah is right also," Mama went on. The smile faded from Alicia's face. "You are the baby in our family, and you always will be."

"When you're ninety and I'm ninety-three you'll still be the baby," Sarah teased.

Alicia looked at her mother, an unspoken appeal in her face, but Mama had turned back to the stove. *This conversation is an unpleasant way to begin my second decade of life,* Alicia thought. She pondered her sister's words for a moment.

"Will I still be the baby when I'm ninety, Mama?" she asked.

Mama lifted the last of the pancakes from the pan and put them on a plate. She handed the plate to Sarah, instructing her to take it to the table and to finish the rest of the breakfast preparations. She then turned her attention to her younger daughter.

"I think," Mama told her thoughtfully, "that when you are ninety and Sarah is ninety-three you might be rather pleased if your sister still called you the baby."

Alicia frowned, failing to see the sense in her mother's logic.

"Aunt Helen is the baby in my family," Mama said. Alicia was surprised by this revelation. She had never thought about whether her aunt was older or younger than her mother.

"Your aunt rather enjoys it when I remind her that she is younger than I am," Mama continued.

"When you were growing up did you tease Aunt Helen the way Sarah teases me?" Alicia asked, trying to envision her mother and her aunt as children.

Mama smiled at the memories Alicia's question stirred up.

"No," she answered. "Your aunt teased me."

"But weren't you the older sister?"

"I was."

47

"I thought all older sisters teased their younger sisters," Alicia told her mother.

"Teasing is more a matter of one's personality than their birth order," Mama told her. "Sarah is fun-loving and free-spirited, like Aunt Helen. One of the ways people like that show they care is by teasing."

Alicia said nothing, but she found it difficult to consider Sarah's teasing an expression of endearment.

"You have a more serious nature," Mama went on, "like your mother."

Alicia smiled. There was no one in the whole world she would rather be like than her mother.

Later that night, lying in bed, Alicia assessed her day. It had been a good birthday, she decided. Her mother had gone to great pains to make the day special for her.

There had been no presents. She had been warned ahead of time that there would not be any gifts this year, but Grandpa, Grandma and Aunt Helen had joined them for supper. Grandma had even made her famous coconut cake for dessert. What a treat that had been!

Alicia decided that Mama must have spoken to Sarah after their early morning discussion. She'd noticed that Sarah had made an effort throughout the day not to tease her, although Alicia could see that it was difficult for her sister. She thought of the conversation she'd had with her mother that morning.

I'll try not to let Sarah's teasing bother me, she decided, *even if she will still be calling me the baby when I'm ninety!*

***

48

The Concert

"Adolph sends news of interest," Daddy commented as he folded the letter from his brother and replaced it in the envelope it had come in. He looked at Alicia and Sarah. "Your uncle's news will be of interest to you also." He smiled. "How would you like to go to a concert?"

"A real concert?" Sarah was clearly delighted by the idea.

"A real concert," Daddy answered, "with a well-known concert pianist."

He mentioned the musician's name, but it meant nothing to Alicia or Sarah.

"The performer is a friend of Uncle Adolph's," Daddy explained. "Your uncle has offered to arrange tickets for us if we would like to go."

"Can he get tickets for all of us?" Sarah asked eagerly.

"Uncle Adolph can get tickets for all of us," Daddy assured her.

"Will we have to take the streetcar to get there?" Alicia asked.

"I believe we might," Daddy answered.

The words brought a smile to Alicia's face. Rides on the streetcar came along about as often as an ice-cream cone, and were a treat she enjoyed almost as much.

"When is this event?" Mama asked.

"The concert is not till next month. I believe Adolph said it will be held on the second Saturday." Daddy took the letter out and checked the date.

"The second Saturday," he repeated, as he handed the letter to Mama.

"That is still weeks away." Sarah's disappointment was evident. "Think how long we will have to wait!"

Alicia said nothing. She did not mind waiting for things. Sometimes the anticipation of an event brought more pleasure than the event itself did.

"The concert tickets arrived in today's mail," Daddy announced a few days before the special occasion.

The weeks had passed quickly since news of the concert first arrived. While Alicia and Sarah had attended school, their mother's days had been filled with sewing. She had made a new dress for Alicia, using a bolt of material that she'd been saving for something special. Good material had been taken from one of Mama's worn dresses to provide Sarah with a new outfit and Mama had crocheted a lace collar to complement her own plain navy dress. She had even turned the collar and cuffs on Daddy's white shirt to give it a fresh look.

All the activity puzzled Alicia. Her mother kept a spotless house, and her physical appearance was always neat and tidy, but she had never placed a great emphasis on anyone's outer looks.

"Your clothes are not who you are," she had reminded Alicia and Sarah many times. "It is who you are inside that matters. People will remember you for your deeds, not for what you wear."

Yet in spite of those oft repeated words, Mama had spent countless hours these past weeks making certain her family would be properly attired for the musical performance.

Alicia and Sarah had been sent to the barber for haircuts the previous Saturday, with instructions as to the appropriate cut.

"Do you remember what to tell the barber when you get there?" Mama asked them before they left the house.

"Yes, Mama," the girls had replied, then repeated in unison, "I'd like it half-way up my ears and shingled at the back, please."

Satisfied that they would come home with a proper haircut, Mama handed Sarah the money for the barber and the girls had gone on their way.

There had been a line-up at the small shop and they had been forced to wait for their turn. Alicia had noticed her sister fidgeting while they waited, but it was not until they were on their way home that she'd learned why.

"I think I'll ask Mama if I can let my hair grow," Sarah commented as they walked home. "I'm tired of going to the barber.

I think we must be the only girls in the whole city that get their hair cut by a barber."

Alicia had noticed that they were the only girls in the shop, but she had thought nothing of it. They always got their hair cut at the barber.

"Where do other girls go?" she asked Sarah.

"I don't know about all of them, but my friend Eunice gets her hair done at a beauty salon."

Sarah thought for a moment.

"Of course, a beauty salon would cost a lot more than a barber. I'll just ask Mama and Daddy if I can let it grow."

Remembering the incident, Alicia wondered if Sarah had asked their parents yet. If she had, the answer must have been no. If it had been yes, Sarah most certainly would have told her!

She forced such thoughts from her mind, and turned back to the situation at hand. Their hair was cut and their clothes were ready. Now the tickets had arrived. The day of the concert was almost here!

Alicia felt excitement course through her as she stood with her family and waited for the streetcar to arrive. She did not know what it was about riding on the streetcar that thrilled her so much, she just knew she loved to go on it.

Perhaps it is because we don't have a car, she thought, *and it is just nice to ride somewhere instead of walking. Or maybe it is because when we go on the streetcar I know we are going somewhere special, and that is exciting.*

Maybe it is because I get to ride for the children's' fare, while Sarah needs an adult fare, she thought. *I wonder how long it will be before I have to pay the adult fare too?* She looked at Sarah, trying to remember how old she had been when she'd reached fifty-one inches in height.

"Get ready, it's coming," Sarah said, poking her sister in the ribs to be certain she was watching.

Daddy and Mama took the girls' hands as the electric car approached, holding them back. When the doors opened they boarded and made their way to the back, hoping to find seats near the coal-fired stove.

"Three and one," Daddy told the conductor as he deposited their tickets in the fare box.

Though they seldom rode the streetcar, he always purchased tickets in advance. A penny saved was a penny earned, and tickets bought at the price of four for a quarter was a good savings over the cash fare of seven cents each. Children's tickets could be purchased seven for a quarter. Now that Sarah required an adult fare, the children's tickets lasted the family a long time. Today, in fact, Daddy was using the last of the children's tickets he had purchased more than a year ago.

Mama and Sarah moved ahead and found seats for all of them. Alicia was about to join them when a hand on her shoulder stopped her. She looked up to see the conductor standing beside her.

"We'll get the little lady to step back to the pole for a moment, sir," he told Daddy.

Alicia felt a sense of alarm. This had never happened before.

"Do as the man says, Alicia," Daddy instructed. Bending down he reassured her. "It's all right. He just needs to check your height."

Alicia beamed. The conductor needed to check her height! Maybe she had reached the fifty-one inch mark! She moved to the pole, delighted that she was tall enough that the conductor wanted to measure her.

"Fifty-one inches!" the conductor announced. "I thought she might require the adult fare, sir."

"I'm afraid I don't have another ticket," Daddy said quietly, fumbling in his pocket as he spoke. "I'll need to purchase a single fare."

Alicia's smile faded as she realized the extra burden this would put on her parents.

The elderly conductor assessed the situation. At first glance the family had seemed to be well off. He noticed, however, that though their clothes appeared new enough their shoes showed obvious signs of wear, in spite of the extra layer of polish that had been applied.

"Perhaps I measured incorrectly," he told them. "If you'd let me check again, miss?"

Alicia returned to the pole obediently.

"It was my mistake," the conductor informed Daddy with a smile. "I forgot to allow an inch for her shoes. The young lady is fine."

He waved them to their seats.

I wish this could last forever, Alicia thought as the second half of the concert began. She had enjoyed every minute so far, and had stayed rooted in her seat during the intermission, unwilling to chance missing even a single note of the beautiful music when it began again.

Alicia smiled as the curtain rose and the music resumed. She was delighted that Uncle Adolph had been able to arrange seats near the front for them, where she could both see and hear the performance. She loved to watch the pianist's hands as he played. At times they flew back and forth across the keys, moving so quickly they were a blur. At other times his hands moved slowly, caressing the keys so lightly she marvelled that the touch was enough to produce any sound at all.

It seemed the second part of the concert had just begun when suddenly it was over. What a disappointment it was to find that the second half of the concert was shorter than the first. *It was not really a half at all,* Alicia told herself. *It was more like a quarter or a third.*

The music ended, and Alicia rose from her seat with the rest. As the crowds began to leave, she moved with her family to the exit. Outside, they began walking. Lost in the memory of the music, Alicia did not even notice that her father had chosen to walk rather than take the streetcar until they arrived home.

As they entered the house, tired but happy from the excursion, Daddy spoke.

53

"Did everyone enjoy the concert?"

"It was wonderful, Daddy." Alicia answered before Sarah had an opportunity to speak. "I never knew anyone could make such beautiful music on a piano."

"The piano is a marvellous instrument," Sarah told her.

Daddy laughed.

"The piano is only a marvellous instrument when it has talented hands to draw the music out," he reminded Sarah.

"When I grow up," Alicia informed them, "I'm going to play the piano."

"That list of things you plan to do is getting awfully long," Sarah teased. "You're going to have to live a long time to accomplish it all."

Alicia looked at Sarah.

"Someday," she told her emphatically, "I'm going to be able to play the piano."

***

Candies at Grandma's

"I'm going with Mama to visit Grandpa and Grandma this afternoon," Alicia informed her sister proudly.

She was excited about the outing and was very much looking forward to it. Though she did not say so, she was particularly pleased that she was the one who had been chosen to go with Mama today instead of her sister.

A visit alone with her mother at Grandpa and Grandma's was a rare event. Usually they visited as a family, although on occasion Mama would go by herself while Alicia and Sarah were at school.

"That's all right," Sarah answered airily. "I have other plans."

She did not say what those plans were, and Alicia wondered if her sister really did have an activity planned or if she just wanted Alicia to think she did. It really didn't matter what Sarah was doing, she decided. She was looking forward to having the afternoon out alone with her mother.

When the noon meal was over and the dishes were done, Alicia went upstairs to get ready. She brushed her teeth, changed into the dress Mama had laid out for her, and groomed her hair carefully. When she was finished she stepped back, looked in the mirror and smiled, certain that Mama would approve of her efforts.

She went downstairs, where she found her mother waiting in the living room.

"I'm ready, Mama."

Mama nodded.

"Sit down for a moment, Alicia," she instructed. "There is something I wish to speak with you about before we leave."

Alicia took a seat across from her mother, wondering what was amiss.

"Yes, Mama?"

"I do not want you to ask for anything when we are at your grandparents' house today. Do you understand?"

Alicia nodded, trying to recall the last time she had visited Grandpa and Grandma's. Had she done something wrong?

"I understand, Mama," she answered.

"The last time you were there you asked your grandmother for a candy," Mama told her. "Do you remember?"

Alicia blushed as she recalled the incident.

"Yes, Mama."

"I do not want you to do that again."

"I only asked because she forgot to offer me one," Alicia told Mama.

She was always given a peppermint candy or a humbug when she visited her grandparents. Waiting for the candy to be brought out was one of the best parts of the visit.

"If you are offered a candy you may have one," Mama informed her, "but it is rude for you to ask."

"I'll remember that, Mama. I promise I won't ask."

They left the house and walked the short distance to her grandparents' home. Grandpa was in the front yard when they arrived, working in his flower bed. He rose when they got there, and greeted them both warmly.

"It's nice to see one of my two favourite granddaughters," he told Alicia as he hugged her, "accompanied by one of my two favourite daughters."

Alicia smiled. She liked Grandpa. He was always cheerful and was fun to be with. She liked Grandma too, but she had always found her grandmother more reserved.

"What kind of flowers are these, Grandpa?" Alicia asked, stooping to touch one of the multi-petalled specimens.

"They are cosmos, Alicia," Grandpa answered. "I have pink and white ones here, and there are some bright yellow ones in the back garden."

"They're very pretty."

"If you'd like, I can cut some and send a bouquet home with you when you go," Grandpa offered.

"I'd like that very much," Alicia answered. She turned to her mother. "Would that be all right, Mama?"

"That would be fine," Mama said, smiling.

"Your grandmother will be pleased to see you," Grandpa told Alicia as they followed her mother into the house.

They found Grandma inside, seated in the living room. She looked up and smiled when they entered. Setting her embroidery aside, she rose to greet them, then moved to the kitchen to boil water for tea. Alicia followed her grandmother to the kitchen, hoping to be of assistance.

"Would you like me to help you, Grandma?"

"That's very kind, Alicia. I would be happy to have your help."

Alicia watched in silence as Grandma bustled about getting things ready. She had offered to help, but it appeared that her grandmother had no intention of letting anyone else take over in her kitchen. It was not until the tea was made, and the cookies were placed on a plate that she turned to Alicia.

"Perhaps you would like to get the cups and saucers, dear," she suggested.

Alicia nodded and moved to the cupboard, grateful to have finally been assigned a task. She smiled as she took four cups and saucers from the cupboard. That was another special thing about coming to Grandma's house. At Grandma's she was served tea, just like the adults. She always suspected that Grandma added more milk to her cup than the others, but she never complained. A china cup filled with milk and a taste of tea was a treat that she didn't get at home.

Alicia made two trips to the living room, carrying a cup and saucer in each hand. She smiled as she passed through the dining room and saw the dark wine cloth covering the table. Her grandmother was in the habit of preparing the table ahead of time for each meal, then covering the dishes with the maroon coloured cloth.

When they were all seated in the living room and Grandpa had asked a blessing on their refreshments, Grandma poured the tea.

That was something else that was different about Grandpa and Grandma, Alicia thought. At her home a blessing was asked before each meal, and there were always evening prayers, but at Grandpa and Grandma's not even a cup of tea was drank without saying a blessing before partaking of it.

She sat quietly, sipping her tea, only partially listening to the conversation around her. Her mind wandered to the candies in the cupboard and she wondered how long it would be before they came out.

It's not that I mind waiting, she reminded herself, but what if Grandma forgets like she did last time?

Alicia glanced at her mother. It would never do to ask after promising Mama that she wouldn't.

She looked at the cupboard. The candies were so close she could almost taste them! She wondered if there was some way to get Grandma's attention and discreetly remind her about the candies without actually asking.

She turned her gaze on her grandmother, hoping that to the others in the room it would appear she was merely interested in what Grandma was saying. It would be terrible if Mama realized she was up to something. When Grandma noticed her and smiled, Alicia smiled back, then turned and gazed longingly at the cupboard where the candies were kept.

She repeated the action several times, then waited. When there was a lull in the conversation, Grandma rose. She went to the cupboard, opened it and took out the covered bowl that held the candies.

"Would anyone care for a mint?"

"Thank you, Grandma, that's very kind of you," Alicia said as she accepted the candy that had been offered. She smiled. She had kept her promise. She had not asked for anything. She looked up to see her grandmother smiling back at her. Then, as she turned away, Alicia was almost certain her grandmother winked at her!

As they strolled home later, Alicia's arms filled with the colourful bouquet of flowers from her grandfather, Mama looked at her.

"I was pleased with your behaviour, Alicia," she told her. "I'm very glad you didn't ask for anything today."

Alicia smiled. Today's experience had taught her that there was more than one way to communicate.

**

False Accusations

"I hate that Billy Hawthorne," Alicia sobbed.

"Shh, don't say such things," Sarah begged. "I know Billy is mean, but you mustn't hate him."

Almost five years had passed since the Miller family had moved into their new home and in all that time Billy had proven himself to be nothing but trouble. Today Billy had created another incident to cause conflict between the Hawthorne and Miller families.

"Well I sure don't like him very much," Alicia said with a sniffle. "I wasn't even in his yard, and he's downstairs right now with his father telling Daddy and Mama that I put a hole in his tent. How could I tear his tent when I wasn't even in his yard?"

A knock sounded at the door before Sarah had a chance to answer and Alicia went to open it. She knew even before she reached the door that it was her father on the other side. Mama would have come in after knocking.

"I need to speak with you, Alicia," Daddy said sternly.

Alicia nodded.

"Have you been in the Hawthornes' yard?"

"No, Daddy, I haven't," Alicia answered honestly.

Her father looked at her, a serious expression on his face.

"Are you certain?" he asked.

Alicia nodded.

"I'd like you to come downstairs with me and tell Mr. Hawthorne that," Daddy told her. "He believes otherwise."

With fear and trembling, Alicia followed her father down to where their neighbours waited in the living room.

"I'd like you to tell Mr. Hawthorne what you told me, Alicia," Daddy instructed her.

"I haven't been in your yard, sir," Alicia stammered. She was not so intimidated by Detective Hawthorne himself as by the young man who stood by his side scowling at her.

"Billy tells me you were," Detective Hawthorne answered. "Isn't that right, Billy?"

Alicia waited, expecting Billy to rescind his claim.

"It is, sir," Billy answered without flinching.

Alicia wondered how Billy could lie without any show of emotion. *He must have had a lot of practice,* she thought. *If I were ever to lie to Daddy or Mama I would feel so guilty that I am certain they would know I wasn't telling the truth.*

"We have a situation here, Mr. Hawthorne," Alicia's father said quietly. "I believe my daughter and you believe your son.

"In any event," he continued, "your son's tent is torn and my daughter has been accused of the crime."

"All will be forgotten if you are willing to replace the tent," Billy's father stated.

"You know we are not in a position to do that."

The silence that followed this comment was broken by a soft voice from the corner of the room. Alicia had been unaware that her mother was present until she heard her speak.

"I would be willing to mend the tent if you would consider that satisfactory, Mr. Hawthorne. I do not believe Alicia is responsible for the damage, but I would be happy to mend it if you would agree to my doing so."

Alicia watched Billy carefully as her mother spoke. Though he had lied earlier without remorse, a slight flush rose in his face as he listened to Mama's offer. Detective Hawthorne looked from Alicia to Billy, as if trying to decide which one to believe.

"I appreciate your offer, Mrs. Miller," he said finally, "and I will accept it."

He shook hands with Daddy, then planted his hand firmly on his son's shoulder and steered him out the door.

"I didn't do it, Mama. I really didn't," Alicia said when the two were gone.

"I know you didn't, Alicia," her mother told her.

"Then why did you offer to fix the tent if you knew I didn't rip it?"

"The Hawthornes are our neighbours. It is always wise to keep good relations with your neighbours," Mama answered.

"If you mend the tent for them, doesn't that teach Billy that it is all right to lie?"

"I think Billy will learn more by me mending the tent than he would by us arguing over it," Mama told her. "Billy will have to live with his conscience. Every time he looks at the tent, he will be reminded of what he did."

Alicia thought about this. She wondered if Billy Hawthorne had a conscience. Then she remembered the flush that had spread across his face when her mother offered to mend the tent. Perhaps Mama's solution was better than any punishment Billy's father might have applied.

***

New Neighbours

"Billy's moving!" Sarah announced as she burst into Alicia's room without knocking.

Alicia looked up from the book she was reading.

"Are you certain?" She was afraid to get her hopes up in case this was another of Sarah's pranks.

"It's true, honest!" Sarah exclaimed. "I wouldn't tease you about something like that – not after the stunt Billy pulled over the hole in his tent last year!"

Alicia grimaced as she recalled the incident.

It was not until her mother had mended the tent so neatly that one would never know it had been torn that Billy finally admitted to puncturing the canvas structure himself while playing in it. Fearing his father's wrath, he had concocted the story about Alicia playing in their yard and damaging the tent. He had stuck by his story for several weeks following the incident.

Sensing that his son was truly the one at fault, Mr. Hawthorne had devised a plan that had finally encouraged Billy to confess.

"Now that summer vacation is here, you'll be able to sleep in your tent every night," Mr. Hawthorne had informed his son.

When Billy protested, his father had replied. "It wouldn't do for Mrs. Miller to think we didn't appreciate her fixing the hole her daughter put in the tent. Using the tent every night will let her know her efforts are appreciated."

It had taken several weeks of sleeping in the mended tent before Billy's conscience finally convinced him to come clean. A loud knock had sounded at the door mid-way through the summer, interrupting the Miller family's evening meal. Daddy had opened it to find Mr. Hawthorne and a shame-faced Billy standing outside. Alicia had been summoned and Detective Hawthorne had apologized profusely for doubting her word. Billy's apology had been less wordy, but Alicia had no doubt that it was sincere. He had carefully avoided contact with her since that evening, and Alicia had welcomed the reprieve.

Now Sarah was informing her that the Hawthornes were moving.

"I didn't see a *for sale* sign," Alicia told Sarah.

"That's because there wasn't one," Sarah replied. "Mr. Hawthorne has been transferred to another city. He has decided to rent the house in case they choose to come back, but it doesn't seem likely that they will."

"When are they moving?" Alicia asked.

"They're moving right now!" Sarah grabbed Alicia by the arm and led her to the front bedroom, which had a window overlooking the street. From there Alicia had a clear view of the activity going on next door.

"Do you want to go and say goodbye?" Sarah asked.

Alicia shook her head.

"I don't think so," she answered. "I think I'd rather wait and say hello to the new people."

The new neighbours moved in just days after the Hawthornes moved out. Alicia returned from school one afternoon to find a girl about her own age sitting on the veranda of the Hawthorne's home. She waved, and the girl waved back. She encountered her new neighbour again the next morning as she left for school. They were both leaving at the same time and the other girl stopped at the sidewalk to wait for Alicia.

"Hello," she called as Alicia approached. "My name is Martha."

"Hello, Martha. I'm Alicia. Are you on your way to school?"

Martha nodded, and the girls started walking.

"What grade are you in?" Martha asked.

"Grade six."

"So am I," Martha told her. "I wonder if we'll be in the same class."

"I'd like that," Alicia replied, thinking how nice it was to have Martha living beside her instead of Billy Hawthorne.

In the days that followed Alicia and Martha became close friends. They walked to and from school together each day, played at Alicia's house after school, and spent time doing homework together.

The friendship grew as the months passed. Then, without warning, Martha's family disappeared. It happened the second summer that they lived in the house. The family moved while Alicia and her family were on an overnight visit to Uncle Adolph's. When they returned, the neighbouring house was empty and a *house for sale* sign was posted.

"I can't believe Martha left without saying goodbye to me," Alicia told Sarah.

"Something must have happened," Sarah answered. "It seems strange that they left so suddenly."

The explanation of the neighbour's disappearance came a week later when their father received a visit from Detective Hawthorne. Alicia and Sarah tried listening from the kitchen, but were able to catch only bits and pieces of the men's conversation. Finding an excuse to do so, they moved into the dining room, where they were able to hear while still remaining out of sight.

"It's too bad it turned out the way it did," Detective Hawthorne was saying. "They seemed like such a nice family when I rented to them."

"They were certainly good neighbours," Daddy assured the man. "They looked after the place well."

"If only they had paid their rent," Mr. Hawthorne said sadly. "It is a difficult thing to turn people out, Mr. Miller. You do understand that I had no choice?"

Daddy murmured something in response, but the girls were unable to hear his words.

"I can't afford to carry two homes," the detective went on. "I was relying on the rental income from this one to cover expenses in our new home. Unfortunately, that income turned out to be non-existent. I tried negotiating, but in the end I felt I had no choice but to ask them to leave."

"I can see you were in a difficult position," the girls' father responded.

"You'll see that I am now trying to sell the house," Mr. Hawthorne went on. "I am hopeful it will sell quickly, even if I have to take a loss on it."

When Mama entered the dining room, Alicia and Sarah buried their heads in their books, pretending to be studying. Sensing otherwise, Mama sent them both upstairs, leaving the men to continue their conversation in private.

"Do you know where Martha's family went?" Alicia asked her father the following morning.

"All I have been told is that they are staying with relatives in the country," Daddy replied.

"Do you think I'll ever see Martha again?"

Her father looked thoughtful. "It is possible you may meet again sometime," he told her, "but it is doubtful if they will return to this part of the city anytime soon."

Alicia said nothing in response. Though Daddy had not said so, Alicia knew that it could just as easily have been her family as Martha's that had been evicted.

***

Summer Camp

Alicia stared at the piece of paper on the table. Her mind was as empty as the page before her. Idly she wondered why her mother insisted that she write to relatives she had never met. Last time it had been a letter to her aunt in Germany. Today Mama had sat her down at the table with the strong admonition not to get up until a letter to her grandfather in England was completed.

She sighed. What was one supposed to write to a stranger? The twice yearly notes sent for their birthdays and Christmas were easy enough, but a letter was more difficult. It was hard enough to write to people she knew, like Aunt Elizabeth or Uncle Adolph.

Resolutely, she picked up the pencil.

Dear Grandfather.

She wrote the words neatly. If her handwriting were sloppy, Mama would make her do it all over again. *What should I write next,* she wondered, staring at the paper again.

"How is your letter coming along?" Mama asked, choosing that moment to enter the room to check on her progress.

"Not very well," Alicia told her. "I don't know what to write."

"Let me see what you have so far." Mama looked at the two words Alicia had so carefully penned. "I see you have a good start," she teased.

Alicia smiled. "I'm trying, Mama, but it's hard to write to someone I've never met."

"I know it is," her mother agreed, "but remember how much it means to your grandfather and your aunt to receive your letters."

"But what is there to write about?" Alicia asked.

"Just write about everyday things," Mama told her. "Your grandfather is interested in how you spend your time; in what you do and where you go. You must remember that your relatives overseas know you only through your letters."

Alicia sat for a time after her mother left the room, thinking about what she had said. For the first time, it occurred to her that it might be just as hard for her grandfather and her aunt to write to her as it was for her to write to them. She thought about the letters that came to her parents from England and Germany. Often they included personal notes for Alicia and her sister.

Grandfather's letters were always formal, expressing the hope that the children were healthy and that they were working hard and doing well at school. His letter always ended with the reminder that the girls should be good and that they should obey their parents.

Alicia sighed. Grandfather's letters were always the same. She wondered if her grandfather found the letters she wrote to him stiff and formal also.

Her thoughts turned to the letters her aunt wrote from Germany. She and Sarah loved getting letters from their aunt. Aunt Hilda's letters read like a good book. They were well written and were filled with funny stories and incidents. Aunt Hilda had a way of taking the most ordinary event – a walk in the park, a journey by train or bus, even a cup of tea with a neighbour – and turning it into something worth writing about. When you read her letters, you felt as if you were right there with her experiencing the situations she described in them.

Alicia remembered commenting once to Sarah that their aunt lived such an interesting life.

"I don't think Aunt Hilda's life is any more interesting than our own," Sarah had replied. "I think she just knows how to make it sound interesting."

Alicia thought about her sister's words. *I think she just knows how to make it sound interesting.* What could she write to Grandfather to make her own life sound interesting?

I will write this letter as if I were writing a story for school, Alicia decided as she picked up the pencil once more. *I will write as if I were trying to earn an 'A' on an assignment.*

The words flowed easily as she told Grandfather about her school and her friends.

I like school, she wrote, *but I can hardly wait for summer vacation. This year, for the very first time ever, Sarah and I will be going away to camp. Mama told us that if we worked very hard at school and did really well this term, we would earn the opportunity to go to camp. The Big Sisters Association has a summer camp north of Toronto, and Sarah and I have been selected to go this year.*

I will write you again when I return from camp and tell you all about it.

Alicia set the pencil down and re-read the words she'd written. Satisfied that it was the best letter she had ever written, she signed her name at the bottom of the page and folded it carefully. The letter was ready for Mama to mail.

"I can't wait to go to camp," Sarah told Alicia enthusiastically. "I'm so excited I could almost burst."

Alicia did not answer. She just continued drying the dishes in silence.

"Aren't you excited, Alicia?" Sarah persisted.

"I suppose so," Alicia answered reluctantly.

"What do you mean you suppose so?" Sarah asked. "You can't just suppose that you're excited about something. You're either excited or you're not."

"I'm a little excited then," Alicia told her, although secretly she thought it might be more fear she felt than excitement.

"What's the matter, 'Licia?" Sarah asked. "I thought you wanted to go."

"I did want to," Alicia said quietly, "when I thought we were going together."

"We are going together. We leave here together tomorrow morning, we travel to camp together, and we spend a whole week there. We can't be together much more than that!"

"We won't be together when we get there," Alicia reminded Sarah. "I'll be in the junior camp and you'll be in the senior camp."

"I'll be close by if you need me," Sarah told her. "Besides, you'll have more fun without me around to tease you."

Alicia smiled. Her sister did tease her more than she liked, but she was also quick to defend her and to cheer her up when she felt down.

"I'd rather have you there teasing me than be there all by myself," she told Sarah.

"I'm sure I'll be close by. The junior and senior camps can't be far apart," Sarah said.

"The junior and senior camps are quite a distance apart," Alicia informed her. "Clarissa told me. She was there last year, so she knows. You'll be all the way across the water from me. If I need you I'll either have to walk forever to get to you, or go in a boat."

She shuddered at the thought of going in a boat. She might fall out and drown! Walking forever to reach Sarah would be preferable to going in a boat.

"You really don't want to go, do you?" Sarah asked.

Alicia shook her head.

"It's too late now to change my mind, though," she said sadly.

"You'll have fun, 'Licia, honest you will," Sarah assured her.

Alicia wondered how Sarah could make the proclamation with such certainty. How did she know it would be fun? She had never been to camp either!

"There'll be sports, and swimming, and crafts, and cooking food over campfires," Sarah enthused.

"I know," Alicia told her. The only thing Sarah had mentioned that interested her was the crafts.

"There'll be singing and dancing," she went on.

Alicia stared at her sister.

"You better not let Mama hear you say there might be dancing," she warned, "or neither one of us will be going!"

"We won't really be dancing," Sarah said. "We'll just move a bit to the music."

"Isn't that dancing?" Alicia asked.

"Not really," Sarah answered, and Alicia chose to believe her.

The entire Miller household rose early the next morning. Sarah was eager to be on her way and was ready to leave the house an hour ahead of time, while Alicia prolonged the moment of departure as long as she could. She made each morning activity last as long as possible, dawdling while she ate breakfast, taking her time as she got dressed, and working her way in slow motion through brushing her teeth and combing her hair.

"If I didn't know better, Alicia, I'd think you didn't want to go to camp," Mama commented, after she had encouraged Alicia several times to move more quickly.

"Just think how much fun you will have there," Mama told her. "It will be far more enjoyable for you than staying here alone with Daddy and me while Sarah is off experiencing new things."

I wish I could tell Mama that I'd rather be here alone with her and Daddy all week than be in the junior camp while Sarah is across the lake at the senior camp, Alicia thought.

I'll try to make the best of it, she decided as she bid her mother goodbye, *but I sure will be happy when the week is over.*

The ride to camp was a noisy one. A group of campers travelled together, accompanied by several counsellors. When the singing began, Sarah joined in and sang heartily, but Alicia sat silently. They arrived at their destination much too soon for her liking, and she and Sarah were separated.

Alicia looked at the swarm of tents spread across the open field, wondering which one she would be in. She hoped it would be near the end of a row. There were so many of the identical portable shelters that she feared she would wander into the wrong one by mistake.

"Is this your first time at camp?" The voice came from behind her. Alicia turned to see a girl standing a few feet from her.

"Yes," she answered shyly. "It is."

"It's my first time too," the girl told her. "I'm Edna."

"My name is Alicia."

"I like it here," Edna commented, looking around as she spoke. "It's nice."

71

Alicia surveyed the camp, wondering what Edna saw that she didn't. Looking beyond the tents in one direction she saw endless trees. In the other direction she saw water.

She felt something touch her arm, and looked down to see an ant crawling across her skin. She brushed it off, trying not to squirm as she did so. No one had warned her that there would be bugs! The ant was further evidence that camping might not be as exciting as she had been told it would be.

"Isn't it wonderful to be out of the city?" Edna asked.

Alicia was uncertain how to respond.

"I like the city," she answered quietly.

"Not me!" Edna told her. "I'd live in the country if I could." She looked around. "I'm so happy to be here, out in the country, away from all the noise and confusion of the city."

"I didn't realize the city was that noisy," Alicia said.

Edna laughed.

"Maybe the city isn't," she told Alicia, "but it's always noisy where I live. I have seven brothers and sisters, so it's never quiet at my house."

"Seven!" Alicia exclaimed. "I only have one."

"Are you the oldest?" Edna asked.

"No. I'm the youngest."

For the first time she was glad that Sarah was not in the same camp as her. She was certain that Sarah would have told Edna that she was the baby.

"You're lucky," Edna told her. She sighed. "I'm the oldest."

Alicia stared. She could not imagine what it would be like to live in such a large family. She tried to picture her home with seven younger siblings, but it was more than her mind could fathom. No wonder Edna stood away from the crowd, enjoying the simple pleasure of solitude.

"Do you know anyone here?" Edna asked.

"Just you," Alicia answered, and they both laughed.

"Since you're alone and I'm alone, do you want to ask if we can share a tent?" Edna asked her. "It might be nice to camp together. I don't know anyone else either."

"I'd like that." Alicia was pleased Edna had suggested it. She had made a new friend already! She turned and looked at her fellow campers. Most of them seemed to be in pairs or small groups. Few seemed to have come alone like she and Edna. It would be nice to be paired with Edna for the week.

The girls left and went in search of Miss Hawkins to see if they could be placed together. When they found her, she agreed, and a short time later Alicia and Edna were officially camp buddies.

Together with her new friend, Alicia immersed herself in the activities the camp offered. To her surprise, she found that she thoroughly enjoyed them. She felt guilty at the end of the day when she realized that she had not thought of Sarah once since she and Edna had paired up.

If today is any indication of a typical day at camp, I won't have time to miss Sarah was Alicia's last thought before she fell asleep.

When the bugle sounded the next morning, Alicia stirred, wondering where she was. Her body ached and her bed felt cold and lumpy.

"C'mon, sleepyhead," a voice urged. "We only have a few minutes before breakfast. I've been trying to wake you up forever!"

Alicia opened her eyes. Edna was up and dressed already, eager to start the day.

"What time is it?" she asked sleepily.

"It's time you were up, that's what time it is," Edna told her.

Alicia scrambled from her bed and, with her new friend's assistance, managed to arrive at the dining hall in time for the morning meal.

The rest of the day, and the week, passed in a whirl. Every minute of every day was filled with activities. There was not an idle moment from the time they rose in the morning to the moment they tumbled into bed at night.

"I never thought camp would be so much fun," Alicia admitted as she collapsed in a tired heap at bedtime mid-way through the week. "I also never thought it would be so tiring."

"I love it," Edna told her.

"So do I," Alicia answered, "although I never expected to."

She looked across to where Edna sat. Her friend's face was barely visible in the evening light.

"I didn't want to come, you know," Alicia confided.

"Really?"

"I did at first," Alicia explained, "when I thought Sarah and I would be together. But when I found out she would be in the senior camp and I would be in the junior camp, I wished I could just stay home!"

She paused.

"I'm glad now that I came."

"So am I," Edna told her. She laughed. "Isn't it funny, Alicia? You didn't want to come to camp without your sister, and I came to camp to get away from mine!"

There was silence for a time. Alicia was almost asleep when Edna spoke quietly in the darkness. "I wish this week would never end."

"Me too," Alicia murmured.

The end of the week came too quickly for both girls. As they packed their bags on the morning of departure, Edna looked at Alicia.

"I'll miss you," she said quietly.

"I'll miss you too," Alicia told Edna.

"Maybe we'll both come back next year," Edna said hopefully.

"Maybe," Alicia answered.

Before they parted the two girls hugged. Neither said goodbye. To say goodbye would be to admit they might not see each other again; that they might not return the following year. Their hug was their silent goodbye.

At home the next day, Alicia approached her mother, asking for a piece of paper.

"What do you need paper for?" Mama asked.

"I'd like to write a letter," Alicia told her.

"A letter?" Mama sounded surprised.

"Yes, Mama. I told Grandfather last time I wrote that I would write again when I got back from camp and tell him all about it."

Mama smiled. Her little girl was growing up. This was the first time she had ever offered to write a letter without being prompted.

Seated at the dining room table, pencil firmly in hand, Alicia began.

Dear Grandfather,

She smiled. She had so much she wanted to tell her grandfather. This was going to be the easiest letter she had ever written!

***

House For Sale

"Don't forget you have to dry the spoons," Sarah told Alicia.

"I won't." Alicia wondered why Sarah reminded her every time. It was not as if she was likely to forget. For as long as she could remember they'd had a rule that the one that washed the dishes had to dry the cutlery. She was still trying to think of a good retort for Sarah's comment when her sister nudged her.

"You're closer to the door than I am," Sarah whispered. "Can you hear what Daddy and Mama are saying?"

Alicia listened for a moment.

"Daddy's talking about some man selling a house," she reported. "But we shouldn't be eavesdropping on their conversation."

"Just listen!" Sarah insisted and Alicia obeyed. A moment later she turned to face her sister.

"I think it's this house that's for sale!" she whispered. Sarah's eyes widened at the news.

"You keep washing and making some noise. I'll see what I can find out." Sarah inched toward the door with the dish towel and a plate in her hand. If Mama or Daddy approached she could honestly say she was still drying the dishes.

Alicia had finished her portion of the after dinner cleanup and was starting on her sister's by the time Sarah returned.

"We need to talk," Sarah whispered. "I'll finish here, then I'll meet you upstairs. Okay?"

"Okay."

Alicia took off her apron and went up to her room to wait. When Sarah arrived moments later, her face was flushed. Alicia wasn't certain whether the tinge of colour was from exertion or excitement. Her sister entered the room and closed the door quietly behind her.

"Well?" Alicia asked when Sarah was seated. "Is it our house that's for sale?"

Sarah nodded and Alicia's hand flew to her mouth.

"I don't think it's for sale yet," Sarah went on, "but the owner has told Daddy that he plans to sell it."

"Where will we go when he does?" Alicia asked, remembering what had happened to her friend Martha's family.

"I don't know," Sarah answered slowly. "I think it might be nice to move again."

"I don't want to move," Alicia protested. "I like it here!"

"Let's wait and see what happens," Sarah consoled her. "Maybe we won't have to move."

Alicia looked at her.

"Remember when we moved here Daddy told Mr. Hawthorne that maybe he would buy the house someday?"

"That was a long time ago," Alicia reminded Sarah.

"It was," Sarah agreed. "And if the owner had wanted to sell it back then, we couldn't have bought it. Now that Daddy is working again, maybe we can."

"Maybe," Alicia agreed, but she sounded unconvinced.

Sleep came slowly to Alicia that night. Her parents never discussed their finances with her, but she knew the family was not well off. Even with Daddy working, they still relied on assistance from the Big Sisters' Association frequently. Many of Alicia and Sarah's clothes and necessities for school were purchased through the Association. How could her parents possibly buy a house when they needed to rely on such assistance just to meet their basic needs?

Would they end up being evicted like Martha's family?

Days went by without any mention of the house being sold. Alicia was beginning to think that Sarah had misunderstood their parents' conversation when she came home one day and found a *For Sale* sign posted.

She entered the house and went in search of her mother.

"Are we moving, Mama?" Alicia asked when she located her mother in the cellar.

"We may be moving," Mama replied calmly. "We don't know yet."

When Alicia pressed for further information, Mama looked up from her work.

"Your father is considering possibilities," she stated, in a voice that told Alicia in no uncertain terms that their conversation was finished.

When Sarah came home, Alicia told her about the conversation she'd had with their mother.

"Mama said Daddy was considering possibilities," she told Sarah. "What do you think she meant by that?"

"I don't know," Sarah answered thoughtfully. "I guess we'll just have to wait till they tell us."

In the weeks that followed Alicia watched carefully. She noticed that her parents held frequent conversations in their bedroom behind closed doors. On occasions when they were talking downstairs, the topic of their conversation seemed to change as soon as they were aware of her presence. She further noted that her parents had taken a special interest in the daily mail deliveries, though Alicia could not think of any reason for their interest.

More than a month passed before Alicia learned what the possibilities that her father had been considering were. She arrived home from school to find the sign had been removed from the veranda railing. Sarah was not far behind her, so Alicia waited for her. When her sister approached, she pointed to the place where the sign had been.

"Do you think this means the house is sold?" she asked. Sarah chewed her lip.

"It might mean that," she answered, staring at the spot where the piece of wood had hung.

"Let's go ask Mama." Alicia started to mount the steps, but Sarah's hand on her arm stopped her. "What's wrong?"

It was unlike Sarah to hang back. Usually Sarah was the leader and she was the follower.

"I think we should wait till Mama and Daddy tell us themselves," Sarah said. "They've been pretty quiet about what's going on so far. There must be a reason for it. I think it's better to let them tell us what's going on in their own time."

When supper was over that night, the girls asked to be excused, but before Mama could respond Daddy held up his hand.

"Your mother and I have some news to share," he informed them. The girls waited. "Perhaps you noticed that the sign was missing from the front porch."

Alicia and Sarah nodded.

"The sign is gone because the house has been sold," Daddy told them with a smile.

Why is Daddy smiling if our house has been sold? Alicia wondered. *Where are we going to live?*

"When will we be moving?" Sarah asked. "Should we start packing?"

"I don't think that will be necessary," Daddy answered.

"Are the new owners going to let us stay here?" Alicia asked.

Daddy smiled again. It was one of the happiest expressions Alicia had seen on her father's face in a long time.

"Your mother and I are the new owners," he answered.

"Really?" Alicia asked, hardly daring to believe such good news.

"Really," Daddy responded.

"But how-" Sarah started to ask. She stopped mid-sentence, knowing her father would consider her question inappropriate.

"My father has assisted us in the purchase," Daddy replied.

The statement was the most information their father had ever divulged about the family's financial affairs, Alicia thought. It explained her parents' increased interest in the mail delivery. They had been watching the post for word from England.

"I'm happy we don't have to move, Daddy," she told her father earnestly.

"So am I, dear," Daddy replied. "I look forward to calling this place home for a long, long time."

An Unforgettable Christmas

"There's a man coming up the walk, and he's carrying a great big box," Sarah announced as she entered the kitchen.

Mama looked up from the biscuits she was rolling. Setting her work aside, she removed her apron and washed her hands. She was still drying them when the doorbell rang. Alicia followed as Mama went to the door.

Her eyes opened wide when she saw the box sitting outside on the porch. Sarah had been right. It was huge! She wondered how the man had ever managed to carry it alone.

"Good day, ma'am." The chap standing on the porch greeted Mama. "I have a delivery for you."

Mama looked at the box. It was obvious from the size of it that it was not one of her husband's Rawleigh orders.

"We are not expecting anything. Are you certain you have the right address?"

The man bent and turned the box around. He inspected the label, then read the address aloud.

"That is this address," Mama agreed.

"The package is addressed to Mr. Paul Miller and family," the man informed her as he straightened. "Would you be Mrs. Miller?"

"I would," Mama replied.

"Shall I put the parcel inside for you then, ma'am?" the man asked.

"Yes, please do."

Alicia stepped back into the shadow of the hallway and watched as the man lifted the box and set it inside the front door.

"What is it, Mama?" she asked, as soon as the door shut behind him.

"I don't know, dear," Mama answered, eyeing the box as she spoke. "It is addressed to your father. We will find out what is inside when he arrives home."

With that comment, Mama returned to her duties in the kitchen.

"I've never found it so hard to wait for anything in my whole life," Alicia complained to Sarah an hour later.

"I know," Sarah moaned. "Why is it that the first time something exciting happens to us, it happens on a day when Daddy is gone all day?"

"Complaining won't make the hours till your father gets home go by any more quickly," Mama reminded them. "I suggest you find something constructive to do while you're waiting."

The subtle implication that Mama would find work for them if they could not find anything to do on their own was enough to stimulate Alicia and Sarah. They went upstairs and found a game they could play together to help occupy the time until their father returned. They played half-heartedly, both listening intently for the sound of the front door opening. The moment they heard it, they rushed from the room and were downstairs before their father had time to get his coat off.

"A man came with a package for you today," Sarah burst out, eager to be the first to share the news. She had, after all, been the one who had seen the man coming up the walk and alerted the others to his presence.

"It's really, really big," Alicia added. She was determined not to let Sarah be the only one with news.

Daddy laughed.

"What ever happened to a proper greeting like *Hello, Daddy* or *How was your day?*"

"Hello, Daddy," Alicia said.

"How was your day, Daddy?" Sarah asked.

"That's better," their father told them. "Hello, Alicia. Hello, Sarah. My day was fine, thank you."

He paused.

"Now what were you telling me about a delivery?"

"A man came with a box," Sarah started.

"It's really big," Alicia added.

"The parcel is addressed to you, and Mama said we had to wait till you got home to find out what is inside," Sarah told him.

"The man came this morning," Alicia informed her father. She sighed. "It was really hard to wait, Daddy. It was an awful long day."

Daddy smiled.

"Let me talk to your mother for a few minutes," he told the girls. "Then we will see what is inside this mysterious box." He bent and lifted the large package, carrying it into the kitchen.

When the family assembled around the kitchen table a few minutes later, Alicia and Sarah clasped hands in excitement. They watched their father cut the string that was tied around the package and hand it to Mama. They waited as she wound it and put it in a drawer, then watched as Daddy slit the box open.

"It is from my sister in Germany," Daddy commented as he surveyed the label.

Alicia and Sarah pressed forward as their father pulled back a flap on the box, revealing the contents. They gasped! Inside were gifts wrapped in brightly coloured paper! Alicia looked at Sarah. She had never seen anything so wonderful.

"It looks like she has included a letter," Mama commented. She reached into the box and withdrew a white envelope. Mama's eyes widened as she opened the envelope and saw the contents. There was silence as she handed it to Daddy. He peeked inside.

Alicia and Sarah watched as their parents looked from the envelope to each other. Not a word was spoken as their father folded the envelope in half and put it in his pocket. He closed the box up again, looked at his daughters and smiled.

"Perhaps your mother and I should have opened this in private," he told them. "I believe your aunt intended that we surprise you with the gifts on Christmas morning."

"It's still a surprise," Sarah said. "Everything was wrapped, so we don't know what is inside."

"I'm sure you will have great fun imagining what the packages might hold," Daddy said.

"And in six more days we will find out!" Alicia declared.

"That's right," Daddy told her. "Until then, this will be kept out of sight." With those words, he picked up the box and carried it down to the cellar.

"I'm so excited I don't think I'll be able to sleep tonight," Sarah confided to Alicia on Christmas Eve.

"I think we should stop talking and go to sleep right now," Alicia told her.

Their uncle had arrived earlier in the day for the holidays, and had been given Sarah's room to sleep in, so the girls were bunking together in Alicia's room.

"Do you really want to sleep?" Sarah asked, and Alicia laughed.

"Not really," she answered, "but I think going to sleep now might make tomorrow come faster."

"Are you excited about Christmas this year, Alicia?"

"I sure am!" Alicia thought of the box that had arrived a week earlier. She had seen nothing more of it since her father had taken it to the cellar, nor had there been any mention of it. "I can hardly wait to see what's in the packages that Aunt Hilda sent."

"Aunt Hilda sent us more than wrapped presents," Sarah told her. "Don't forget about the envelope."

"I wonder what was in it," Alicia said, remembering her parents' reaction when they'd looked inside. "It was definitely more than a letter."

"It was money," Sarah informed her.

"I suppose it might have been," Alicia said thoughtfully.

"It was."

"How do you know?"

"I know," Sarah's voice dropped to a whisper, "because I heard Mama talking to Aunt Helen about it. That's why I can hardly wait for morning. This isn't going to be any ordinary Christmas. It's going to be the best Christmas we ever had!"

"What did Mama tell Aunt Helen?" Alicia asked, feeling guilty for asking, yet longing to know.

"Mama told Aunt Helen that Daddy's sister in Germany – that would be Aunt Hilda – sent gifts for everyone and that she sent enough money for a *real Christmas.* Apparently Aunt Hilda told Daddy that she wanted you and I to have the kind of Christmas she and Daddy had when they were children, and she sent enough money to be sure it happened."

"Are you sure?" Alicia asked.

"I'm certain," Sarah responded. "I don't know how much money she sent, but it must have been quite a bit. Mama told Aunt Helen that she and Daddy had a long talk about the money. They both thought that with circumstances what they are there were a lot of other ways the money could, and maybe should, be used, but they decided that when it was a gift from Aunt Hilda they had to use it in the way she had requested. So Mama went shopping."

Sarah paused.

"She told Aunt Helen she felt like a rich lady buying all the things she did, but that she also felt sad thinking that so much money was being spent for just one day."

"What did Aunt Helen say?" Alicia asked.

Sarah laughed. "You know Aunt Helen. She told Mama to stop worrying. She said that God had used Aunt Hilda to provide us with a marvellous Christmas and that she should be grateful for it and enjoy it.

"She said that God had taken care of them in Scotland, that He was taking care of them now, and that He would continue to take care of us in the years ahead – maybe not as well as He did this Christmas – but that He would still take care of us."

"But Mama said that if things didn't get better next year and there wasn't enough food, she was worried that we wouldn't understand how we could have so much at Christmas and so little the rest of the year."

"That makes sense," Alicia said.

"And Aunt Helen told her that twenty years from now we won't remember the lean meals the rest of the year — all we'll remember will be the feast we had this Christmas!"

"Ooh, this is so exciting," Alicia told Sarah. "I think we should stop talking and go to sleep, or tomorrow will never come."

"You're right, 'Licia. We're not going to talk no more, more, more!"

Both girls giggled as Sarah's words brought back memories from their younger years.

Alicia was almost asleep when Sarah spoke again.

"Alicia."

"Uh-huh."

"It's nice to be sharing a room again."

Alicia smiled. It was nice, but she got more sleep when she slept alone.

When Alicia wakened on Christmas morning, Sarah had already risen and gone downstairs. She dressed quickly and hurried down to join the others. The aroma that greeted her as she descended the stairs made her mouth water.

"What are you cooking, Mama?" she asked, after she had wished her mother a Good Morning and a Merry Christmas.

"I'm cooking the Christmas goose," Mama replied; a radiant smile lighting up her face.

"It smells wonderful!" Alicia could not remember the last time they'd had a goose for Christmas. Perhaps they'd never had a goose before. She wasn't sure.

"You can have Muffets for breakfast," Mama told her. "The rest of the family have already eaten. We let you sleep in."

Alicia blushed. She was probably the only young person in the entire city who managed to sleep in on Christmas morning.

"The rest of our relatives should be here soon," Mama went on. "We'll open the gifts when they arrive, then have our big dinner at noon."

Sarah came into the kitchen as Alicia was finishing her breakfast.

"Merry Christmas, Alicia. You were certainly a sleepyhead this morning," she teased.

"I wouldn't have slept in if you hadn't kept talking all night," Alicia informed her. She looked around to see if anyone else was listening. "I'm glad you told me what you did."

Sarah nodded. "Have you looked in the living room yet?" she asked, changing the subject.

When Alicia shook her head, Sarah grabbed her arm. Tugging gently, she led her to the doorway of the room. Alicia gasped in delight.

"It's beautiful!" she exclaimed. "I've never seen anything like it, except in the window at Eaton's or Simpson's."

She stared at the scene before her. Where there had been an empty corner yesterday, a tree now stood. It was lit with candles, decorated with strings of popcorn, and adorned with ornaments.

"No wonder we were sent to bed early last night," Alicia commented. Their parents and Uncle Adolph must have been busy for hours constructing the elaborate display.

"The candles and the ornaments on the tree came from Germany," Sarah told her. "And guess what? The ornaments are chocolate, so when Christmas is over we get to eat them!"

Alicia looked at her sister, wondering if she was teasing again. She went over and touched one of the foil wrapped ornaments. She had never heard of anything so wonderful. Her eyes moved from the decorations on the tree to the presents stacked beneath it.

"They're not all for us. I checked," Sarah informed her.

Alicia laughed.

"I would hope not," she told her sister. "There are far too many gifts there for just our small family."

The ringing of the doorbell interrupted their conversation, and Alicia and Sarah moved together to answer it.

The remainder of the day passed in a whirl. The house echoed with laughter as the families blended together – Grandpa and Grandma Mitchell and Aunt Helen, Aunt Elizabeth, Uncle Andrew and Cousin James, and Uncle Adolph, together with the four of them.

As Mama had promised, the presents were opened before dinner. The gifts sent from Germany included porcelain dolls and books for the children, embroidered hankies and dresser scarves for the ladies and hand-knit socks for the men. Alicia and Sarah received new nightgowns from their parents, a book from Aunt Helen and a hat and mittens from their grandparents.

The goose Mama served at noon was cooked to perfection, and was complemented by creamy mashed potatoes, yams, and canned green beans. Mama's homemade tea biscuits rounded out the main course, followed by raisin pie for dessert. It was more food than Alicia had ever seen in one place!

Dinner was followed by carol singing and games of checkers and crokinole. In the afternoon Mama surprised them by bringing out a small wicker basket filled with oranges, and a bowl full of assorted nuts.

The leftovers from the noon meal were more than sufficient to feed them all again at supper time, although Alicia felt certain that no one would have complained if there had been no supper that night.

When the day was over and the guests had all gone home, a weary Alicia tiptoed upstairs to bed. Sarah was engaged in a game of checkers with Uncle Adolph, but Alicia was too tired to wait for her. Her sister would tease her again in the morning about being a sleepyhead, but she was too tired to care.

Alone in her room, Alicia changed into her soft, flannel nightgown and climbed into bed. A knock sounded at the door as she reached to turn out the lamp, and Mama entered.

"Did you have a good day, Alicia?"

"I had the best Christmas ever, Mama. Thank you so much!"

She frowned when she saw the look on her mother's face.

"What's wrong, Mama?"

"I don't want you to expect every Christmas to be like this one, Alicia," Mama told her. "This was a very special Christmas. We can't expect any more like it."

"I know, Mama," Alicia told her. "I understand."

And thanks to Sarah, she did.

***

Music Lessons

"Trudy has offered to give me music lessons," Alicia announced excitedly one Sunday as the family were finishing their noon meal. An uncomfortable silence followed her proclamation.

"I'd like to learn to play the piano," she continued, when no one commented. Her parents looked at each other.

"Your mother and I will discuss the idea and will give you our decision later," Daddy told her.

"You know they're not going to let you do it," Sarah informed Alicia after dinner.

"Why not?" Alicia asked.

"I can think of two good reasons," Sarah responded. "We don't have a piano for you to practice on and we don't have any money to pay Trudy for teaching you."

"I don't think she wants money," Alicia said. "I think she just wants to see if she can teach."

The older girl had confided her dream of being a music teacher to Alicia that morning after church.

"My mother used to teach music you know," she'd informed Alicia. "I think I might like to teach too."

"You could start by teaching me," Alicia answered. The two girls giggled, then Trudy paused and looked thoughtful.

"Maybe I could," she answered. "Do you really want to learn?"

"I want to learn someday," Alicia told her, remembering the music she'd heard at the concert when she was younger. She might never be able to play like a concert pianist, but it would give her pleasure to try.

"Why not ask your parents if I can teach you now?" Trudy suggested.

"I will," Alicia had answered.

She'd never dreamt that wanting to take music lessons would cause a stir at home. Now she and Sarah sat on the veranda waiting while Daddy and Mama discussed the idea indoors.

"It shouldn't take this long to decide something so simple," Alicia moaned to Sarah.

"They won't be much longer," Sarah told her.

"How do you know?" Alicia asked.

"Because," Sarah answered with a grin, "if they are, we will be late for Sunday School. Daddy won't allow that to happen."

The words were scarcely out of Sarah's mouth when the door opened and Daddy summoned Alicia inside.

"Your mother and I have discussed your idea," he told her when the three were together. "We are not opposed to you learning to play a musical instrument."

Alicia smiled. Sarah had been wrong! Daddy and Mama were going to let her take piano lessons.

"However..."

With sinking heart, Alicia realized that Sarah had been right after all. Daddy went on to explain in detail the reasons they could not permit her to take lessons at this time. In addition to the two that Sarah had given her, Daddy and Mama had a third one.

"Even if we were in a position to provide you with music lessons, Trudy is too young to be able to teach you properly. Perhaps in time you will be able to learn from someone more qualified to teach."

Alicia nodded, trying hard to hide her disappointment.

The mile long walk to Sunday School did little to ease the sadness she felt over her parents' decision. She felt it was unfair, but she would never have voiced her feelings to her parents.

"Are they going to let you?" Trudy asked eagerly the moment Alicia entered the classroom.

Alicia shook her head.

"Why not?" Trudy whispered.

"I'll tell you after Sunday School," Alicia whispered back. There was not time to get into a discussion now.

When the lesson was finally over and the class was dismissed, Alicia and Trudy met in the hall. Disappointment edged Alicia's voice as she repeated to Trudy the things her father had said earlier.

"I wouldn't think of charging money to teach you!" Trudy exclaimed. "I just want to try teaching so I can see if I'd be any good at it."

"I know," Alicia answered, "but I still don't think Daddy will agree. Besides, we don't have anywhere for me to practice."

She deliberately left out the argument her father had made that Trudy was not qualified to teach.

"Isn't there anyone you know that has a piano you could practice on?" Trudy asked. "A relative maybe, or a neighbour?"

Alicia shook her head. "Grandpa and Grandma don't have a piano," she answered.

"Maybe there's someone else," Trudy encouraged.

Alicia frowned, trying to think of someone she knew well enough to ask if she could practice piano lessons at their home.

"My Aunt Elizabeth has a piano," she said slowly, "but I don't think I could ask to practice there."

"Do you want to learn or don't you?" Trudy asked impatiently.

"I do." Alicia was still not convinced her father would allow it, even if she did find somewhere to practice.

"I'll get my father to talk to your father," Trudy told her. "It might work out yet."

Alicia never knew what was said in the conversation between Trudy's father and her own, but when Daddy returned from the evening service that night, he sought her out.

"I have given the matter of your music lessons further thought," he told her. Alicia waited, hardly daring to hope she would hear the news she wanted so badly to hear.

"Your mother and I are prepared to let you learn from Trudy," he informed her. "You will have weekly lessons at her house after school on Thursdays. On Tuesdays and Saturdays you will practice your lessons at Aunt Elizabeth's house."

"Thank you, Daddy! Thank you!" Alicia exclaimed. She could hardly wait for Thursday to arrive so she could have her first lesson.

"There is one other thing," her father told her. "In return for practising at her home, you will help Aunt Elizabeth with her housework for one hour each Saturday."

Alicia nodded.

"Your music lessons will end immediately if we find that they are interfering with your school work," her father concluded. "Do you understand?"

"Yes, Daddy."

When her father left the room, Alicia lay back on her bed, considering all that had happened. When she left for church this morning she'd had no thought of learning to play the piano till she was older. Now, just hours later, everything was arranged.

She frowned as she considered the trade she was making – one hour of housework for the privilege of practising the piano at her aunt's. She also had to make sure her school work was kept up.

I'm up to the challenge, she thought with a smile. Thursday could not come soon enough.

"How are your music lessons working out?" Sarah asked Alicia a few weeks after her first lesson.

"Pretty good," Alicia answered. "Trudy is a good teacher." She was amazed at how much her teenage friend had taught her already.

"How do you like cleaning for Aunt Elizabeth?" Sarah asked her with a teasing smile.

"It's all right," Alicia answered, and Sarah laughed.

"You don't have to be so discreet, Alicia," she told her. "I've cleaned for Aunt Elizabeth too."

"It's nice to have a little spending money," Alicia reflected, trying to find something positive to say about the situation.

When her aunt had asked her to go from the hour they had originally agreed she would work each Saturday to working three hours each week, she'd had reservations, but the quarter Aunt Elizabeth gave her at the end of each session was a nice compensation for her efforts.

"I thought Mama was a good housekeeper," Alicia told Sarah, "but Aunt Elizabeth is even better."

She laughed as she recalled an incident that had happened the previous Saturday. She had been dusting in the hallway at her aunt's when she heard her name.

"I'm in the hall, Aunt Elizabeth," she called back.

Her aunt entered the hallway.

"You forgot to dry the kitchen floor, Alicia."

Alicia looked down from her perch atop the stool. From that location she was able to reach high enough to dust the tops of the door frames, as her aunt required.

"I'm sorry, Aunt Elizabeth. I don't think I heard you correctly." Alicia stepped down from the stool as she spoke. "Did you say I forgot to dry the kitchen floor?"

"That is exactly what I said, Alicia," her aunt responded.

Alicia stared. She had never heard of drying a floor before. Mama was an excellent housekeeper and she had taught her daughters well, but even Mama didn't dry the floor after she washed it.

"I'm sorry, Aunt Elizabeth," Alicia apologized. She reached to take the drying cloth her aunt held out.

"I wasn't being neglectful," she explained. "It's just that I've never heard of drying a floor before."

"I expect your mother does the same thing at home, even if you are unaware of it," Aunt Elizabeth answered. "It is the only way to ensure that no one slips on a wet floor."

Sarah laughed as her sister recounted the episode to her.

"Mama is thorough," she informed Alicia, "but Aunt Elizabeth is meticulous!"

"I'm finding that out," Alicia laughed. "I'm finding that out!"

***

93

Pineapple Pie

Alicia stared at the bills in her hand, wondering how best to spend them. She counted them again. She had three dollars – three whole dollars! She had never seen that much money before, much less been entrusted with such a large sum.

She glanced at the clock. Her parents' train would be leaving from Union Station any minute now. They were going on a holiday. It was the first holiday they had taken in their entire married lives!

She frowned, wondering if their occasional visits to Uncle Adolph's counted as a holiday.

They don't, she decided. The trips to her uncle's were only overnight excursions, whereas this trip would last an entire week.

Daddy and Mama had given her the money before they left, instructing her to use it wisely.

"This is not just your food allowance," Daddy told her as he handed her the bills. "It is enough for your groceries for the week, plus extra in case of an emergency."

"Be sure you lock the door behind you when you go out," Mama reminded her. "Keep your key with you at all times."

"I will, Mama," Alicia assured her.

"Don't forget to be at Grandpa and Grandma's before dark every night," Mama added.

"I won't, Mama," Alicia replied.

"If only Sarah were here to stay with you," Mama fretted.

Sarah was engaged for the summer working at a camp north of the city and would not return until late August. Meanwhile, an opportunity had arisen for Daddy and Mama to spend a full week with friends in Montreal, but Mama had been reluctant to leave Alicia on her own.

At last a compromise had been reached. Alicia would spend the nights with Grandpa and Grandma Mitchell and Aunt Helen, but would be allowed to spend the days on her own.

The clock on the mantle struck two, and Alicia turned to look at it.

I have hours yet before I need to go to Grandpa and Grandma's, she thought. She looked around. The house seemed big and empty without the presence of her parents or her sister. *Perhaps I should go for a walk.*

She started to pack an overnight bag, then changed her mind.

I'll come back here before I go to Grandpa and Grandma's, she decided.

Alicia left the house with no particular destination in mind, turned at the corner and wandered along Danforth Avenue. She strolled along, window shopping and enjoying the sunshine on her face and the luxury of being out alone.

She stared at the merchandise displayed in the store windows, wondering just how far three dollars would go if she decided to go on a spending spree. She recalled the time that her grandfather had taken her shopping when she was younger. Grandpa had given her a nickel with the promise that she could buy anything she wanted with it. He had expected her to request candy or ice-cream, but Alicia had asked if she might buy grapes instead. The nickel had purchased a pound of grapes, providing a treat for the entire family.

If five cents could buy a pound of grapes, Alicia thought, *I wonder just how far three dollars would go if I wanted to spend it all.* She pictured herself struggling home, arms laden with the purchases she might make.

I can't do that, she chided herself. *This money has to last all week.*

She was about to turn from temptation and go to the park when her senses were captured by a pleasant aroma. Thoughts of an afternoon at Withrow Park were abandoned as she followed the scent to the bakery down the street.

The wondrous assortment of baked goods displayed there, coupled with the aroma drifting out through the open door, made Alicia's mouth water. She went inside to survey the goods offered. A clerk came forward.

"Are you shopping for your mother, lass?"

"No, ma'am," Alicia answered, looking at the goods as she spoke. "I'm mostly just window shopping today."

"Window shopping is usually done through the window," the lady replied, a broad smile creasing her plump face. Alicia smiled back.

"That's true," she said, "but something smelled so good in here that I just had to come in and find out what it was."

"Would you like to try one of our cookies?" the clerk asked.

"No, thank you, ma'am, I couldn't," Alicia responded, embarrassed. "But I thank you for the offer."

"We offer broken cookies as samples," the clerk explained, indicating a plate of partial cookies nearby on the counter.

Alicia blushed. She had misinterpreted the woman's offer.

"Help yourself," the lady encouraged her.

Alicia reached for one of the crumbled cookie specimens and popped it into her mouth. The buttery shortbread sample melted in her mouth.

"That was delicious," she told the clerk when she finished it. "Thank you."

"I'm glad you liked it. Perhaps you would like a dozen to take home?"

"I don't think I'll buy cookies today," Alicia answered, thinking that Mama and Daddy would not be pleased if she spent her food allowance on cookies. "I think I will buy a loaf of bread today."

She smiled. A loaf of bread was a purchase Mama would approve of.

Alicia handed the lady one of her bills and watched carefully as she counted out ninety-four cents in change. She was leaving the store when she spotted a pineapple pie in the window. She had never had pineapple pie before, but this one looked so good it made her want to try it. It looked absolutely scrumptious. She turned back to the clerk.

"How much is the pineapple pie?"

"Twenty-five cents."

Alicia thanked her and left the bakery. She stopped at two more stores on her way home to purchase meat and cheese to go with her loaf of bread.

This sandwich is good, Alicia thought as she ate supper at home before going to her grandparents' house, *but I'd rather be eating a pineapple pie!*

The thought of the pie she had seen plagued Alicia all week as she went back and forth to Grandpa and Grandma's house. She longed to buy it, but found it hard to justify spending so much money on just one item. Why, that one pie cost more than four loaves of bread!

But I bet it tastes better than four loaves of bread, she thought with a giggle. She sobered. *I'll wait and see how much money I have left at the end of the week,* she decided. *Then, if I have enough left, I might buy a pineapple pie if they still have one.*

When she woke from her last night at Grandpa and Grandma's house, Alicia counted her money before setting out for home.

Daddy and Mama will be pleased, she thought.

She still had most of the money they'd given her. She had taken breakfast with her grandparents each morning and Grandma had invited her back for supper a few evenings. This meant that she had more money left than she had expected.

I think I'll walk by the bakery on my way home, she decided. *They just might have a pie that wants to go home with me.*

A short time later she left the bakery, the boxed pie held securely in her hands.

This will be a nice treat for Mama and Daddy when they come home, she thought. She envisioned the three of them enjoying the pie while her parents told her all about their week away.

I'll just have a little taste to see what it's like while I wait for them to get home, Alicia decided when she arrived back at the house. She untied the string on the box, opened it and cut into the pie.

Her parents returned hours later to find Alicia lying on the lounge in the living room looking pale. When she complained of a stomach ache, her mother bundled her off to bed.

"I knew we shouldn't have gone and left you alone, with no one here to care for you and to ensure that you had proper meals," Mama commented as she tucked her in.

Alicia sighed. There was no way she would ever admit to her mother that her stomach ache was not from lack of food, but from eating an entire pineapple pie by herself in one day!

***

Polio Epidemic

"I think things are getting a little better, don't you Sarah?" Alicia asked her sister.

The girls were sitting on the porch enjoying the early morning sun. Sarah had returned from her work at the summer camp three weeks earlier than expected, after a child there had been struck with *infantile paralysis.*

"Daddy's new job must pay well," Alicia continued. Their parents still made it a policy not to discuss their father's earnings with the girls, but there were obvious signs that things were a little easier for them. Mama served meat several times each week now instead of just on Sunday, and they had begun using butter instead of bacon drippings on their bread.

"I don't think it's Daddy's new job, although I'm sure that helps," Sarah stated bluntly. "I think it's the inheritance they got."

Alicia's eyes grew big at her sister's words.

"Where would Mama and Daddy get an inheritance from?" she asked.

"One of Mama's relatives in Scotland died," Sarah explained, "and left Mama some money. I don't know how much it was, but I heard Mama say it was a nice little nest egg and that if they were careful it would see them through till times got better."

Alicia wondered how it was that Sarah always seemed to know what was going on and she didn't. How was it that Sarah overheard so much and Alicia never overheard anything of importance?

"You just have to keep your ears open wide and your mouth closed tight," Sarah commented, making Alicia wonder if she also read minds. "It's amazing what you find out that way."

"Why wouldn't Mama tell us if one of her relatives died?" Alicia asked, still trying to absorb what Sarah had told her.

"She didn't tell us because we never knew them," Sarah responded.

Alicia said nothing, but privately she questioned the wisdom of Sarah's words. Surely their mother would feel sad if a relative had died. Wouldn't it help to share it with her family and allow them to comfort her?

"How did you think they were able to take that holiday this summer?" Sarah asked. "Daddy didn't even start his new job till after they got back."

Alicia considered what Sarah said. It made sense. She had wondered why Mama and Daddy had suddenly chosen to go away, when they had never done so before, but she had not questioned it. Now she was beginning to understand.

"So when did this happen?" she asked.

"I don't know," Sarah shrugged. "Sometime last year, I guess."

"And you're just telling me now?" Alicia looked at Sarah, wondering why she was always the last to know everything.

"I honestly never thought to tell you," Sarah answered. "I wasn't keeping it a secret. I'd forgotten all about it till you said things were better."

"Does Mama know you know?" Alicia asked.

"No."

"I won't say anything then," Alicia assured her. She would have liked to tell Mama she was sorry about the relative that had died, but she couldn't do so without revealing what her sister had just told her.

And that would never do!

"I believe the time has come for our girls to experience the C.N.E." Daddy announced at supper that evening. The look of concern that registered on Mama's face at the words made it obvious to Alicia that their father had not discussed his idea with their mother before presenting it.

"Do you really think that's wise, Paul?"

Alicia and Sarah exchanged glances. Mama never called their father Paul when they were around! Alicia resumed eating, remembering her sister's advice to keep her ears wide open and her mouth closed tight if she wanted to find out things.

"I think the girls are old enough to appreciate the exhibits," Daddy answered. "We've never been able to take them before. I think this year would be a good time to go."

He turned to the girls, completely unaware that he had misread his wife's concern.

"What do you think, girls? Would you like to go to the Canadian National Exhibition this year?"

"Oh, yes Daddy, please," Sarah answered.

"Can we really?" Alicia asked. She had heard about the wonders of the C.N.E. from her school mates, but had never dreamt that she might actually get there herself.

"Paul!"

All heads turned to look at Mama. Alicia had never heard her mother speak in such a manner. She wondered what objection Mama might possibly have to them attending the exhibition.

Perhaps it is the money, she thought. *That is what has always kept us away in the past.* School aged children were admitted free, but her parents never would have considered allowing the children to go alone. A trip to the C.N.E. would involve the cost of at least one adult admission, as well as the transit fare there and back.

She thought of the inheritance Sarah had told her about. Maybe it was gone, or was running low. Perhaps it had not been as large as Sarah had thought. Maybe Daddy's employment was unstable again.

Her attention was drawn back to the table when Mama spoke again.

"I have no objection to Sarah and Alicia attending the C.N.E., Paul. I might even enjoy going myself." She attempted a smile. "My concern is over the crowds that will be at the event."

"I'll keep the girls with me at all times," Daddy assured her. "I'll see that nothing happens to them."

Mama sighed. It would be necessary to be more specific about her concerns.

"I am afraid the girls might be exposed to polio," she said quietly. "One never knows how many infected people may be present at such a venue."

She turned to her daughters.

"Your father and I will tell you later whether or not you will be going."

Alicia stared. It was all she could do to keep her mouth shut. This was the first time in her entire life that she had ever seen Mama overrule something Daddy said. This polio thing must be serious indeed if it had her mother so frightened.

"It looks like we won't be going to the C.N.E. after all," Sarah commented a few days before the event started. Public advisories had been issued, encouraging parents to keep their children away from the exhibition. She sighed. "And this was supposed to be the best year ever!"

"I don't mind missing the C.N.E. so much," Alicia replied. "After all, we've never been before, so it's not really such a big thing if we miss it. What bothers me is that school might not be starting on time this year!"

"I don't mind if school is late starting," Sarah remarked glibly. "A few extra days off are fine with me."

"What if it isn't just a few days, Sarah? What if it's weeks?"

"It won't be weeks, 'Licia. They can't keep the schools closed for weeks! We'd have to continue right through the summer next year if they did."

"This polio epidemic is pretty serious," Alicia commented.

Sarah nodded.

"It scares everyone because they don't know how to prevent it." She looked at her sister. "Mama is terrified one of us will get it."

"I know."

Their lives had become greatly restricted of late. Mama insisted that they stay at home, away from possible exposure to the disease.

"She even kept us home from church last Sunday! I don't think that has ever happened before. Usually we have to be really sick to miss Sunday services."

"If this keeps up there may be no services anyway," Sarah told her.

"Why not?"

"It's been recommended that there be a ban on public gatherings," Sarah explained. "A church service is considered a public gathering."

Which meant, Alicia thought, that Sarah's prediction of school being delayed only a few days could be wrong. If there was talk of prohibiting public gatherings, the fear of polio still loomed large.

"It's just not fair that this would happen the year I begin high school," Alicia moaned.

They were mid-way through the month of September and still there was no word of when school would start. Alicia was disappointed over the delay. She had looked forward to her first day of high school all summer, and felt cheated now that it had been postponed.

"There are some things in life that we can change," Mama reminded her, "and other things that we have no control over. It is always wisest to concentrate our energy on the things we can change, rather than fretting over the things we cannot do anything about."

"I know, Mama," Alicia said. "I can't help feeling disappointed though."

Her spirits lifted when her father came home that night with news that they might soon resume lessons, even though there was still no date set for the schools to re-open.

"How is that possible?" she asked.

"The school board is working to set up a system whereby students could work on their own at home, doing assignments that will be printed in the newspaper," Daddy informed her.

It was near the end of September that Daddy came home with a newspaper in his hand.

"Your assignments are here," he told Alicia and Sarah.

The girls took the paper from him eagerly, and moved to the table to search for their work.

"You'll need these also," their father informed them, handing them the necessary textbooks for their studies.

As the newspaper assignments continued, Alicia and Sarah finished each one quickly, then wished there were more.

"I can't believe how quickly we can do these assignments at home," Alicia told her sister, "when it takes all day to do the same work at school."

Sarah laughed.

"We're not doing the same thing we would be doing at school," she told Alicia. "We're doing condensed work. There'll be a lot more work waiting for us when we get back to school."

"I wondered how high school could be easier than public school," Alicia laughed.

When word came that school was finally ready to open, both girls cheered. They were more than ready for their holiday to end!

"I never thought my first day of high school would be the day after Thanksgiving instead of the day after Labour Day!" Alicia told Sarah as they walked to school on the first day of the revised school year.

"I expect we will remember the summer of '37 as the longest summer ever," Sarah commented.

"I expect we will," Alicia agreed with a laugh.

***

Renewed Acquaintances

Alicia's knees trembled as she started up the steps to her new school. Whether it was from excitement or fear, she wasn't certain. Either way, she was grateful for the presence of her older sister.

Sarah had been attending high school for three years now, and knew her way around every part of the large brick building. Though Sarah's classes would be in a different area than her own, it was nice to know she was not far away if she were needed.

They entered the building together, and Sarah escorted Alicia to her classroom before leaving her on her own. She felt out of place as she stood in the hallway waiting to enter the room. She noticed a few others standing alone, as she was, but most of those around her were in groups of two or three.

There were some familiar faces from her old school, but there were more that were strangers. Of those that she knew, there were none she counted as friends.

I guess I've been careful about forming friendships since Martha left, Alicia thought. She was thinking that high school might be a good time to build new relationships when she was bumped from behind.

"Oh, I'm so sorry, really I am."

There was something familiar about the voice issuing the apology.

"It's all right," Alicia assured the other party, turning as she spoke. A smile lit her face as she found herself staring into an old friend's eyes.

"Edna!"

"Alicia?"

Alicia nodded.

"My old camp buddy." Edna stared at her. "You've changed."

"I've grown taller," Alicia answered. She was unaware of any other changes.

"I'm sorry I bumped you," Edna told her. "I was just so excited about getting back to school that I didn't think about where I was going."

Alicia smiled. "I'm sort of glad you bumped into me. If you hadn't, we might have both been finished high school before we met again."

They looked at the crowd milling about them.

"Grade school wasn't like this!" Edna agreed.

The door to the classroom opened.

"Is this your room too?" Edna asked.

"It is," Alicia told her. "It looks like we're going to be in the same class."

They entered the room and were able to find seats close together, but had little opportunity to talk again till the end of the day.

"I'm really glad you're in my class, Edna," Alicia told her when the school day was finished.

"So am I."

The noise in the hallway made it difficult to hear, so the girls waited till they were outside before continuing the conversation.

"Did you go to camp again?" Edna asked, as she stood with Alicia while she waited for Sarah.

"No," Alicia answered. "I only went that one summer. Didn't you go back?"

Edna shook her head sadly.

"I wanted to," she explained, "but I couldn't. It didn't seem fair for me to go two years in a row, when no one else in the family had ever gone. When the next summer came, I asked my parents to let my sister go in my place."

"That was nice of you," Alicia told her, remembering how much Edna had loved camp.

Edna shrugged. "You'd have done the same thing. It's just what sisters do."

"How many brothers and sisters do you have?" Alicia asked, trying to recall what her friend had told her three years earlier. "I think it was seven. Am I right?"

Edna laughed. "You have a good memory. It was seven."

"You said *was*, not *is*." Alicia wondered if something had happened to one of Edna's siblings, but she was afraid to ask.

Edna nodded.

"There's two more now!" she told her. "You'd think my mother was trying to win the baby race, but she wasn't."

Sarah came along before Alicia had opportunity to answer. She introduced her sister to Edna, then bid her friend goodbye and started walking with Sarah.

"Have you ever heard of a baby race?" Alicia asked Sarah as they walked.

Sarah looked at Alicia.

"No," she answered slowly. "Why?"

"It was something Edna said," Alicia told her. "It sounded funny to me, but I didn't have time to ask her about it. She told me there were two new babies at their house since I saw her at camp. Then she said you'd think her mother was trying to win the baby race."

"Maybe it's just a figure of speech that we aren't familiar with," Sarah answered.

"It could be," Alicia agreed. "I'll ask her tomorrow and find out."

The following morning Alicia and Edna met outside the school.

"Do you mind if I ask you something?" Alicia asked, after the two had exchanged greetings.

"Of course not," Edna replied. "What is it?"

"You said something yesterday that I'm curious about," Alicia told her. "I don't know if what you said is just an expression that I've never heard before, or if it really means what it sounds like."

Edna looked puzzled. "What did I say?"

"You said something about a baby race," Alicia said. "What did you mean by that?"

Edna laughed.

"I guess you haven't heard. There's some lawyer who died a while back. I don't know what his first name was, but his last name was Miller."

Alicia stared. "The same as my last name?"

"Exactly," Edna told her, "although I doubt that you are related.

"Anyway, this lawyer was an interesting man with a strange sense of humour. For some reason when he died he left most of his money to the woman in Toronto who would have the most babies in the ten years following his death."

"That's a strange thing to do."

"It is," Edna agreed, "but a lot of women wanted to win. I think he was pretty wealthy."

"So that's what you meant when you said a baby race?" Alicia asked.

"That's what I meant," Edna told her.

The bell rang, summoning them to class. Alicia smiled. She was grateful she hadn't shared her thoughts about the baby race with anyone. Her sister would have teased her if she'd told her she pictured a group of babies lined up in their prams, being raced through the street. Even Edna would have laughed. *Sometimes it is better to keep one's thoughts to oneself,* she thought with a smile.

***

Family Secrets

"Mama, are we related to a lawyer named Mr. Miller?"

Without even pausing to consider Alicia's question, Mama responded. "No, dear. We are not related."

Alicia wondered how her mother could be so sure.

"Perhaps we are a distant relation?" she persisted.

"No, dear," Mama replied. "Mr. Miller is not a relative of ours."

"How do you know, Mama? You didn't even ask what his first name was."

"What is Mr. Miller's first name, Alicia?" Mama asked patiently.

"I don't know," Alicia admitted. "I just thought you couldn't know whether or not you are related to someone if you didn't even know their first name."

"We have no Miller relatives in Canada, dear."

Mama smiled as she said the words, but it was clear she considered the conversation finished.

Alicia considered asking her father the same question just to be sure, but decided such a move would not be wise when Mama had seemed so certain. As it turned out, her father was the one who sought her out later in the day.

"I understand you were asking Mama if we are related to a Mr. Miller," he told her.

"Yes, Daddy, I was," Alicia answered. "Mama told me we aren't related."

"Your mother is correct." He looked at her for a moment. "How old are you now, Alicia?"

"I'm thirteen," she responded, thinking it was a strange question for her father to ask.

"Yes," Daddy answered. He looked thoughtful. "You are thirteen and Sarah is sixteen."

"That's right."

This is one of the strangest conversations I've ever had with Daddy, she thought.

"Fetch your sister, Alicia," Daddy said suddenly. "Then come to the living room. I have something I wish to tell you both."

Alicia hurried off to do as he had requested.

"Daddy wants to see us both in the living room," she told Sarah when she located her. "Something strange is going on."

"Why do you say that?" Sarah asked. She looked at her. "Did you do something bad, Alicia?"

Usually it was Sarah who was summoned to speak with their father.

"I don't think so," Alicia answered. "All I did was ask Mama if we were related to that lawyer named Mr. Miller, and now Daddy wants to talk to us both."

"That doesn't sound too serious," Sarah told her. "Let's go find out what this is about."

"It sounds serious to me. You didn't see the look on Daddy's face when he told me to get you."

Alicia followed her sister down the stairs. Their father was waiting for them in the living room. He stood in front of the mantle, staring thoughtfully at a picture of his childhood home. He turned when they entered the room.

"Sit down, girls."

They did as their father instructed, expecting him to do the same, but Daddy remained standing. His gaze turned once more to the picture above the mantle.

Alicia and Sarah exchanged glances. Their father looked troubled. They wondered why, but they both knew better than to ask. Instead they waited silently. Daddy would speak when he was ready.

Time ticked by slowly. Alicia was beginning to wonder how much longer Sarah would be able to wait, when their father turned. He took a seat across from them, and began to speak.

"No doubt you are wondering why you have been summoned, Sarah," he said to his elder daughter.

110

Sarah nodded.

"And you, Alicia, are likely wondering how the simple question you asked your mother earlier could lead to this meeting now."

It was Alicia's turn to nod.

"Alicia asked Mama today if we were any relation to a lawyer named Mr. Miller," Daddy explained to Sarah. He turned to Alicia.

"I assume you are speaking of the lawyer who died some years back, leaving a large inheritance to the woman in the city who would have the most babies in the next decade?" he asked.

Alicia nodded.

"First," Daddy told them, "we are not related. That Mr. Millar spelled his name with an 'a', ours is spelled with an 'e'.

"Mr. Millar was an interesting man," he went on. "Some people have labelled him as eccentric. The stork derby, as I have heard it called, was only one of a number of strange provisions Charles Vance Millar made in his will.

"None of which we will discuss," he added, noting the looks of interest his comment brought to his daughter's faces.

"In fact," he told them, "we are not here to discuss Mr. Millar at all. Alicia's question about him has simply brought on a discussion I have put off far too long."

There was a lengthy pause.

"What I am about to tell you," their father said firmly, "will be discussed today and then forgotten. There is no need to ever speak of it again. Do you understand?"

"Yes, Daddy," Sarah answered promptly.

"Alicia?"

"Yes, Daddy."

Alicia watched as her father rose and moved back to the mantle. Staring at the picture above it, he asked, "Have you ever wondered why my name is different than your grandfather's?"

"I've never really thought about it," Sarah answered.

"It is different," their father went on, as if Sarah had not spoken, "because I changed my name."

He turned to face them. Still standing, he said, "I was not born Paul Miller. I was born Gottlob Müller."

Sarah gasped.

"I changed my name before you were born, Sarah. It was during the war and it was a difficult time. I believed at the time that it was a wise move to separate myself from anything of German origin, including my name. I still believe I made a wise choice. And that," he told them, "is why your mother was able to say with such certainty that we were not related to Mr. Millar. We bear no relation to anyone with the Miller surname, in Canada or elsewhere."

Alicia and Sarah stared as their father left the room. It really hadn't been a discussion, at all, Alicia thought, but it certainly had been a revelation!

***

Important News

"Can you keep a secret?" Sarah whispered. Alicia nodded.

"What is it?" she whispered back.

"I think Grandpa and Grandma are going to move in with us."

Alicia stared in surprise.

"I overheard Daddy and Mama talking," Sarah went on. "Mama said that if they did, it would only be temporary, but Daddy said that given their age and the state of their health, he expected the move to be a permanent one."

"Would Aunt Helen come too?"

"I don't know." Sarah thought for a moment. "I expect she would. She's lived with Grandpa and Grandma all her life. I can't imagine her living anywhere else."

"Unless she decided to get married," Alicia whispered. Both girls giggled. Neither of them could imagine their aunt ever marrying.

"Why are they moving?" Alicia asked.

"Grandpa and Grandma are getting older and they need someone to help care for them," Sarah told her.

"But they have Aunt Helen," Alicia protested.

Sarah shook her head.

"Aunt Helen works. She can't be with them all the time," she told Alicia, repeating the words she had heard her mother say a short time earlier. "Mama is home all day and could care for them while Aunt Helen is working. I expect Aunt Helen would help in the evenings if she came with them."

"We're old enough to help too," Alicia said. "Mama and Aunt Helen shouldn't have to do all the care giving. I wouldn't mind spending time with Grandpa and Grandma and helping them if I could."

"It's more likely you and I will get stuck with the extra dishes and the cleaning than spending time with our grandparents," Sarah retorted.

"Where will everyone sleep?" Alicia asked, ignoring the sharp remark.

"That's the problem. This house isn't big enough for seven people." Sarah sighed. "Mama plans to give Grandpa and Grandma the big room at the back of the house overlooking the garden. I expect Mama and Daddy will take my room and I'll move in with you.

"I heard Mama tell Daddy she was certain we wouldn't mind sharing a room again."

Alicia looked around the room. Hers was the smallest of the three bedrooms. She remembered how Sarah had teased her when they'd moved into the house, telling her that because she was the little one she got the little room. It was hard to imagine sharing this space with her sister.

"It will be crowded, but I guess it will be okay," she told Sarah, secretly wishing there were some other option.

"It shan't be for long," Sarah replied.

"I thought you said the move was likely to be permanent." Alicia said the words in a way that sounded more like a question than a statement.

"I expect it will be."

"Then how is it that we wouldn't be sharing a room for very long?" Alicia questioned.

"Because I expect to be leaving soon." Sarah's words hit Alicia like a splash of cold water.

"Do you mean you're moving out?"

Her sister nodded.

"On your own?"

"On my own," Sarah stated firmly.

"Why?"

"Because it's time," Sarah told her. "I'm seventeen years old. It's time I was on my own earning my way in the world and living by my own rules instead of someone else's."

"But you haven't finished high school yet," Alicia protested. She chose to ignore her sister's reference to the tension that arose occasionally between Sarah and her father over household rules.

"I don't need to," Sarah informed her. "I've learned everything I need to know already. I'd rather be working."

Sarah looked at Alicia and her voice lost some of its bravado.

"Please don't tell Mama and Daddy what I said," she begged. "I'll tell them myself when the time is right."

"When will that be?" Alicia wondered how long she would have to keep her sister's secret.

"I'll wait till I have a job, so I can pay for room and board someplace," Sarah answered. "Promise you won't say anything. Please, 'Licia."

"I promise." Alicia was uneasy about the idea of keeping such information from her parents, but she was unable to resist her sister's plea. She looked at Sarah and nodded.

"I won't say a word," she vowed. "I'll let you tell them when you are ready."

The look of relief on Sarah's face was evidence to Alicia that she was doing the right thing.

"I'll keep your secret, but you have to promise me something too, Sarah. You have to promise that you won't leave until you have a good job and a nice room to rent," Alicia told her.

"I promise."

"I'm going to miss you when you leave, Sarah," Alicia said earnestly.

"If Grandpa, Grandma and Aunt Helen all move in, the house will be so full you won't have room to miss me," Sarah told her with a laugh.

"It won't be the same without you here," Alicia protested.

"Things aren't supposed to stay the same, 'Licia," Sarah informed her. "Life is all about growing and changing."

I wish it weren't, Alicia thought as Sarah left the room. *I'd like things to stay like this forever.*

Word of the change about to take place in their household was announced that evening at supper. After the conversation with her sister, Alicia was not surprised when Daddy informed them that their grandparents and their aunt would be moving in to the house. What came as a surprise were the planned sleeping arrangements.

"Grandpa and Grandma will have the big room at the back of the house," Mama informed them. "Aunt Helen will have the room at the front and you girls will share Alicia's room."

"But where will you and Daddy sleep?" Alicia asked.

"Your father and I will be sleeping in the living room," Mama replied. The statement was made in a matter-of-fact tone that implied that it was normal for the heads of the household to sleep on a davenport in the living room while everyone else in the house had the luxury of a bed.

"When will they be coming?" Sarah asked.

"They will be here by the end of the month," Mama answered.

Alicia nudged Sarah. The end of the month was only a week away!

"We have much to do to prepare for their arrival," Mama told them. "I will be counting on both of you to help me get ready, and to make them feel welcome when they arrive."

***

Cramped Quarters

"I never realized how tiny this room was, 'Licia."

Sarah was standing in front of her sister's closet, struggling to find hanging space for her dresses. The days had been filled with activity since the decision to move their grandparents in had been announced.

"It wouldn't be so bad if Aunt Helen wasn't coming too."

"That's an awful thing to say, Sarah!" Alicia was shocked at her sister's words.

"Why?"

"If you think about what you said, you'll know why, Sarah." It was not often that she stood up to her older sibling, but a comment like this one could not be ignored.

"I said it wouldn't be so bad if Aunt Helen weren't coming too," Sarah repeated. She looked at Alicia. "What's wrong with saying that?"

Alicia said nothing, giving her sister time to think it over.

"Oh!" Sarah's hand flew up to cover her mouth and her cheeks reddened as she realized how the words had sounded.

"I didn't mean it that way, 'Licia. I love Aunt Helen."

"I know you do," Alicia said quietly. "You and Aunt Helen have a special relationship."

She sounded wistful.

It isn't that I'm jealous, she thought. *It's just that sometimes I feel left out when Aunt Helen and Sarah are together.*

Of all their relatives, Aunt Helen was the one most like Sarah, and the one who understood her best.

"I have Aunt Helen and you have Aunt Sadie," Sarah answered. Alicia nodded. She did have a special bond with Aunt Sadie. It was not the same as Sarah and Aunt Helen, nor could it be when Aunt Sadie lived so far away.

"What I meant," Sarah went on, "was that because Aunt Helen is coming too we are merging two entire households into one. It's not that I don't want Grandpa and Grandma or Aunt Helen here. It's not them I mind, it's all the stuff they'll bring with them!"

"I never thought about that part of it," Alicia said. "Do you think they'll bring everything?"

Her mind whirled as she considered the possibility. Grandpa and Grandma's home was the same size as their own; and it was just as full of furniture! How could they possibly fit it all into the house along with what they already had?

"I expect they'll bring everything," Sarah answered.

"Where will we put it all if they do?" Alicia looked around. There was no space for anything extra to be placed in her small room.

"Uncle Andrew and James are going to help Daddy move some of our furniture to the cellar," Sarah informed Alicia. "When the other bedrooms are empty, you and I get to help Mama clean them."

Alicia sighed.

"It won't be so bad with the three of us doing the work," Sarah encouraged.

"I know," Alicia responded. "It isn't the idea of cleaning that makes me feel sad. It's the idea of storing all our furniture in a cold, damp cellar to make room for someone else's belongings."

She sighed again. Her father had built most of the furnishings for the three bedrooms. It didn't seem right that they should be put in storage.

"I guess we should be thankful we have a cellar to store it in," Sarah commented. "Besides, it can't be that bad a place to keep things. If it was, Mama would never have packed all our extra clothes and put them down there."

"I suppose you're right," Alicia agreed.

In preparation for their houseguests, their mother had gone through all the girls' clothing with them. Anything out of season had been set apart. After it was neatly folded, it had been packed in boxes and labelled before being taken to the cellar.

"Do you think we'll be ready in time?" Alicia asked.

"Of course we will," Sarah answered confidently. "How could we not be ready when Mama is in charge of packing and sorting at both houses?"

They laughed. If anyone could get things done quickly and efficiently, it was Mama.

Sarah was right, as usual, Alicia thought as she watched her aunt and her grandparents' belongings being unloaded two days later. *Everything is ready!*

She glanced across the room at her grandmother, wondering if she should attempt to start a conversation with her. Grandma was seated in the rocking chair by the window, keenly observing all the activity. Alicia's grandfather stood on the porch outside.

He was eager to assist but, like a small child, he seemed to be getting in the way more than he was helping. Occasionally one of the men would hand Grandpa one of the lighter boxes and he would carry it proudly up the stairs, happy to be given something to do.

Alicia looked around the living room. At a glance, one would never know they were sitting in her parents' bedroom. The only evidence that the room might be used as sleeping quarters was a small wardrobe for her parents' clothes, which Daddy had discreetly placed in a corner.

"This will be our last move," Grandma said, breaking the silence that hung over the room.

Alicia was surprised by her words.

What do I say in response? she wondered. Alicia rose from her seat and moved to the window. She pulled the small footstool over and sat down beside her grandmother.

"I'm glad you're here, Grandma."

The words seemed inadequate, but it was the only response she could think of. Grandma reached down and took Alicia's hand. She patted it softly.

"So many moves," she murmured. "So many moves."

Before Alicia could think of an answer, Aunt Helen bustled into the room, followed more slowly by Mama. They had been upstairs, supervising the placement of the furniture in the two bedrooms.

"How are you doing, Mother?" Helen asked gently.

"I'm fine, dear," Grandma replied. "I am in good company."

She patted Alicia's hand again.

"Alicia is good company," Mama agreed. She smiled at her daughter, then turned back to her mother. Her voice was soft as she spoke. "I know how hard this is for you, Mother."

"I much prefer doing the work myself to watching someone else do it," Grandma told her.

Helen laughed.

"There's still plenty of work to be done, Mother. Getting the furniture moved was the easy part. There are still all the boxes to unpack."

"Perhaps there is something I can help with?" Grandma's face brightened at the thought.

"Helen and I thought Alicia might assist you with the unpacking," Mama suggested, glancing at Alicia as she spoke.

"That would be lovely." Grandma turned to Alicia. "Would you mind, dear?"

"I'd be happy to help you, Grandma," Alicia told her. She held out her arm to assist her grandmother in getting up. Slowly the two made their way to the hall and ascended the stairs.

The large bedroom at the back of the house looked strange to Alicia now that it was filled with Grandpa and Grandma's belongings instead of her parents. It had seemed open and spacious when her parents occupied it. In comparison the room looked cluttered now, although Alicia supposed that it might have been under-furnished before.

Grandpa and Grandma's bed had been placed on the wall opposite to where Daddy and Mama's had been. Two upholstered chairs sat facing each other by the window, with a small table between them. Other pieces of furniture had been placed wherever they could fit.

I wonder how they will ever manage, Alicia thought as she looked around the room. There was little room to move without bumping into something. Her gaze stopped at a large item that filled most of one wall and she suppressed a giggle. Grandma had even brought her china cabinet!

"It won't look so bad when we get the boxes all unpacked," Grandma commented.

Alicia said nothing. She was too busy helping her grandmother make her way through the narrow path to think of a response.

When Grandma was seated in a chair by the window, Alicia began bringing in the boxes. The hours flew by as she opened each box and unpacked it, following her grandmother's instructions as to where the contents should be placed. By the time Mama summoned them for supper, everything was unpacked but the china.

"We'll leave that for another day, dear," Grandma told Alicia as they began making their way downstairs.

The meal that night was simple, but it was enjoyed by all. Mama served it in the dining room, as there was not enough room for seven people around the kitchen table. The dining room table, normally reserved for special occasions, could be stretched to accommodate ten people. Tonight, however, the room seemed crowded with only seven of them.

I guess we'll get used to it, Alicia thought as she looked at the large group. She had a sudden vision of Edna's family of twelve crowded into a house no bigger than their own. She smiled. Suddenly seven didn't seem like such a large number after all.

***

Rumours of War

"Hitler has invaded again. First he took back the Rhineland, now it is Austria. I don't know where it's going to end if he isn't stopped. If things continue, we'll be drawn into another war before you know it."

Alicia listened to the conversation taking place between Uncle Andrew and her father in the next room.

"It appears the German leader has no plans to stop until he takes over the world," Uncle Andrew said.

"Such a thing could never happen," Alicia's father replied calmly.

"I fear it may, unless someone stands up to him," her uncle said soberly.

"The man will listen to reason," Daddy said. "He is, after all, just reclaiming land that once belonged to Germany."

"I beg to differ, Paul," Uncle Andrew asserted. "I believe there is more to Hitler's agenda than reclaiming lost land for Germany. He will not be happy until he controls all of Europe. And after Europe, the world!"

"You exaggerate, Andrew." Daddy's words were harsh, but his tone was soft.

"I don't, Paul. The Führer has absolute control in Germany. His word is law. Surely you know that. I tell you, Paul, we could be on the brink of another war."

"Chamberlain would never allow Britain to be drawn into another war," Alicia's father stated. "He will do everything possible to prevent such an occurrence."

"That may be true," Uncle Andrew replied, "but I fear the day for negotiating may already have passed."

Alicia shuddered. She had learned about the horrors of the Great War at school. Her teacher had told the class that the Great War had been the war that would end all wars. Now her uncle was talking as if there might be another such war.

Was it possible she would someday have stories to tell her children of living through the war years, just as her parents did?

She frowned, trying to recall stories that her parents had told her about the war. Now that she thought about it, she realized they'd told her very little. The only time her parents ever mentioned the war was the day her father had revealed the truth about his name change. She had learned more about the war at school than she had ever heard from her parents.

I'll ask Mama and Daddy about it sometime, she decided as she put her needlework away.

"Do you think there's going to be another war, Daddy?" Alicia asked after Uncle Andrew was gone.

Her father looked up from the book he was reading. He thought for a moment before answering.

"I don't know, Alicia, but I sincerely hope not. I admit there are stirrings in Europe, but I remain hopeful it will all come to nothing."

Alicia nodded, satisfied.

"Thank you, Daddy."

She fell asleep easily that night, reassured by her father's comments. If Daddy expected the friction in Europe to end soon, it was nothing to concern herself over.

As the unrest in Europe continued and rumours of war grew stronger, Alicia decided to get her mother's opinion.

"What was it like during the Great War, Mama?" she asked one day as she worked with her mother in the kitchen. Mama stiffened at the question, and Alicia wondered what memories her words had stirred up.

"It was a difficult time for everyone, Alicia. People suffered everywhere – at home and abroad. The worst suffering, of course, came through the loss of lives."

She stopped speaking, reflecting.

"It is an era I would prefer not to discuss, dear," she told her daughter firmly.

"I understand, Mama."

They worked in silence for a time, then Alicia spoke again.

"May I ask you another question, Mama?"

"Certainly," her mother smiled at her.

"Do you think there's going to be another war, Mama?"

Mama's smile faded at her words, and a sombre look replaced it.

"I fear there may be, Alicia. I pray it will be prevented, but I fear this is one time God may not answer my prayers in the way I would choose."

***

1939-45

The Second World War

Changes

Alicia was not present when Sarah told their parents that she was moving out, so she was unaware of the words that were exchanged. Sarah chose not to share the information with her, and she, in turn, chose to respect her sister's privacy by not asking. The move happened quietly, with just a few days notice before the event.

Perhaps it is better this way, Alicia reflected.

"I'll be back to visit often," Sarah assured Alicia before she left.

"I hope so," Alicia told her. "I sure will miss you!"

The first night without her sister was the hardest. She had grown used to once again sharing a room and found it difficult to get to sleep without Sarah lying beside her. The room seemed suddenly too big, and it was far too quiet.

I've slept alone in this room for years, Alicia thought as she lay in the dark with her eyes wide open. *I welcomed the solitude here. I resented having to share it with Sarah when Grandpa and Grandma moved in. Now I wish she were here.*

A tear escaped and ran down her face. She had never thought she would miss her sister so much.

She saw Sarah the following Sunday at church and was delighted when Mama invited her to join them for dinner. Sarah spent the afternoon with the family, and for a few blessed hours it was as if she had never left.

The girls walked to the young peoples' meeting at church together that evening, and Sarah walked home with Alicia when it was over.

It was not until they reached the walkway that Alicia realized her sister was not coming in with her.

"I'll see you again soon, 'Licia," Sarah told her.

"Aren't you coming in?"

"Not tonight." It was obvious Sarah was eager to be on her way.

"Don't you want to say goodbye to Mama and Daddy?" Alicia asked.

"I said goodbye to them before we left for the service," Sarah responded.

When Alicia started to speak, Sarah broke in.

"I need to go, 'Licia," she said. Her voice dropped to a whisper. "I'm meeting someone and I'm late."

"I see," Alicia answered although, if truth be told, she didn't see at all. Who could her sister possibly be meeting at this hour of the night?

"I'll see you soon, 'Licia," Sarah said again. "I promise." She was gone before Alicia had a chance to respond.

Weeks passed without any contact from Sarah, and Alicia began to grow concerned. She wondered if her sister's absence had been noted by the rest of the family. If it had, no one commented on it. Alicia was disappointed, but not surprised, when Sarah stopped attending the regular Sunday services, but she could not understand why she no longer dropped by the house to visit. Surely her new job did not demand all her time!

She began to wonder if something was amiss and was looking for a way to contact Sarah when she came out of school one day and found her sister waiting for her.

"Sarah!" she exclaimed. "I'm happy to see you again!"

"I'm happy to see you too, 'Licia," Sarah told her.

"Where have you been?" Alicia asked. "It's been a long time since you came by the house. I was beginning to think you'd forgotten all about us."

"I've been busy," Sarah informed her, a slight tinge of red coating her cheeks as she spoke.

"Your work can't keep you that busy!" Alicia answered. "Surely you must get some time off."

"I do," Sarah agreed.

"Then why haven't we seen you?" Alicia demanded. "You said you'd see me soon last time you left," she added reproachfully, "and you didn't!"

"I have other ways to occupy my time off than visiting with family," Sarah told her defensively.

"I'm sorry, Sarah," Alicia said. There was no sense upsetting her sister. "I didn't mean to make you feel bad. I know you're busy and I'm glad you're here now. Are you coming home with me?"

Sarah shook her head.

"I'll walk you part-way," she told her, "but I don't want to come to the house right now."

Alicia longed to ask why, but something about her sister's attitude warned her to wait till Sarah was ready to explain. They walked in silence for a block.

It's strange, Alicia thought, *that after all this time I can't think of a thing to say to Sarah.* The thought saddened her. Were she and her sister drifting apart?

"I want to talk to you about something, Alicia," Sarah said finally. She paused. "But I don't want you to tell anyone else. Can I trust you?"

Alicia nodded. "You know you can," she told her.

"I haven't been home much because I've found someone else I'd rather be with," Sarah confided.

Alicia stared. Whose company could her sister possibly prefer to that of her own family?

"In fact," Sarah went on, "I think I've found the person I want to spend the rest of my life with."

Alicia stopped walking. She looked at Sarah, an unspoken question in her eyes.

"I'm getting married, 'Licia!" Sarah told her excitedly. "I wanted you to be the first to know."

There was a long pause. Alicia grasped for something to say, but her mind was numb. How could Sarah be getting married? She was too young. She was too...her mental list of objections was cut short by her sister's next words.

"I want you to meet him!"

"Meet him?" Alicia asked. She wondered why Sarah had chosen her to be the first person to meet her new friend. Wasn't she supposed to bring him home and introduce him to the family? Wasn't the young man supposed to ask their father's blessing before anything definite was decided? She sighed. Sarah never had done things the conventional way!

"When do you want me to meet him?" she asked.

"Right now," Sarah informed her. She pointed down the street to where a young man stood waiting by a lamp post.

There was no time to compose herself, no time to think of the right things to say or the manner in which to say them before they reached Sarah's friend.

Later, walking home alone, Alicia assessed the situation. The young man seemed very nice, and Sarah appeared happier than she had been in a long time. Both had promised Alicia that she would not have to keep their secret long, and assured her they would speak with her parents soon.

"I don't want a big, fancy wedding," Sarah had commented with a laugh. "I just want to get married."

And if Daddy agrees, Sarah will soon get her wish, Alicia thought. She frowned, wondering what her sister would do if their father didn't agree to the union. *We'll cross that bridge when we get to it,* she decided. She hoped their father would agree. More than anything, she wanted her sister to be happy.

"I can't believe you're really getting married!" Alicia exclaimed, observing her sister as she spoke. Sarah's gown was simple and the guests at the wedding were few, but the smile on the bride's face was radiant.

"I know," Sarah answered. "Just think, 'Licia, in a few minutes I'll be Mrs. Jacob Snider."

"Sarah Snider – Sarah Elizabeth Snider," Alicia said, trying the name out to see how it sounded. She squeezed her sister's arm. "You're sure, Sarah?"

Sarah laughed. "I've never been more sure about anything."

"I'm still trying to figure out how you got Daddy to agree," Alicia whispered.

Sarah smiled. "It took a little persuasion, but he finally consented."

I wonder what Sarah said to change Daddy's mind, Alicia thought. At first their father had been adamant that Sarah was not marrying until she was of age. Then, for no apparent reason, he'd had a change of heart. He had declared that he accepted the idea and had publicly given his blessing.

Now, just weeks later, here they were at Aunt Elizabeth's, surrounded by their family and waiting for the ceremony to begin.

Alicia peeked into the living room, where her aunt had assembled three rows of chairs. Grandpa, Grandma and Aunt Helen were seated in the middle row, while Jake's parents and Mama sat in the front one. Aunt Elizabeth, Uncle Andrew and James were in the back row. Uncle Adolph was in position at the piano, waiting for his signal to start playing.

Jacob stood waiting nervously with the minister by the mantel.

"It's time to take your seat, Alicia."

Alicia turned to see her father standing behind them. She nodded and moved silently to the back row, where she slipped into place beside her cousin.

The music started and all heads turned to the doorway. Daddy extended his arm to Sarah, and slowly escorted her into the room. Together they walked the short distance to where Jacob stood waiting. Alicia watched as her father let go of Sarah's arm and stepped back. She noticed that Daddy waited close by until the minister spoke, asking who gave the bride away.

"I do," her father answered, then solemnly took a seat.

So that's all there is to getting married, Alicia thought as the minister pronounced Jake and Sarah husband and wife moments later. All the time spent fussing and preparing for the event, and it was over almost as quickly as it had begun. It had taken longer to get Sarah properly attired and to fix her hair than it had for the minister to perform the brief ceremony. *I wonder if all weddings are like this,* she thought. Sarah's wedding, simple yet meaningful, was the first she had ever attended.

A family dinner followed the ceremony. When it was over, Sarah and Jake thanked everyone and left for their accommodations a few blocks away. Alicia was disappointed that Sarah was not going on a honeymoon, but her sister seemed untroubled by the fact.

As Alicia helped her aunt clean up, she found herself hoping once again that Sarah had made the right choice.

In the weeks following Sarah's marriage, things settled into a normal routine in the Miller household. Alicia found her life busier than it had ever been and, at moments, found it difficult to cope with it all.

"I feel like I can't keep up with everything," she confided to Edna one day at school.

"Surely your life can't be that busy," Edna answered.

"It really is," Alicia told her. "In addition to my school work, I help Mama with the housework, and I try to spend as much time with Grandpa and Grandma as I can."

She frowned.

"They really aren't very well, you know," she told Edna. "Grandpa is still able to get around fairly well and likes to go for walks with me, but Grandma spends nearly all her time in the house. I try to spend the same amount of time visiting with Grandma as I do going for walks with Grandpa, because it doesn't seem right to spend more time with one of them than the other."

"So you have homework and housework to do, as well as spending time with your grandparents," Edna told her. "That doesn't sound so bad."

"That's not all I do, you know," Alicia reminded Edna. "I have piano lessons, cleaning at Aunt Elizabeth's and my church work."

"Maybe you do have too much going on," Edna reflected. "Maybe you should drop something. If it were me I'd drop the church work."

"Oh, no!" Alicia exclaimed, horrified at the thought. "I could never do that."

"Why couldn't you?" Edna asked. "You've told me yourself how many hours it takes each week."

"I know," Alicia said quietly, "but I still don't want to give it up."

She thought of the preparation she did for her children's Sunday School and mid-week classes. It was time consuming, but what pleasure it brought her to work with the little ones!

"I'd give up anything else before I'd give up my church work," she stated emphatically.

"All right," Edna said. "Let's analyze this. You can't give up school, or helping your mother with the work at home."

Alicia agreed.

"You won't give up your church work."

"That's right," Alicia affirmed.

"Then there's only two things left. If it's really too much for you to keep up with everything, you'll either have to spend less time with your grandparents or give up your music lessons."

Alicia nodded thoughtfully. One of the things she appreciated most about Edna was her practical nature. Whether it came from helping younger brothers and sisters solve their problems or was an inborn quality she did not know, but Edna always had a way of evaluating a situation and helping her sort her priorities.

"I guess," she said slowly, "my music lessons will have to end."

She thought for a moment.

"Yes," she stated firmly, "it will have to be the music lessons that go. I'll tell Trudy on Thursday."

***

Declaration of War

"What day is it today, Alicia?" Grandpa asked, looking up as she entered the room.

"It's the second day of September, Grandpa," Alicia replied. Summer was over and school would begin again in a few days.

"The second of September," Grandpa repeated slowly. "Yesterday was the first."

She nodded.

"Remember that date, Alicia," Grandpa instructed. "September first, nineteen hundred and thirty-nine." He folded the newspaper he had been holding and set it on the table beside him.

The newspaper, once considered a luxury in their household, now appeared daily. Each morning Grandpa would make his journey to the store to purchase it, and every afternoon he would share vital news from it with his granddaughter.

"I'll remember, Grandpa," Alicia assured him, "but why is it so important?"

She watched as her grandfather rose from the chair. His body was slowing with age, but he was determined to remain active, and still walked without the assistance of a cane. When he was standing, he spoke.

"Would you care to go for a walk, Alicia?"

She smiled. She had grown used to her grandfather answering her questions in his own time.

"I'd like that," she told him. "I'll just let Mama and Grandma know we are going out."

Moments later, the two left the house together. It was not until they had reached the end of the street and turned at her old elementary school that Grandpa spoke again.

"I told you to remember the first of September, Alicia," he informed her, "because I believe that is the date that will go down in history as the beginning of a major war – so major, in fact, that it may someday be known as a second world war."

Alicia felt a chill at the words, but she said nothing in response. Her walks with her grandfather had taught her that she learned far more by listening than she did by talking.

"The news today," Grandpa went on, "is that Germany invaded Poland yesterday."

"The first of September," Alicia commented, realizing now the significance of the date.

"The first of September in the year of our Lord nineteen hundred and thirty-nine," Grandpa affirmed.

"I believe," he went on, "that single event will be the one that finally pushes Britain into action. I believe Germany's invasion of Poland will cause Britain to declare a state of war."

He shook his head sadly.

"I never thought I would live to see the day."

Alicia said nothing. She continued walking with him in companionable silence.

Grandpa reached over and took her arm. Whether it was because he was tired physically and needed the support, or simply because he wanted the touch of her hand on his, she wasn't sure. She waited, knowing he had more to tell her.

"We were fortunate, you know, Alicia," he said. "We took the opportunity to emigrate when it was given."

There was a long pause.

"We almost didn't come, you know."

Should I say something in response? Alicia wondered. *Or does Grandpa have more he wants to say?*

Grandpa patted her arm. In that moment she knew there was no need for her to say anything. Her grandfather was disturbed by the news of the day and simply needed a listening ear. She was pleased that she had been the one chosen for the purpose.

"No," he repeated. "We almost didn't come to Canada. We had no money for such a journey. When my brother-in-law offered to pay for our passage, I almost refused. I was a proud man. It was difficult enough to be dependent on my daughters – I had no wish to be beholden to another party as well."

They continued walking. Alicia waited patiently, knowing her grandfather would resume his story when he was ready.

"I consented because I knew how much it meant to your mother and your aunt to come here. Your grandmother and I would have been quite content to live out our days in Scotland."

He looked at her and a warm smile creased his wrinkled face.

"Just think what we would have missed out on if we hadn't come," he said, patting her arm again. "Your parents would never have met if we'd stayed in the old country, and we would never have had you and your sister."

"I'm glad you came, Grandpa," Alicia told him.

Grandpa nodded absentmindedly, and she could see he was lost in his memories again.

"The timing was right," he told her. "We came at a good time, two years before the war. Of course, we didn't know when we came that there would be a war."

He paused, reflecting. "Life in the United Kingdom was much more difficult during the Great War than it was here in Canada.

"It affected us here," he murmured. "Your uncle and your father can attest to that, but not in the same way that it did back home. There were difficult times here, but the war itself was far removed. There were no bombs dropped on our cities. There was no need to take city children from their parents and place them with strangers in homes far away to protect them."

Alicia listened, spellbound as her grandfather rambled on. The things he was sharing had never been spoken of in her presence before. She was afraid to speak, for fear she would break the mood and Grandpa would stop talking.

"For most of us here the war was an inconvenience," he told her. "There was some shortage of foods and supplies, but for those of us who did not have sons fighting overseas the war seemed far away.

"This one, I think, will be different. If my instincts are correct, the war that is about to break out will affect every man, woman and child across this great nation."

He stopped.

"I've rambled on too long, my dear."

He smiled at her.

"You are a good listener. I think we've walked far enough for one day. We should return to the house now."

The walk home was a quiet one, with both of them reflecting on the words that had been spoken.

Britain declared war two days later and little more than a week passed before it was announced that the Dominion of Canada had joined them. Alicia was shocked when she went to school the following Monday to find a number of her male classmates absent.

"A lot of the boys are enlisting," Edna informed her.

"How can they?" Alicia asked. "They aren't old enough."

"The boys will say they're of age, and no one will question them."

"They'll know by looking at them that they're too young," Alicia protested. It did not make sense to think of boys her age going to fight.

"It's war time, Alicia." Edna laughed. The sound was harsh, as was the tone of her voice. "Those in authority will turn a blind eye when boys our age say they are eighteen."

She looked at Alicia.

"I wish I was a boy," she stated boldly. "I'd sign up in a minute."

Alicia frowned. The thought of enlisting for the war had never occurred to her.

"If my grandfather is correct," she told Edna, "this war could be a long one. Both men and women may be needed before it is over."

"That's true," Edna agreed, "but they'll give the women the boring jobs. They won't let us go and fight."

Alicia suppressed a sigh. There were times when she wondered how she and Edna could be such good friends when they were so different. The thought of helping the war effort while remaining safely at home in Canada did not frighten her at all, but the idea of serving in any capacity overseas terrified her. Yet here was Edna, wishing she were a boy so she could enlist and go to war!

***

A Double Loss

Alicia watched in silence as Daddy and Uncle Andrew carried her grandfather down the stairs. She stood back, longing to be near him, but reluctant to risk getting in the way. She had grown close to Grandpa in the months since he and Grandma had come to live with them. It broke her heart now to see him in this weakened condition.

Sensing her presence, Grandpa turned his head as he neared the door and saw Alicia standing in the shadows. He laid a hand gently on his son-in-law's arm, motioning him to stop. He beckoned and Alicia moved forward. Grandpa tried to speak, but his voice was little more than a whisper. Alicia bent and took one of her grandfather's aged hands in her own.

"It's all right, Grandpa," she whispered, even though she knew things were far from all right.

"Be good till I see you again, Alicia," Grandpa whispered.

A tear ran down Alicia's cheek at the familiar words. Her grandfather's way of saying goodbye never changed. He had been saying the words to her each time they parted since she was a toddler.

"I will, Grandpa," she promised, forcing herself to smile as she spoke.

"It might be," he paused to draw a breath.

"It might be a long time, Alicia," he told her.

"Don't say that, Grandpa. You'll be back soon."

He shook his head slightly and drew another feeble breath.

"I may not come back, Alicia. But I'll see you again." He paused. "I'll see you again. Be good till then."

"I will, Grandpa, I will."

Reassured, her grandfather let go of her hand, a silent indication that he was ready to leave.

The wait for her parents to return from the hospital seemed endless. At her mother's request, Alicia went to Grandma's room to wait with her for news.

"It's a shame a young girl like you has to spend time with an old woman like me on such a nice day," Grandma told her. "You should be outside with your friends."

Alicia smiled. Her grandmother did not see her as the teenager she was, but still thought of her as a little girl who spent her spare time skipping or playing hopscotch outdoors.

"I want to be with you, Grandma," she assured her.

It's the truth, she thought. *I'd be here even if Mama hadn't asked me to be.*

"Your grandfather is going to a better place, you know," Grandma said quietly.

"Don't say that, Grandma, please," Alicia begged. "I'm sure that after a little time under doctor's care Grandpa will be well again and will come back home."

Her grandmother shook her head.

"No, Alicia," she said firmly. "It is best to accept the facts. Your grandfather will not be back."

She softened when she saw the tears her words brought to her granddaughter's face.

"You are young, Alicia. You have not seen death visit as often as I have. When you have been on this earth for most of a century, you begin to long for your real home. We are only visitors here, dear, just passing through on our way to our heavenly home."

"I know, Grandma," Alicia sobbed. "I'm just not ready to let Grandpa go there yet. I want him here with me."

"None of us are ever truly ready to let someone go," Grandma told her. "But there comes a time when we must think about what is best for the other person. Do you want Grandpa to live a long time in this state? How happy will he be if he can't go for walks with you anymore? What will it be like for him if he lives another ten years, but can't get around or isn't able to see?"

"I'll help him," Alicia vowed. "I'll be his eyes, his ears and his legs if I have to. I just don't want him to die, Grandma."

Grandma reached for Alicia's hand and held it in both of her own.

"Neither do I, darling," she told her. "But I have accepted what must be. It's time for you to do the same."

Alicia ran from the room in tears. The guilt she felt over leaving her grandmother alone was nothing compared to the pain Grandma's words brought her. In the stillness of her room, she knelt by her bed. With tears streaming down her face, she prayed.

"I can't imagine life without Grandpa, God," she told her heavenly father. "It hurts so much to think of losing him. But it hurts to see him suffering too. I'm going to have to trust you, God, to do what you know is right for my grandfather."

She rose from her knees, knowing she needed to get back to her grandmother. As she reached for the doorknob, she added a post script to her prayer.

"If you take Grandpa to be with you, God, I'm sure going to need your help. I'm going to be awfully lonely without him."

A week passed during which Grandpa lingered between life and death in the hospital. Aunt Helen and Mama visited daily. Alicia begged to go along, but hospital regulations regarding visitors were strict.

"I'm sorry, Alicia," Mama told her on the sixth day. "I spoke with the nurse, but they simply will not allow children to visit."

"I'm not a child, Mama," Alicia insisted.

"I've explained that to the head nurse," Mama replied, "but she insists that you must be over sixteen to visit."

"I'll be sixteen soon," Alicia reminded her.

Mama smiled. "I know you will, dear, but the matron is unwilling to bend the rules, even for a young lady who is almost sixteen."

"Tell Grandpa I love him, Mama," Alicia requested. The words were seldom spoken in their home. It was believed that such feelings were understood without voicing them, but today she felt it was necessary to say the words.

"I'll tell him," Mama promised.

Mama and Aunt Helen were late returning that evening. Visiting hours at the hospital were long over when Alicia heard the door open. She ran down the stairs, eager for news, but the expressions on her mother and aunt's faces told that her grandfather was gone. Silently, she turned and walked back to her room. At times like this a person just needed to be alone.

The weeks following her grandfather's death were difficult for everyone, but were particularly hard for Alicia's grandmother.

Knowing how lonely Grandma was, Alicia took to spending evenings in her room with her. With her mother's permission, she ate supper each night with her grandmother, then spent the rest of the evening with her. Sometimes they talked, other times Alicia read to her. If she had homework, she did it in Grandma's room. Even when she was busy with school work, her presence was company for her grandmother.

"I always thought I'd go before your grandfather, you know," Grandma commented one evening as they ate their meal together.

In a way, Alicia thought, *I guess we all expected that Grandma would go before Grandpa.* Grandma had been bed-ridden for some time now, while Grandpa had been in good health prior to suffering a stroke.

"Why did you think that, Grandma?" Alicia asked.

"Your grandfather was younger than me," Grandma told her, "and he always seemed to be in better health. I guess it just goes to show you that none of us really know the number of our days on this earth."

"Always remember, Alicia, that when God closes a door he opens a window," Grandma told her another day.

Alicia frowned. She had heard the expression all her life, but she'd never really understood what it meant. Summoning her courage, she asked, "What exactly does that mean, Grandma?"

"It means," her grandmother replied, "that our plans are not always God's plans. Sometimes he needs to close a door that we had planned to walk through in order for us to see the window of opportunity he has opened for us."

"I'll remember that Grandma," Alicia promised. She had no way of knowing it would be the last conversation she would ever have with her grandmother.

The next day Mama met Alicia at the door when she returned from school. Her red eyes and swollen cheeks alerted Alicia to the fact that something was wrong even before Mama said a word.

"Grandma passed away today," Mama told her, fighting back tears as she spoke.

Alicia was stunned by the news. Somehow she found the right words to say to Mama. With an aching heart she listened as Mama told her arrangements for the funeral. As soon as she could respectably do so, she excused herself.

Her feet felt like lead as she climbed the steps to her room. The door to Grandma's room was closed. She didn't know whether she was grateful or disappointed. An open door and an empty room would have caused fresh pain, but a closed door made her feel that if she knocked and entered Grandma would be sitting in bed, waiting eagerly for her daily visit.

Alicia passed the closed door and went to her own room. Not until she had shut the door behind her and knew she was alone did she allow the tears to fall.

First Grandpa, she thought, *and now, just as I was really getting to know her well, Grandma is gone.*

Less than six weeks had passed since Grandpa's passing. It wasn't fair. No one was supposed to lose both their grandparents in such a short time!

She sat down on the bed, thinking of the time she had spent with her grandmother these last few weeks. Not a day had gone by that Grandma hadn't told her how much she missed Grandpa, or how eager she was to see him again.

A smile formed in the midst of her tears. Grandpa and Grandma were together again.

***

Baby William

"You look happy, Sarah," Alicia commented. "Motherhood suits you."

It was her first visit with her sister since the baby's arrival, and her first opportunity to meet her new nephew.

"I am happy," Sarah told her, looking down at the tiny infant nestled in her arms. She bent and kissed his soft, downy head.

"I'm glad," Alicia said. "I couldn't bear it if you were unhappy."

Sarah looked at her. Her expression changed as she realized the meaning behind her sister's words.

"This is what I wanted, Alicia," she assured her. "Jake and I both knew from our first date that we would marry someday. We'd already talked about it before we knew about the baby." She laughed her carefree laugh. "William's early arrival was simply the device we used to convince Daddy to let us marry on our schedule instead of his."

Alicia stared.

"Did you plan this, Sarah?" she whispered.

She regretted the words the moment they were out of her mouth. If Sarah had planned her pregnancy or had used it to manipulate their father into agreeing to things on her terms, it was none of Alicia's business.

"I'm sorry, Sarah," she apologized. "I should never have suggested such a thing."

"It's all right, 'Licia," Sarah told her. "I don't mind answering your question. Jake and I talked about marriage and we planned to have children. The fact that William came along earlier than we might have planned for doesn't bother us."

She caressed her son.

"In fact, we are already talking of making him a big brother."

Sarah laughed at the look of shock on her sister's face.

"Not yet," she quickly told her, "but we do want our children to be close in age."

"Closer than us?" Alicia asked and Sarah nodded.

"Yes," she murmured. "Three years is a big age difference between children. I think eighteen or twenty-four months would be better."

"Did you find it hard, Sarah?" Alicia asked. "The difference between us, I mean."

When Sarah admitted that she had, Alicia was surprised.

"Didn't you find it difficult, 'Licia?'"

"No," Alicia told her. "I really didn't."

"The age difference between us seems like nothing now," Sarah said, "but growing up it seemed pretty big to me. Why, I was ready to start school by the time you were ready to walk."

"And I wanted to go with you," Alicia said.

They both laughed, recalling the story Mama had told them of two-year-old Alicia trying to follow her sister to school.

"I never thought of the age difference," Alicia told Sarah. "I knew you were older, and more adventurous. I believed everything you ever told me, and I wanted to be exactly like you!"

"Did you really?" Sarah seemed surprised.

"Oh, yes," Alicia told her. "There was nothing you said that I didn't believe, and nothing you did that I didn't want to do."

"But you never liked any of the things I did," Sarah protested.

"You're right," Alicia admitted, "but I wanted to like them."

"Why?" Sarah asked.

"Because I wanted to be just like my big sister," Alicia answered.

The baby stirred, and Sarah rocked him. With her eyes still on her son, she spoke gently to Alicia.

"Maybe three years between children isn't so bad after all."

Alicia smiled. She doubted that Sarah would wait three years before making William a big brother, but it was nice to know that she approved of such a difference in age.

***

National Registration of 1940

"Have you heard the news?" Edna asked Alicia excitedly. It was a warm Saturday afternoon in early July. The girls were meeting for the first time since school let out for the summer.

"What news is that?" Alicia responded. She had grown used to such greetings from Edna. Usually the news Edna had to share was of little consequence, but she always listened regardless.

"There's to be a registration of everyone age sixteen and over," Edna told her.

"What is everyone registering for?" Alicia asked.

Edna laughed.

"It's sort of like a census, I guess," she told her. "Every Canadian our age and older has to register."

"But what is it they are registering for?" Alicia asked again.

"I don't know, exactly," Edna answered, "but I do know it's because of the war. My father said it was nonsense that both men and women have to register, when only the men would be called up to fight if there was another conscription.

"Then my mother said that this is a different time period than the last war and that maybe some women would want to fight right alongside the men, and my father laughed.

"He said no woman in her right mind would want to fight, and that a woman's place was in the home caring for her family, not in the workforce or on the battlefield. Then Mama reminded him that things are changing, and that it wasn't all that long ago that women couldn't even vote..."

"Whoa...Edna, slow down," Alicia begged, interrupting her friend's monologue. She laughed. "You can talk faster than I can think. I'm still trying to figure out what conscription is."

Edna laughed with her.

"I'm sorry," she told her. "I guess it comes from being part of a big family. Sometimes I talk fast because it's the only way I get a chance to say everything I have to say."

"It's all right," Alicia assured her.

"Conscription," Edna explained, "was a method used in the last war to force men to enlist for military service."

"Oh," Alicia said. "I see. I've never heard of such a thing."

"You should ask your father about it," Edna told her. "I'm sure he would have had to enlist."

"Maybe," Alicia answered, "but if he did, he's never talked about it."

"Some people don't like to talk about it," Edna commented. "Anyway, my father believes this registration is happening so that everything will already be in place if the government decides to pass a law enforcing mandatory military service."

"Do you think that might happen?" Alicia asked.

"It might," Edna told her. "If it does, I hope they take women as well as men. I'd hate to be left sitting at home cooking and cleaning while the men are overseas fighting for our freedom."

Alicia frowned. This was the second time Edna had expressed her desire to join the fight overseas. She shuddered. Thoughts of the war troubled her. Daily she prayed that it would soon be over.

"When does this registration take place?" she asked.

Edna shrugged. "Sometime next month, I think."

The conversation moved on to other topics, but Alicia did not forget the information Edna had shared. That night, at home, she mentioned the registration to her parents, but neither of them had heard anything about it.

Two weeks passed before official word of the registration was received. Alicia's father arrived home from work a day or two later with the newspaper tucked under his arm.

"I believe you will find this of interest," he told his daughter, as he handed her the paper.

Alicia stared. There, listed on the front page of the paper, was the list of questions every Canadian sixteen and over would be required to answer the following month. She looked at the list ... name, address, age, date of birth, marital status etc.

This looks simple enough, she thought as she folded the newspaper. *I'm not sure what all the fuss is about.*

When the nineteenth of August arrived, Alicia made her way to the registration station early. Public announcements stated that the registration sites would be open from eight in the morning till ten at night.

I could have waited and come with Mama and Daddy tonight, Alicia thought, *but I want to do this by myself. If I am old enough to register, I am old enough to do so on my own.*

She felt a sense of nostalgia, as she walked up the steps of her old public school, where the registration for her district was being held. There were few people around at this hour, and her footsteps echoed in the empty hallways as she made her way to the room she was to register in.

She did not have long to wait before her interview. The registrar was a middle-aged woman with a quiet voice; so quiet that at times Alicia had to strain to hear the questions she asked.

It would have been easier if she had just given me the paper and let me fill it out myself, she thought.

Politely she answered each question – full name and address, age and date of birth, marital status (she blushed at the question – why the very idea that she might be a married woman at her age!)

"Do you have any dependants?" the registrar asked.

"No, ma'am" she answered.

"Were you born in Canada?" she queried.

"I was."

"And your parents?" she asked. "Are they Canadian?'

"My father was born in England and my mother in Scotland," Alicia answered.

"When did they immigrate?"

Alicia answered, grateful that she had gone over the questions ahead of time with her parents. Further questions regarding the languages she spoke, her education, general health and occupation followed.

When the form was complete, the registrar reviewed it with her, then asked her to sign verifying the information was correct. The woman then took a small card and filled it in. She handed it to Alicia, asking her to sign it.

When she had done so, the lady placed the card in a small vinyl case. Solemnly she handed the case to Alicia, instructing her to guard it carefully and keep it with her at all times.

"I will, ma'am. Thank you," Alicia told her. Clutching the brown case in her hand she exited the building. It was not until she was outside in the bright sunlight that she opened it and looked at the certificate inside.

The small piece of cardboard was about two inches high and three inches wide. Across the top were printed the words "Dominion of Canada" followed by "National Registration Regulations, 1940, Registration Certificate".

The words "This certificate must always be carried upon the person of the registrant" were printed beside the name and number of the electoral district and polling division. Her name and address followed, along with the date and the registrant's signature. Her own signature ran vertically down the left side of the card.

I'm still not certain why this is so important, Alicia thought as she tucked the case safely into her purse. *Nevertheless, I will keep it with me at all times as I have been instructed. Perhaps it will prove to be of significance someday.*

***

Thwarted Plans

"It's so nice to have the family all together for Sunday dinner," Mama commented, as she placed the last of the food on the table.

"It certainly is," Daddy responded.

Alicia looked at the group assembled. Her parents were in their respective spots at opposite ends of the table. Aunt Helen was seated beside her, while across from them sat Jacob and Sarah. Young William was perched on his father's knee. Her parents were right. It was good to have everyone together again. Sarah's visits these days were far too infrequent, and Jake was so busy with his work that they seldom saw him.

"We don't see nearly enough of your family, Sarah." Aunt Helen added her comment to the others. She looked at the baby and smiled. "William is growing so quickly."

Hearing his name, the lad looked up and grinned, then babbled a happy response.

"I believe William is answering you, Helen," Daddy said, and they all laughed.

Cheerful conversation flowed throughout the meal. By the time it was finished, William was ready for a nap. Alicia expected Sarah and Jake to excuse themselves and leave, but to her surprise Sarah asked if she might put William down for his sleep in Alicia's room.

While Sarah settled the baby, Alicia helped her mother and aunt with the after-dinner cleanup. They had just finished when Sarah re-entered the room.

"I'm sorry, Mama," she said. "I had intended to help Alicia with the dishes and give you and Aunt Helen a break."

Mama smiled. "You were occupied with other matters," she answered kindly.

The ladies left the kitchen and moved into the living room, where Daddy and Jake sat talking. When there was a lull in the conversation, Sarah leaned forward eagerly.

"Jake and I have some news to share," she told the family. After a quick look around the room, Sarah took Jake's hand.

Alicia smiled. *This is it,* she thought. *Sarah is about to announce an addition to their family.* She waited eagerly, but the words that came out of her sister's mouth were not the ones she expected.

"My husband," Sarah informed them, "is about to enlist in the armed forces."

When Sarah's statement was greeted by a stunned silence, she nudged her husband.

"Sarah and I have discussed the matter," Jake told them, "and we are in agreement." He spoke slowly, thoughtfully. "It is impossible for me to sit idly by, when there are forces at work to destroy the world as we know it."

"Those forces have posed little threat to Canada," his father-in-law reminded him.

Jake nodded. "That is true," he agreed, then added ominously, "thus far."

"They may never threaten Canada," Mr. Miller said quietly.

"Perhaps not," Jake answered, "but there are those who thought the situation we face today would never happen either. In light of the happenings in Europe and the situation in the Orient, I find it hard to believe that Canada may not also be a target someday."

"You have a wife and child to consider," his father-in-law told him. He looked at Jake. "I wish you had discussed this matter with me privately, Son."

A cry sounded, interrupting the conversation, and Sarah rose. Alicia followed her upstairs, grateful for an excuse to leave the room.

"Are you really going to let Jake join the army, Sarah?" Alicia asked when they were alone in her room.

Sarah nodded. She reached down and picked up William, cuddling him close.

"I don't want him to go," she told Alicia. "I'm terrified I'll lose him." She burrowed her face in the baby's neck, muffling her words.

"But he feels so strongly about it that I don't really have any choice. He says he won't use his wife and child as an excuse to shirk his duty to his country."

"It might have been better if Jake had told Daddy privately," Alicia commented.

Sarah raised her head and looked at Alicia. Her eyes were misty.

"He didn't tell Daddy privately because he knew Daddy would try to talk him out of it! Jake's already had to battle his own parents over the decision; he shouldn't have to battle mine too."

"I'm sorry, Sarah," Alicia said sympathetically. The words seemed so inadequate. She wanted to say she understood, that she knew how her sister must be feeling, but she didn't.

When they re-entered the living room with William, the conversation had moved on to other topics. It was not until Sarah and Jake were leaving that the subject of Jake enlisting was mentioned again. As they reached the door, Daddy pulled Jake aside.

"I trust you will give this matter serious thought before making a final decision, Jacob," he told his son-in-law.

"I already have, sir," Jake answered firmly. "The decision has been made. I am sorry if you are unhappy with it, but it is something I have to do."

An awkward moment followed Jake's answer, then his father-in-law extended his hand.

"I pray God will go with you then," he said sincerely, "and bring you safely home again."

Two weeks passed before Sarah's next visit to the house. She came alone with William on a Saturday afternoon. When her father asked how Jake was, Sarah appeared subdued.

"Jake is fine," she answered quietly. "You will be happy to know he will not be going overseas. In fact, he will not be going anywhere."

It took some questioning before she finally revealed that Jake had been turned down by the armed forces. An injury he had suffered as a child had resulted in a slight limp. Those who knew Jake thought nothing of it, but the impediment was cause enough for the army to reject him.

"I'm sorry," Daddy told Sarah.

Sarah looked at him.

"Are you really sorry, Daddy?" she asked.

Alicia stifled a gasp. The question was bold indeed.

"Yes, Sarah, I am," her father responded. "I know how much this meant to Jake. As a father and a grandfather I am relieved to learn that my son-in-law will not be going to war, as a man I understand his need to protect his country and those he loves."

There was a lengthy pause before he continued. "For Jacob, I am sorry."

***

New Beginnings

"I wonder why it is that we finish school in June, but we don't graduate until November," Alicia commented. Only three weeks remained of her high school years. "I would have preferred to graduate in June."

She turned to her mother. "Wouldn't it make more sense for us to graduate the day that we finish school, Mama, instead of months later?"

"The time will pass quickly," Mama assured her. "I'm sure we can find a way to put it to good use."

"It troubles me that I don't have a job yet," Alicia told her mother. "A lot of my classmates already have something lined up for when school ends."

"We've talked about this before," Mama said firmly. "You have nothing to be concerned about. You can begin looking for work in the fall."

"What if I can't find work then?" Alicia asked. "What if all the good jobs are taken? Wouldn't it be better to start looking now?"

"Your father and I want you to have this summer free to enjoy yourself. You have a whole lifetime of working ahead of you," Mama reminded her. "This is your last summer of freedom."

My last summer of freedom. Alicia contemplated the words her mother had spoken. She had never thought of it that way. She had been eager to finish school, graduate and take her place in the world.

"Perhaps I should enjoy this summer," she said slowly. "I never thought about it that way."

"After this you will have responsibilities," Mama told her. "Once you start work you will have bills to pay and obligations to meet. You may have holidays, but it is doubtful you will be given an entire summer off."

"You're right, Mama," Alicia answered.

155

The remaining weeks of school passed quickly. When the final day of classes arrived, Alicia was grateful her graduation ceremonies did not take place till the fall. It made it easier to say goodbye to her classmates, knowing she would see them all again in a few months.

"It doesn't seem like we're really finished high school, does it?" Alicia commented to Edna as they prepared to part.

"I don't think it will seem real to me until September," Edna told her.

"You don't know how lucky you are, Alicia," she added wistfully. "I wish I could have the whole summer off."

"I know," Alicia answered sympathetically. Edna had been working after school and on weekends all through high school. She had obtained full time work the previous summer, and had even considered dropping out of school her final year in order to keep the job. In the end she had chosen to complete her education, and had now been able to procure an even better position as a result.

"I feel a little guilty knowing most of my classmates will be working while I am playing," Alicia admitted.

"Don't feel guilty," Edna told her. "Enjoy it while you can. Next summer you will be wishing you could do it again."

"I expect I will," Alicia responded with a laugh, "but right now I'd be grateful for something to occupy the months ahead."

The summer Alicia had thought would be endless passed more quickly than she would have believed possible. She spent countless hours in the park and at the beach with Sarah and young William. The little fellow was growing faster than the plants in Daddy's garden. He was walking now and making attempts at talking. The fact that his words were seldom understood did not bother the young lad. He was a happy child and Alicia enjoyed every moment she was with him. In addition to the time she spent with Sarah and William, Alicia devoted several weeks to helping with the children's summer programs run by her church.

When her father took his annual vacation, she went away with her parents for a week. They made a visit to Uncle Adolph's, then went on to the conference centre run by their church for a few days.

It was not until the Labour Day weekend in September was over that Alicia began actively searching for work. She had enjoyed the summer and was grateful to her parents for encouraging her to delay her entry into the labour force till the fall. Weeks passed, however, and she was unable to find work in her chosen field. She began to grow troubled over her lack of employment.

"It's not that there isn't work to be had," she moaned to Sarah. "It's just not the type of work I've been trained to do. There are plenty of jobs in the manufacturing industry, but Mama and Daddy want me to wait till I find office work."

"Something will come along," Sarah assured her. "You just have to be patient."

The evening of her graduation arrived, and Alicia still had not found a suitable position.

I hope the something Sarah talked about comes along soon, Alicia thought as she began to dress for the ceremony. She took the gown her mother had made for the occasion from its hanger and ran her fingers over the material before slipping it on.

I feel like a princess, she thought as she surveyed herself in the mirror. The dress was pale blue, her favourite colour, and was edged with lace on the bodice and the cuffs. It fit her trim figure perfectly.

Her eyes travelled from the dress to her hair. She smiled at the sight of the soft curls. Mama had treated her to her first permanent wave and she was pleased with the results.

A knock sounded on the bedroom door, and her mother entered. She stopped just inside the room.

"You look lovely, dear," she said, smiling at Alicia.

Alicia beamed. Such compliments were rare.

"Thank you, Mama."

"There is only one thing missing."

Alicia looked concerned. She checked her reflection again.

"What is missing, Mama?" she asked.

Her mother reached into her pocket, then held out her hand. Alicia stared at the silver locket in the outstretched hand.

"It's Grandma's locket." She looked at her mother. "Are you sure you want me to wear this, Mama?"

A tear formed in her mother's eye, but she nodded.

"Aunt Helen and I have discussed it," she told Alicia. "We both agree that Grandma would want you to have it."

As her mother moved closer, Alicia bent down to allow her to fasten the chain around her neck. When it was secure she straightened. Mama stood back and surveyed her.

"Now," she pronounced, "you look ready to graduate."

It seemed that one minute she was walking out the school doors on her last day as a student and the next she was walking back in for her graduation ceremonies, Alicia thought as she entered the building an hour later with her parents.

It all passed in the blink of an eye, she thought, then laughed at herself for using one of her grandmother's expressions.

In spite of the festive occasion, a sombre mood hung over the auditorium where the ceremonies were taking place. It was more than reverence for the occasion, Alicia thought as she looked around. Most of the young men who should have been present at the event were absent. Many of them were already serving overseas. Some of the boys who had enlisted but had not yet shipped out had been granted leave to attend the commencement. Dressed in uniform, the small group stood proudly erect as they accepted their diplomas. A hush descended over the auditorium as the principal stood at the end of the ceremony and announced the names of two young men who had died serving their country. There was not a dry eye in the room as he praised their bravery and the lads' fathers stepped forward to accept the awards for their sons posthumously. It was a solemn reminder to all of the difficult times they were living in.

The ceremony was over and Alicia was leaving the building with her parents when Edna caught up with her.

"Miss Richards is looking for you," she exclaimed. She lowered her voice. "I think she wants to talk to you about a job. She asked me to send you to her if I saw you."

Alicia looked from Edna to her parents.

"You go and see what Miss Richards wants, dear," Mama told her. "Your father and I will wait here."

Excitement stirred in Alicia as she retraced her steps with Edna. Was it possible the teacher knew of a suitable position for her?

"There she is," Edna said as they neared the auditorium.

Alicia looked ahead to where her former teacher stood. A younger woman stood beside her and the two were deep in conversation. They looked up and smiled as Alicia approached.

"Good evening, Miss Richards. Edna told me you wished to speak with me."

Alicia hoped that the nervousness she felt was not evident in her voice.

"Yes, Alicia. I did ask to speak with you," Miss Richards responded. "I was wondering if you have found employment?"

"No, ma'am, I haven't," Alicia answered.

The teacher smiled.

"I may know of something suitable," she told her. "I'd like to introduce you to Gwendolyn Finch."

She indicated the lady standing at her side.

"Miss Finch is also a former student of mine.

"Miss Finch, this is Miss Miller." She paused. "Miss Miller, Miss Finch."

"Please, call me Gwen," the other lady told Alicia, smiling warmly. Alicia looked into Gwen's laughing brown eyes and smiled.

"And I am Alicia," she told her.

"Miss Finch," the teacher went on, as if the two had not exchanged first names, "is in need of an office assistant. I have recommended you for the position, Alicia."

"That's very kind of you, Miss Richards," Alicia told her. "I certainly appreciate it."

She turned to Gwen.

"Are you taking applications for the position?" she asked. "Would you like me to come for an interview?"

She waited, hoping she was not appearing too eager.

Gwen laughed. "No application or interview will be necessary, Alicia. If Miss Richards has recommended you, I am certain you are well qualified for the position. Are you able to start next week? I realize it is short notice, but I am in need of someone right away."

Alicia beamed. This was turning out even better than she had anticipated.

"I could start Monday if that is suitable to you."

"Monday would be perfect," Gwen responded. She took a card from her purse and handed it to Alicia. "This is the location. Are you familiar with the area?"

Alicia looked at the address. She nodded.

"Yes," she answered slowly. "I am."

"Come at nine on Monday," Gwen instructed her. "I'll show you what is required and we will arrange your schedule then."

She turned back to Miss Richards and Alicia knew she had been dismissed. She found Edna waiting for her as she made her way back to her parents.

"Did you get it? Did you get it?" Edna asked the moment she drew near.

"Did I get what?" Alicia asked innocently, but the grin on her face betrayed her.

"Oooh, I'm so happy for you, Alicia," Edna told her. She gave her a hug. "I hope this job will be exactly what you've been wanting."

Alicia laughed.

"I hope so too," she told Edna. "I guess I'll find out on Monday."

***

Gwendolyn

Determined to make a good impression, Alicia arrived fifteen minutes early for her first day at her new job. To her dismay she found the door to the building locked. She looked around for an appropriate place to wait, but finding none she stood patiently outside the address she had been given.

When her watch indicated five minutes past the hour of nine, Alicia began to wonder if she was at the wrong location. She pulled the card Gwen had given her from her purse and verified the address. The number on the building matched that on the card, but there was no sign marking it as a place of business. She checked her watch again. Where was her employer?

Perhaps she had misunderstood and she was to start the following Monday instead of this week, she thought. No, she was quite certain she had the date and time correct. A sense of dread washed over her as it suddenly occurred to her that the whole thing might be a hoax. Maybe there was no job!

I won't allow myself to think like that, she decided. *Miss Richards would never partake in such a ruse.*

Another glance at her watch revealed that it was now a quarter past the hour. She was about to leave when the sound of footsteps approaching at a fast pace caught her attention. She looked around. There was no one in sight yet, but the steady rhythm of fast-moving heels clicking on concrete told her someone was just around the corner. And that someone was in a hurry!

She stepped back into the shelter of the doorway. Her new position was not in the best part of the city. In fact, her father had threatened to make her quit her job even before it began when he'd learned of the location.

"No respectable business would be located in that neighbourhood," he had insisted. "And even if there is, no daughter of mine is going to work there!"

Some soft spoken words from Mama had resulted in a compromise. Alicia would be allowed to go and check out the position. If it proved to be legitimate and she liked the work, she could continue, provided there was another woman in the office with her at all times, and that she was only in the area during daylight hours.

The footsteps slowed, indicating the party was drawing near. She shivered. Her father certainly would not approve of the situation she was in now, cowering in the doorway of an unmarked office building. She pulled further back into the shadows, making herself invisible from the street. The figure came into view, and Alicia breathed a sigh of relief.

"Miss Finch!" she cried, forgetting her new employer's request that she call her by her given name. "I sure am happy to see you!"

"Alicia!"

The woman was out of breath and her hair and makeup were a mess. Even her clothing looked wrinkled, as if it had been slept in, or hastily pulled from the line and put on without the benefit of being ironed first. "I forgot you were coming today. I apologize for my lateness. It's always hard to get back into routine again after the weekend."

Her hand was fishing in her purse for keys to the building as she spoke. Alicia wisely said nothing, but waited silently while the older woman unlocked the door.

The office Gwen led her into was spacious enough, but it had a run-down look, much like the building it was housed in and the neighbourhood surrounding it. A row of filing cabinets lined one wall and there was a large desk on the opposite wall. Two smaller desks were evenly spaced in front of the large one.

Gwendolyn Finch moved swiftly to the desk at the back of the room. She flung her coat over the chair and deposited her purse in a corner, then picked up the phone. Alicia stood just inside the door, uncertain what to do.

"Yeah, Harry, it's Gwen...I'm in the office." Miss Finch's voice carried throughout the entire room. Embarrassed, Alicia turned to face the door. She fumbled with the buttons on her coat, trying not to overhear what should have been a private conversation.

"I just got here," her employer went on. "I haven't had time to check yet. Yeah, yeah...I'll let you know. I have to go, Harry. The boss could be in any time...Okay...Okay...I'll see you tonight." She hung up without saying goodbye.

Alicia turned to face Gwen, forcing herself to smile.

"Sorry about that, kid," Gwen told her. "Make yourself at home." She pointed to the less cluttered of the two small desks. Alicia moved toward it, her coat still in her hand. She laid it neatly over the back of the chair, wondering what had happened to Miss Gwendolyn Finch. The woman in charge of this office bore little resemblance to the sophisticated lady Miss Richards had introduced her to three days ago.

Give it time, she cautioned herself. *Things are not always as they appear.*

"I use the big desk when the boss isn't in," Gwen informed Alicia, sitting down at it and crossing her legs. She laughed. "When he's here – which thankfully isn't often – I take the small desk."

"I see." Alicia knew it was the wrong thing to say, but she was at a loss for words.

She took a seat at her desk, following Gwen's example. Automatically her hands began moving, making neat piles of the papers that lay scattered across the desk. If this was to be her work space, the first thing she needed to do was tidy it.

Gwen laughed again.

"Relax, kid," she told Alicia. "Things are pretty informal around here."

"Yes, ma'am," Alicia answered, continuing her self-assigned task. When the job was finished to her satisfaction, she turned to face Gwen. The lady sat unmoving at the large desk, watching Alicia intently.

"What would you like me to do first?" Alicia asked.

"There's paperwork to be done," Gwen told her nonchalantly. "The files need to be organized," she pointed to the mass of filing cabinets behind her, then her voice dropped to a conspiratorial whisper, "but do you know what I need you to do more than anything else, Alicia?"

"No, ma'am," Alicia answered respectfully.

"Call me Gwen," her employer ordered. "I don't want to hear you address me as Miss Finch or ma'am any more. Do you understand?"

"Yes, Gwen," Alicia answered.

"That's better," Gwen told her with a smile. "What I need you here for most of all is to help keep the boss in his place."

Alicia suppressed a gasp.

"You mean there really isn't much work to do?" she asked politely.

"That's right," Gwen told her. She sighed when she saw the look on Alicia's face. "I'm sorry, kid, really I am, but I could hardly tell you that before. Why, you'd never have come if I'd told you. Besides, how would it have sounded to Miss Richards if I'd said that I really didn't have much work for an assistant, but I sure would like to have another woman around so the boss would keep his hands off me?"

"I thought you said the boss wasn't in very often," Alicia said.

"He isn't," Gwen told her, "but when he is here, he seems to forget that I'm an engaged woman and he's a married man."

"I'm sorry, Gwen," Alicia told her. "I really don't think this is the right position for me."

She started to rise, reaching for her coat as she did so.

"Don't go, Alicia, please." Something in Gwen's voice caused Alicia to stop. She sat back down.

"I know it's not the best job in the city and it's certainly not in the best neighbourhood," Gwen went on. "But I sure would appreciate it if you would at least give it a try."

Alicia hesitated.

"I can't accept payment for work I don't do," she told Gwen firmly. "And I'm afraid keeping the boss from chasing you doesn't count as work."

"That's what you think!" Gwen retorted. Alicia's initial reaction to the comment was shock, but she soon found herself laughing along with Gwen.

"I'm willing to give it a try," Alicia told her.

There was something about Gwen that reminded her of Sarah. She was fun-loving and free-spirited, but she also seemed warm and kind-hearted. It was obvious she was in a difficult position with her boss. If Alicia could alleviate the situation by her presence, she was willing to give it a chance.

With an understanding in place, the two set to work re-organizing the filing cabinets. The project was going well and they had made significant progress when the door opened and a man entered. A quick glance at Gwen's face told Alicia the boss had arrived.

"Well, well, what have we here?" The man's deep voice echoed in the room as he took in the scene before him. "Have you company, Gwen, or has my business suddenly expanded so much that it takes two people to run the office?"

The words were polite enough, but there was a harshness to the tone that told both the girls the man would have preferred to find Gwen alone.

"I've taken on an assistant, Joe," Gwen informed her boss. "It's just temporary, till I get everything running smoothly. You needn't worry about the expense. Her pay will come out of my pocketbook, not yours."

She nudged Alicia, who turned to face the man. "Joe, this is Alicia," Gwen introduced them. "Alicia, this is my boss, Joe."

Alicia noted that Gwen had used the words *my* boss, not *our* boss.

"I'm pleased to meet you, sir," she said politely.

"I'm very pleased to meet you too, Alicia," Joe told her, holding out his hand. Alicia extended her own hand, though she would have preferred not to. Joe held it a little too long, caressing her fingers slightly.

165

"Perhaps my words were a little hasty." he apologized. "Perhaps this office is big enough for two assistants; although I would have preferred it if you had consulted me before you took it upon yourself to hire someone, Gwen."

He smiled at Alicia.

His mouth is smiling, she thought, *but his eyes are as cold as a block of ice.* She thought of her father's strict provision that she was never to be alone with a man in the office. It was advice she would gladly adhere to where Joe was concerned. Her heart went out to Gwen, and she was glad she had chosen to stay.

Joe remained in the office less than an hour, but the time dragged by slowly.

I feel like it should be time to go home now, Alicia thought when at last the door closed behind him. She looked at her watch and was surprised to see that it was not even break-time yet!

Little work had been accomplished in the time that Joe was present. He had flirted shamelessly with both Gwen and Alicia. His passes at Gwen had been more obvious, but Alicia noticed that he took every opportunity to brush her arm or shoulder when he was near her. She quickly learned to work with her back to the wall, enabling her to somehow keep her eyes on both her work and the boss.

"I'm thankful he isn't here often," Alicia whispered to Gwen when the two of them were alone. "I don't think I could stay on if he was."

Gwen's pleading eyes stopped her from saying more.

The rest of the day passed quickly. Alicia proved herself to be a quick and efficient worker.

"I'm glad you were here today, Alicia," Gwen told her as she locked the door behind them at the end of the day. "I really hope you'll stay on."

Alicia hesitated.

"Tell me you'll be here at nine o'clock tomorrow," Gwen pleaded.

Alicia sighed.

"I'll be here at nine tomorrow," she said in resignation.

Gwen grinned.

"And the next day, and the day after that?" she teased.

Alicia laughed.

"Let's take this one day at a time," she told Gwen. "For now I can promise I'll be back tomorrow."

How long I stay at this job will depend entirely on how frequently the boss is in, Alicia thought as she walked home. She could work with Gwen indefinitely, but it would be difficult to stay on in a position where she neither liked nor trusted the man who ran the office.

To Alicia's surprise and Gwen's relief, Joe was seldom in the office in the weeks that followed. He appeared briefly each morning at first, but when Gwen continued to give him the cold shoulder and Alicia ignored his advances, he began to stay away.

"How does he ever get anything done when he's never here?" Alicia asked Gwen one day.

Gwen laughed.

"Joe comes in and does his work at night, after we go home," she told Alicia.

"Why would he do that?" Alicia asked.

"He tells me he's more productive without us here," Gwen informed her. "But if you ask me, I think he just doesn't want to be home at night."

Thoughts whirled through Alicia's mind at the comment, but she said nothing. Things went smoothly for several weeks. Alicia was beginning to think the job might work out after all, when she arrived at the office one morning and found it locked. She waited patiently, knowing Gwen was not always on time. Almost an hour passed, and still Gwen had not arrived.

I wonder if something is wrong, Alicia thought. *Even Gwen isn't usually this late.*

She was about to leave when a boy rode up on a bicycle.

"Are you Miss Miller?"

Alicia nodded and the lad handed her an envelope. She took it and the boy was gone before she could thank him. She turned the envelope over. As soon as she saw the writing she knew the note was from Gwen. Eagerly she tore it open and took out the paper inside. The words were brief and to the point.

Dear Alicia,

By the time you get this I will be a married woman. Harry has finally stopped talking about marriage and is ready to commit. We are leaving for Niagara Falls.

I'm sorry I couldn't tell you in person. I've enclosed your wages, plus a little extra to help you until you find a new job.

Good luck, kid.

Gwen

Alicia stared at the paper. Gwen had eloped! She read it again, then slowly opened the envelope. There was a second piece of paper folded neatly inside. She withdrew the paper and opened it. It was a personal cheque, payable to Alicia Miller. Her eyes grew wide when she saw the amount. Gwen had been generous indeed. Tucking the envelope and its contents into her pocket, Alicia started toward home. She had no desire to be present when Joe discovered that his office staff had abandoned him.

***

A New Position

"How do you like your new position, Alicia?" Sarah asked. They were together in Sarah's backyard. Sarah was seated on the ground with her back leaning against a tree trunk, while Alicia and William built roads in the sand nearby.

"It's all right," Alicia answered quietly.

"You don't sound too certain," Sarah told her. She looked at her sister. "Do you like it or don't you?"

Alicia laughed. There was no beating around the bush with Sarah. She was always direct and to the point, and she expected other people to be the same way.

"I like where I work, and I like the people that work there," she told Sarah, "but the work itself isn't very stimulating."

She went on to describe her duties running the address-o-graph machine in the mail room.

"I'd rather I was part of the secretarial group, or worked in the book store," she finished. In addition to printing books and magazines, the publishing company she now worked for ran a small book store.

"Maybe an opportunity will come along in another department later," Sarah suggested.

"It's possible," Alicia answered, "but for now I will just have to be content where I am." She paused. "I don't want it to sound like I'm complaining," she went on. "I'm very grateful to be working where I am instead of in a factory."

"One good thing about the war is that there's no shortage of work." Sarah agreed.

"That's for sure!" Alicia had wondered how long she would be unemployed after Gwen's sudden departure, but it had taken less than a week to find a new position.

"Did you hear that there's going to be another registration?" Sarah's question interrupted her thoughts.

"Yes." Alicia laughed. "It's strange, you know. Because of the way they are doing it, I am too young to register this time, but I was old enough for the registration two years ago."

Sarah nodded. This second nationwide registration was restricted to females between the ages of twenty and twenty-four.

"I have to register," Sarah said soberly.

Alicia looked surprised.

"Surely you won't be required to take a job, Sarah," she protested.

"I might be," Sarah told her. "After all, lots of women with children as young as William are working now."

Alicia nodded. "Edna told me there's such a shortage of workers for the factories that they're transporting hundreds of women in to Ontario from other provinces to work here." She looked at Sarah. "Did I tell you Edna left her office job and went to work in a munitions factory? She said if she couldn't be fighting the enemy overseas she could at least be building equipment to help the men who are fighting!"

Alicia shuddered at the thought.

"I wouldn't mind working in a factory," Sarah said, "if I didn't have William. I'd be happy working somewhere that built ships or airplanes, but I don't think I would want to work in a munitions factory."

She looked thoughtful.

"I'm not sure why I feel that way," she went on. "After all, it really doesn't matter whether you're building boats and aircraft for the war, or weapons. I just don't like the idea of having a part in building weaponry.

"If it weren't for William, I'd be glad to go back to work." She looked at her son, playing happily in the sand. "I sure would hate to leave him every day."

"The government is subsidizing day nurseries," Alicia reminded her. Even as she said the words, she found herself hoping that her nephew would never be placed in such an establishment.

"I know," Sarah replied, "but I don't like the idea of using one."

"If you decide you want to go back to work, Sarah, or if you have to go, maybe Mama would look after William for you."

"Mama probably would be willing," Sarah agreed, "and if the war continues long enough that I am forced to take a job, I will ask her."

She rose and stretched, then walked to where William was playing and scooped him up into her arms. She hugged him close, then tickled him playfully. The joyful sound of mother and child laughing together filled the yard.

Still holding her little one, Sarah turned back to Alicia.

"I'd miss moments like this if I were working."

She looked thoughtful.

"It's strange," she said. "If someone asked me what I do all day or how William and I spend our time, I wouldn't know what to tell them. It seems that there is little that happens in our daily lives that is worth mentioning. And yet, I would miss him dreadfully if I were to go back to work."

"I think you summed it all up a few minutes ago, Sarah," Alicia told her. "After you played with William you said it was *moments like this* that you would miss if you weren't with him.

"Your days are filled with moments." She moved forward and ran her fingers through William's soft, golden curls. "Stay home with him if you can, Sarah. You're already doing more than your share for the war effort through your volunteer work."

Sarah was one of the most dedicated volunteers Alicia knew. Three mornings a week she took William with her to the local Red Cross office, where she assisted with office work and helped pack boxes to be sent overseas.

"It's not just the work you do at the Red Cross office either," Alicia reminded her. "You must have knitted hundreds of socks and mittens to help keep our soldiers warm."

Sarah laughed.

"Dozens," she corrected, "not hundreds."

She hugged William so tightly that the lad protested and begged to be put down. Placing him on the grass Sarah turned to Alicia.

"Thanks, 'Licia," she said warmly.

Alicia looked at her, wondering what it was she was being thanked for.

"Thanks for encouraging me to stay home with William, and for reminding me that even though I'm not working in a factory, I'm still contributing to the war effort."

She sighed.

"I'll go and register next week," she said. "Then I guess I'll just have to wait and see if the people in charge let me stay home with William or not."

Weeks went by, and life settled into a normal routine. *At least as normal as it can be under the circumstances,* Alicia thought. The war had changed life for everyone.

Like the rest of the country, she had come to accept food rationing as a way of life. She had grown accustomed to waiting without complaint in long line-ups for the limited supply of items available at the stores.

It is rather ironic, she thought, *that during all our years of poverty the shops were filled with things that we, and others like us, could not afford to buy. Now, due to the war, there is work for everyone and money for purchasing, but the goods are not available.*

At least our family is not affected by the ration on gasoline, she thought with a smile. *That is one advantage to not having an automobile.*

The sun reflected off something on the sidewalk, causing her to stop. Automatically she bent to pick up the bit of foil that had been discarded by some thoughtless person. It was a small piece, and in another time she would not have thought it worth her effort to pick the remnant up, but in this day and age it was important not to waste such an item. She put it in her pocket, making a mental note to remember to take it out when she got home and add it to their salvage pile.

My grandfather was right, she thought, *when he predicted that this war would not only affect those with family overseas, but would affect every level of our society.*

She sighed. How she wished the war would end. Daily the papers were filled with news of the horrors going on overseas. She had grown accustomed to seeing headlines that told of the battles in Europe and listed the numbers of those lost on both sides. Far more personal, however, were the columns on an inside page of the paper that listed by name those soldiers reported dead or missing in action. Seldom a week went by that she did not see a name she recognized. Her heart ached as she thought of the young men that had given their lives defending the cause of freedom. Many were boys her own age, fresh out of school. It saddened her to think of the tragic loss of life.

Her thoughts replayed the conversation she'd had with Edna on Saturday night.

"We need to be more active," Edna had stated emphatically. "This war has gone on too long. People need to realize the importance of working together to bring it to an end."

Alicia had sighed.

"I don't know what more we can do, Edna," she'd said. "We're already contributing everything we can. Why, when I think of the things we save now that were considered useless before the war, I can hardly believe it.

"Broken glass, papers, tin cans, meat bones, toothpaste tubes – even worn out socks..." she'd paused for effect, "and that's only a partial list!"

"Don't forget about our nylons," Edna reminded her.

Alicia laughed. She could not remember the last time she'd had a new pair of nylons. Most of the women she knew had taken to painting lines on the back of their legs to resemble seams from stockings, but Alicia had never seen the sense in such a practice.

We all know there's no nylons available, she thought, *so what's the use in drawing a line on my leg and pretending I'm wearing them?*

"Collecting things isn't enough," Edna told her. She'd looked at Alicia intently. "We need to do more than that. Every working adult should be buying victory bonds, and every child should be encouraged to purchase war savings stamps.

"Don't forget that every five dollars invested in war stamps will buy one round of anti-aircraft shells!"

Perhaps I will invest in a victory bond, Alicia decided as she entered her place of employment. *It's one more thing I can do to help. I'll look into it when I cash my cheque next Friday.*

She moved through the building, bidding her co-workers a cheerful *Good Morning* as she made her way to the mail room.

Keeping an address-o-graph machine running may not be very challenging, she thought as she set up her day's work, *but I definitely prefer it to working in a factory.* Alicia frowned, once again wondering if she was really doing her part for her country. She wondered if she was being selfish, wanting to work in an office when there was such a need for factory workers.

If you want me somewhere else, I'll go, Lord, she prayed. *I prefer office work to factory work, but if that's what you want, I'll do it.*

Alicia had just begun printing the first set of mailing labels when an aide arrived, looking flustered.

"The boss would like to see you in his office, Miss Miller," she stated. Alicia looked at the woman in surprise.

"If you'll come with me, please," the aide instructed.

I wonder what this could be about, Alicia thought as she followed the aide through the building and up two steep flights of stairs. She was out of breath by the time she reached the top, but there was no time to rest. The quick-moving aide was already approaching a door at the end of the long hallway. Straightening her skirt as she ran, Alicia hurried to catch up to her.

By the time she reached the end of the hall, the woman was standing with one hand on the door handle and the other on her hip. Her foot tapped impatiently on the floor.

"I'm sorry, ma'am," Alicia apologized. "I'm not used to climbing so many stairs." She did not mention that the aide had raced ahead, making it difficult for her to keep up.

"One must never waste time when someone else is paying them for it," the aide responded, causing Alicia to blush. Unable to think of an appropriate response, she murmured another apology and waited for the woman to show her into the office.

The room she was ushered into was smaller than one would expect the head of the company to have, but it was comfortably furnished. A man rose from a chair behind the desk as they entered. After introductions were made, the aide departed, leaving Alicia alone with the boss.

"Sit down, Miss Miller, sit down," the man encouraged. She sat on the edge of the chair he indicated, waiting patiently to learn why she had been summoned.

"You've been with our company several months now, Miss Miller," the man began. He leaned back in his chair and folded his hands across his chest. He peered at her intently. "Do you like it here?"

"I do, sir."

"And your present position with the company – are you content with it?" he queried.

"I am content, sir," Alicia replied, grateful that he asked her if she was content in her position, not happy.

He nodded.

"I see," he said. He paused, looking thoughtful. "I wonder if you would be willing to consider a different type of work, Miss Miller?"

Alicia hesitated.

"May I ask what you had in mind, sir?" she asked cautiously.

He straightened in his chair. "You are a bright young woman, Miss Miller. No doubt you are aware of the great need for workers in factories today to produce goods for use overseas."

"I am, sir."

This is it, she thought. *He is going to ask me to transfer to a job in a factory. I am about to be let go, not because my work is unsatisfactory, but because my labour is needed somewhere else.*

"I enjoy working here, sir, but I am willing to work wherever I am needed," she told him.

He smiled, and she steeled herself, waiting for the words she was certain were coming.

"I'm very pleased to hear that, Miss Miller. You would be willing to take on a different work assignment, then?"

"I would, sir." Her voice did not reflect the disappointment she felt at the thought.

He opened a folder on his desk, and Alicia was aware for the first time that her personal file was sitting in front of him. He studied the contents for a moment.

"I see you have excellent typing skills."

Alicia frowned. Why would the man be interested in her typing skills if she was being transferred to a factory job?

"You also won a bronze medal in shorthand." He looked at her. "Exactly what does that mean?"

"The Bronze Medal was given to students who achieved a level of one hundred and twenty words or more per minute in shorthand class," she explained, causing the man to look impressed.

He nodded.

"I believe I may have just the assignment for you. I mentioned that there is a shortage of workers for the factories. There is also a shortage of good office workers, as many of them are choosing to go and work in factories instead. Whether this is because the wages are higher there, or out of a sense of duty to their country, I am uncertain. In any event we have lost a number of our staff."

He studied the contents of the folder again, then looked at her.

"If you are willing, Miss Miller, I would like to transfer you immediately from the mail room to the secretarial department."

Alicia was stunned at the words, but endeavoured to hide her surprise. "I am quite willing, sir," she assured him.

"You will start at a junior level," he informed her. "However, if you prove yourself as useful as these papers indicate you to be," he touched the folder in front of him, "I have no doubt you will move up the ranks quickly."

I can't believe it, Alicia thought as she followed the aide back through the building to her new posting. *I came into work this morning a mere attendant in the mail room. It is not yet ten o'clock, and I have been promoted to a position in the secretarial department.* She glanced up and noticed that the aide was once again well ahead of her. She quickened her steps, determined not to make the woman wait for her again. A smile creased her face. Things were turning out even better than she had anticipated.

***

Victory in Europe

Alicia stared at the people milling about in the street below her office window. The numbers grew as she watched. People pressed into the crowd from the surrounding roads, and poured out of the downtown stores and office buildings to join the throng in the street. The rumours had been flying for days, but today it was official. The war in Europe was over!

She shook her head, wondering where the mass of people had come from. It seemed that half of the city's population had gathered at the corner of Yonge and Bloor Streets to celebrate the victory. Banners waved above the crowd, car horns blared, and people cheered. The noise was so loud that at times it made the window rattle. Alicia stepped back a pace, fearing the glass might explode.

A hand touched her shoulder, startling her. She turned, and found herself face to face with Miss Williams. The sound of her supervisor's approach had been drowned out by the noise of the crowds below. Alicia flushed, embarrassed at being caught away from her desk.

"I see you were checking out the festivities, Alicia."

Alicia's face turned even redder at the remark.

"I'm sorry, Miss Williams," she apologized. "I'll get back to work right away."

She started toward her desk, but Miss Williams stepped in front of her, blocking the path.

"Your work can wait, Alicia," she told her. "Go and join the celebrations. Most of the girls have already done so."

"Thank you, Miss Williams. I appreciate your offer, but I have work I simply must finish before I leave."

The older woman looked at her.

"You are young, Alicia, and you are witnessing a momentous event in world history. The war is over! Your work will wait. Go and celebrate!" That said, she led Alicia from the room, and locked the door securely behind her.

Downstairs, Alicia inched open the main door of the office building. She was immediately grateful she had not pulled it open quickly, as the crowd on the streets was so great that people were pressed into the doorways of buildings like sardines packed into a can.

Realizing there was little hope she would be able to make her way through the crowd, she eased the door closed again and left the building through a back door. She made several attempts to join the celebrations, but was unable to move more than a few feet in any direction. At last in resignation she turned and headed home. The sound of the crowds celebrating the victory of the Allied Forces in Europe followed her as she made the long walk home.

There was no work the following day. Stores, schools and businesses were closed as the city gathered to officially celebrate the end of the war. Victory celebrations were held at various locations throughout the city – in parks, in churches, in halls – wherever there was room for a crowd to gather there was a celebration.

Alicia and her family left the house early to attend a morning church service. It was one of the best attended services Alicia had ever been at. Ushers packed people into the pews in the sanctuary until there was barely room to move, then brought chairs in from another room and placed them in the aisles. Alicia looked around the room as she waited for the service to begin. In addition to the large number seated, there were rows of people standing at the back.

The preacher rose and took his place behind the pulpit and a hush settled over the congregation.

"This is truly a day of Thanksgiving." The reverend's voice filled the room. "We have much to praise God for; we have much to celebrate."

The sweet strains of the organ sounded, and the congregation rose to sing the doxology. The familiar words of the old hymn by Thomas Ken had new meaning on this day.

Praise God from whom all blessings flow
Praise Him all creatures here below
Praise Him above ye Heavenly Host
Praise Father, Son and Holy Ghost.

Prayers of thanksgiving and speeches followed the singing. When the service went on beyond the expected hour, children began to fidget. Even William, normally content in any situation, threatened to express his discomfort at being forced to sit in cramped quarters for so long.

When it was over, Alicia's parents and Aunt Helen went home, while Alicia went with Sarah, Jacob and William to one of the gatherings in a nearby park. The event was well attended, and well organized. In spite of their late arrival, Alicia's group had no difficulty moving to a location where they could both see and hear all that was going on.

Remembering the crowds she had seen downtown the day before, Alicia applauded the wisdom that had gone into planning numerous events throughout the city, rather than one large gathering.

William tired as the day wore on, and by mid-afternoon Sarah and Jake decided it was time to take him home.

"I hope you didn't feel you needed to leave when we did, 'Licia," Sarah told her sister, as they began walking toward home.

Alicia shook her head.

"No," she replied. "I was ready to go home."

They walked in silence for a block, then Alicia spoke again.

"It's hard to believe it's really over, isn't it?" she asked. "It's been six years since war was declared – six long years."

She looked at her sister and brother-in-law, thinking of all that had happened in those six years.

"It has been a long time," Sarah agreed. "Why, we were still practically children when the war began!"

Alicia suppressed a smile. There was no sense pointing out that Sarah and Jake had already been married when the war started.

"I'm grateful it's finally over," Alicia said.

"But it's not over!"

Alicia and Sarah turned to look at Jake.

"It's not over," he repeated soberly. "The war with Germany has ended, but the war in the Pacific region continues." Seeing the look on the girls' faces, Jake apologized. "I'm sorry, ladies. I didn't mean to throw a rain cloud over your victory parade. I should have kept my thoughts to myself."

"Everyone says that Japan will surrender soon," Alicia reminded him. "They won't be able to hold out much longer."

"That may be so," Jacob agreed quietly. "But even then it will be a long, long time before life returns to normal."

They reached the corner where Sarah and Jake turned off for their house. After brief goodbyes, Alicia walked on alone. She pondered her brother-in-law's words as she walked.

How long would it be before Japan surrendered? And when they did, how long would it take for life to return to normal? And, now that she thought about it, what should she consider normal anyway? Her entire life thus far had been lived in a world ruled by either an economic depression or a global war. As she mounted the steps to her home, she wondered just what direction her life would take in a post-war world.

***

The Post War Years

New Directions

Alicia listened intently to the words coming from the man behind the pulpit. The speaker this morning was a guest in their assembly. He was a missionary home from the field on furlough, telling the congregation of the work he was doing in a foreign land.

She had gone to the service this morning expecting it to be much the same as any other Sunday. She would never have admitted it to anyone, but lately she'd been finding the morning church service rather boring. The guest today, however, held her attention from the moment he was introduced.

What was it about this speaker, she wondered, that made him so interesting? There was nothing in the man's physical appearance to attract one, but the earnestness with which he delivered his message had a strong appeal. His enthusiasm and love for the people he worked with was evident in every word he spoke. Alicia listened, spellbound, as the man told of labouring in an undeveloped country under difficult circumstances.

I'm not sure if I could do what that man did, Alicia thought as she walked home after the service. She couldn't imagine what it would be like to leave behind the comforts of the life she knew and travel thousands of miles to work in primitive surroundings.

That's what Aunt Sadie did, she reminded herself. She smiled as she thought of her attempt years ago to dig her way to China to see Aunt Sadie. The smile faded as she recalled the statement she had made that day, vowing that when she was older she would be a missionary in China herself.

Her childhood desires had dimmed in the years that had passed. Any thought she had once had of going overseas had been put aside due to the war. As time went by, she had forgotten about the idea. The speaker's words today had rekindled the thought. Her steps slowed as she reflected on the man's closing words.

"It may be that there is someone here today that God is calling to labour for him in a foreign country," he told those seated before him. "If God is speaking to you; if he is calling you to follow him and give your life to serving him; I urge you to listen to his call. There is nothing more rewarding than knowing you are doing what God has called you to do."

Alicia thought of the speaker's words often in the days that followed the meeting, wondering if they had been meant for her.

How do I know whether God is speaking to me and calling me into service, or whether I am simply acting on a notion from years past, she wondered?

The thought tormented her until finally one night she added an extra line to her evening prayers.

"Heavenly Father," she prayed. "I don't know whether or not you are calling me to mission work in China. I am willing to go if that is your will for my life, but I need to know that my desire to go is more than just a childhood fantasy and that it is your voice speaking to me. Please show me what your will for my life is."

She fell asleep, satisfied for the first time in weeks that if God was calling her to China he would make it clear to her.

A month passed. Alicia had almost forgotten about the idea of going to China, when it was announced one Sunday at church that a new bible college was opening in her end of the city. She felt a tingle run down her spine when the college was promoted as *the perfect place for young people wishing to prepare for ministry or mission work to study*, and immediately sensed that this was the sign she had asked for. She discussed the possibility of attending the bible school with her parents that afternoon.

"I'm not sure where it will lead," she told them tentatively, "but it's possible it may lead to mission work in China."

She was nervous as she waited for her parents' reaction to her statement. It was the first time she had shared her ambition with anyone, and she had no idea how they would respond.

"You still want to go to China, do you, Alicia?" Daddy asked.

She nodded, and he smiled.

"You said you would go there someday." He paused, and a frown replaced the smile. "I've no objection to you going to bible school, Alicia, but we are not in a position to send you there."

"I don't expect you to pay for my classes, Daddy," Alicia protested. "I have a little money saved. If I'm careful I think I can afford this."

Daddy looked at her thoughtfully. "You really want to do this, don't you, Alicia?"

Alicia thought for a moment before answering.

"It's not so much that I want to. It's more something that I feel I need to do. I'm really not sure how I'll manage," she said honestly, "but I believe it will work out somehow."

"You have my blessing," her father told her. "We will help you as much as we can. I can't promise how much we will be able to give you, or when you will get it, but we will assist you as we are able."

He left the room. Mama had remained silent throughout the entire exchange. Alicia turned to her.

"What do you think, Mama?" she asked. "How do you feel about my plans?"

Mama smiled. She reached over and patted her daughter's arm gently.

"Do you remember when you were little, dear?" she asked. "Do you remember the holes you kept digging in the back yard?"

"I sure do, Mama." Alicia laughed. "I was determined I was going to dig my way to China, and Daddy was just as determined I wasn't!"

"I recall the day Daddy caught you," Mama told her.

Her mother's words brought images from that day to Alicia's mind. She remembered it as if it were yesterday.

"I remember what you told me after Daddy sent you inside," Mama said quietly.

"I said I would go to China someday, and that I would be a missionary there," Alicia stated.

Her mother nodded. She smiled at her daughter. "I've always known you would go to China one day, Alicia. I just didn't know when you would go."

The weeks that followed were busy as Alicia finalized her plans to return to school. She looked at the courses being offered, and the cost of tuition, then carefully reviewed her finances. When the money was counted and the options considered, Alicia knew she could not afford to study full-time.

She decided to approach the school officials and see if they would allow her to attend half days. To her surprise she found that the school administrators were happy to accommodate her. Her employer also encouraged her in her endeavour, and even promised to give her occasional work on Saturday mornings to help compensate for her smaller salary.

With everything in place, Alicia enrolled for the fall semester. She was in her room a few days before school started, when Aunt Helen came looking for her.

"I've spoken with your father," Aunt Helen informed Alicia. "He has agreed to decrease your room and board to five dollars a week as long as you are in school."

Alicia studied her aunt's face, wondering why she was the one sharing this news with her instead of her father.

"I appreciate the offer, Aunt Helen, but I'm not sure Daddy can afford to do that."

Alicia had no idea how she was going to meet her share of the household budget as well as her school expenses on half wages, but she was determined to try.

Aunt Helen smiled.

"It won't be a burden for your father at all," she told Alicia. She moved closer to Alicia and lowered her voice. "I am aware that your parents rely on the board they receive from both of us to keep things running smoothly. My room and board will increase, and yours will decrease."

"Aunt Helen, I can't let you do that for me," Alicia protested.

"You most certainly can," her aunt insisted. "I earn a decent wage, and I think I have been paying less than my share of the expenses around here." She looked at Alicia. "You have enough to concern yourself over without worrying about money too. I am happy to help out."

When her aunt left the room, Alicia sat down at her desk. She recalculated her budget, then sat back with a smile. With the reduction in her room and board, she would be able to balance things quite nicely.

***

Back to School

"I can hardly believe I'm doing this," Alicia commented as she ate breakfast with her parents the first day of the fall semester. "It doesn't seem possible that after working for so long I am now going back to school."

"You'll still be working, dear," Mama reminded her.

"I know." Alicia frowned, wondering if she would be able to juggle working and going to school at the same time. "I hope that I'll be able to keep up with the rest of the class, even though I'll only be attending half days."

"It shouldn't be a problem for you, Alicia," Aunt Helen encouraged. "You always did well in school."

"You'll have evenings for studying," Daddy reminded her.

"No, I won't."

Alicia's protest drew the attention of everyone at the table.

"My evenings will be busy too," she informed them. "Don't forget that in addition to my day classes, I've enrolled in language school at the university. That will be two evenings each week."

She sighed.

"I hope I haven't bitten off more than I can chew."

"It will be fine, Alicia," Aunt Helen assured her. She rose and carried her dishes to the small pantry off the kitchen.

"It's time I was off to work," she informed the family when she came back into the room. She patted Alicia's arm. "I look forward to hearing about your day when I return, dear."

Alicia departed from the house five minutes after her aunt, with a notebook tucked firmly under one arm. Nervous energy flowed through her as she walked to the location where her classes were being held.

It's amazing how it's all come together, she thought as she entered the building where she would be studying for the next two years. *Not long ago the world was at war, and the idea of going to China was nothing more than a childhood fantasy. Now I believe it is God's plan for my life, and today I am taking the first step to formally preparing for mission work.*

When the first week of classes was over, Alicia assessed the situation. She was pleased with how easily she'd been able to settle into her new routine. Each morning, Mama had breakfast waiting for her when she came downstairs. After breakfast she made her way to school, arriving in time for her nine o'clock class.

She left the building promptly at noon when they were dismissed and hurried home. Mama, ever punctual, always had a hot bowl of soup or a fresh sandwich waiting for her when she arrived. After a quick lunch, she caught the street car downtown and went to the office, where there was usually a stack of work waiting on her desk.

Yes, she decided, *things are working out well.* Her only disappointment was that she'd had no time to get to know the other students.

I'll have even less time once I start my language classes, but I'm there to learn, not to socialize, Alicia reminded herself. *Still, it would be nice to get better acquainted with some of my classmates.*

She was leaving school the following week, when two of the female students approached her.

"Are you in a hurry, Alicia?" the taller girl asked.

"I'm afraid I am, Eva." Though she'd had little time to mingle with the others, Alicia had made a point of memorizing their names. "I only have a moment."

She blushed, fearful that her words would be interpreted as a brush off.

"I'm sorry," she apologized. "I'm afraid that didn't come out quite the way I meant it to."

"That's okay." It was the shorter girl, Sally, who answered. She smiled. "We were wondering if you'd like to eat lunch with us today?"

"I appreciate the invitation," Alicia told them, "but I can't today."

"Tomorrow perhaps?" Sally suggested, but Alicia shook her head.

"Thursday?" Eva asked.

"I'm sorry, I really can't," Alicia told them. Eva and Sally exchanged glances, then turned away.

Oh dear, Alicia thought, as she watched them leave. *I've offended them!*

She looked at her watch. There was no time to go after them and explain now. Her apology would have to wait. She left the building and started out at a fast pace for home.

"You're late, dear."

Mama's words greeted Alicia the moment she opened the front door.

"I was beginning to grow concerned."

"I'm sorry, Mama," Alicia told her. "I didn't mean to worry you."

Between bites of her chicken sandwich, Alicia related the conversation she'd had with her classmates to her mother.

"I didn't mean to offend the girls, Mama. I just didn't have time to explain my situation to them."

"I'm sure they will understand when you tell them how things are," Mama reassured her. "Perhaps you should plan to have lunch with the girls one day before you go to work."

Alicia frowned. "I'm not sure I'd have time for that." She did not mention that she also couldn't afford to eat out.

"Why don't you invite the girls to come here for supper one evening?" Mama suggested.

"That's a lovely idea, Mama. Are you sure you wouldn't mind?"

"Your father and I would be happy to meet some of your classmates," Mama assured Alicia. "Why not ask Sally and Eva to join us on Friday evening?"

Excited about the idea of inviting the girls, Alicia took pains to arrive at school early the next morning. She sought out Eva and Sally before classes began and extended the invitation, which they graciously accepted.

When her work was finished on Friday, Alicia hurried home, eager to do her part to help her mother prepare for their company. In spite of her rush to get home early, she found that Aunt Helen had arrived ahead of her, and was already assisting Mama in the kitchen.

"Is there anything I can do to help, Mama?"

"I don't think so, dear." Mama looked up from the gravy she was stirring on the stove. "Why don't you slip upstairs and freshen up before your guests arrive?"

Though she would have willingly helped out in the kitchen, Alicia was grateful for the opportunity to change her dress and comb her hair before dinner. She was on her way back down the stairs, when a shadow covered the glass at the front door, and a knock sounded. She ran down the steps to answer it.

"Eva, Sally – I'm so happy you could come." She ushered the girls into the dining room, where she introduced them to the rest of the family.

When the meal was served and the blessing had been said, conversation between the three girls flowed freely. The older folk ate quietly, allowing the younger generation to become better acquainted.

Alicia learned that Eva lived in a small farming community an hour from Toronto, while Sally had come to the city from northern Ontario.

"What part of the north are you from, Sally?" Daddy asked when there was a lull in the conversation.

"My family lives in Sault Ste. Marie, Mr. Miller," the girl answered.

"I have been through your fair city," Mr. Miller told her. "I passed through there many years ago when I was travelling west to Brandon." He smiled. "You're a long way from home."

"I certainly am," Sally agreed. "One of the things I miss most about home is my mother's cooking."

She turned to Alicia's mother.

"My mother asked me to convey her thanks to you for inviting me this evening, Mrs. Miller," she said warmly. "She and I are both grateful."

Mama looked pleased. "We are happy to have both of you girls here," she assured them. "We hope you will come back often."

The conversation turned to other topics, including Alicia's work. "So now you see why I couldn't have lunch with you," Alicia said, when she had explained her work schedule.

The girls nodded.

"It must be difficult trying to get all your assignments done when you are working too," Sally said sympathetically.

"It helps that I live at home," Alicia told them.

"You are fortunate to be able to do so," Eva agreed. "But it is still a lot to keep up with school and work at the same time."

Alicia laughed. "I expect it will get even more difficult next week when I begin my language classes at the university."

"I didn't know you were taking language classes, Alicia." Sally looked at her in surprise. "What language will you be studying?"

"I'll be taking Chinese classes on Tuesday and Thursday evenings."

"I don't believe it!" Sally exclaimed. "So will I!"

The girls looked at each other.

"Are you planning to go to China?" Alicia asked tentatively.

Sally shook her head.

"No. I've just always had an interest in languages. Are you planning to go to China?"

"I hope to." Alicia's confession brought a touch of red to her face. It was the first time she had spoken of her ambition to anyone other than her family.

"I've always been interested in going to China," she went on. Memories of her ill-fated attempt to dig her way there two decades ago brought further colour to her cheeks, but she continued bravely. "Now I believe God may be calling me to go there as a missionary. That's why I enrolled in bible school."

Eva and Sally had been listening intently.

"Have you met John Hammond?" Sally asked.

"I don't believe I have."

Alicia frowned, trying to picture the man. The name was vaguely familiar, but she was unable to put a face with it.

"Is he in our class?"

Sally nodded, and her eyes sparkled.

"He's not only in our class," she informed Alicia. "He's also planning to do mission work in China."

Alicia gasped. Was it possible there was another student in their little school preparing for work in China?

"I'll introduce you," Sally went on. "John's taking Chinese classes at the university too. Maybe the three of us can go together."

"That sounds like a splendid idea." Alicia's father answered before she had opportunity to. "I would be grateful to have a young man escorting my daughter home from a late evening class, and I expect your father would feel the same way, Sally."

Before Eva and Sally left, it was agreed that Alicia would meet Sally at the university on Tuesday and they would attend class together.

"I'll introduce you to John," Sally whispered to Alicia before she left. "I have a feeling you're going to like him."

***

John Hammond

Alicia felt strangely nervous as she stood waiting for Sally on Tuesday evening. *I don't know which I'm more nervous about,* she thought, *my first language lesson or meeting John Hammond.*

Sally had pointed their fellow student out to her at class, but there had been no time for introductions. Alicia's heart fluttered as she recalled her first impression of John. He was of average height and was rather a stocky build, with wavy blond hair and brown eyes. It was the memory of his smile, however, that caused her pulse to race and her palms to sweat.

She wondered if Sally had pointed her out to John also, for once that morning, in the middle of the professor's lecture, he had turned and looked directly at her, flashing the most engaging smile.

You don't judge a book by its cover, and you don't judge a man by his looks, she reminded herself sternly. It was what was inside that counted. Still, she could not help feeling warm inside each time she remembered John's smile.

Alicia checked her watch. They would be late if Sally did not get there soon. When her friend still had not arrived ten minutes before the class was to start, Alicia decided to wait inside. She took a seat near the back of the class, in a location where there was room for Sally and John to join her when they came in.

The class was about to begin when Sally came rushing through the door, with John close on her heels. They slipped into the seats Alicia had reserved for them, exchanged smiles with her and turned their attention to the instructor at the front of the room.

When class was over and proper introductions had been made, John asked Alicia and Sally if he could treat them to a drink on the way home. Alicia's face must have revealed her surprise at the suggestion, for Sally answered quickly.

"That's very kind of you, John. I think a nice hot cup of tea would be lovely. Don't you, Alicia?"

She nudged her friend gently, and Alicia murmured her agreement.

Over tea at Fran's, they discussed the day courses they were taking, then the conversation turned to their first language lesson.

"I didn't realize the Mandarin language was so complicated," Alicia commented. "I don't know how I'll ever master it."

Sally nodded in agreement.

"It's not just learning the oral language that will be a challenge," she said. "It's the multitude of characters that make up the written language."

"Knowing both the oral and written language is essential if one is to work and live in China," John told them seriously. "In some ways though, I think it may be easier to learn than I had expected, since the three of us are taking the same course. I consider myself fortunate to have found other students from the bible college who are studying Chinese. I had expected to be the only one from our school."

"That's what I'd thought too," Alicia told John. "I could hardly believe it when Sally told me both of you would be in my class!"

"It will be good to have friends to practice our oral work with," John answered. "The written assignments, of course, we will have to do individually, but the spoken language can be practised whenever we are together."

When their drinks were finished, John escorted the girls home. Sally was dropped off first, because she lived the closest, leaving Alicia to walk several blocks alone with John.

The house was well lit when they approached, indicating to Alicia that her parents were awaiting her arrival, and no doubt were hoping for an introduction to John. She invited him in to meet her parents, hoping that he would not read more significance into the meeting than she intended.

When her father shook John's hand and thanked him for walking Alicia home, John answered that he was happy to do so.

"I don't like the idea of a young woman out on the streets alone at night," Daddy told John. "I'd have been happy to go and meet

Alicia myself, but Sally assured me that the girls would come to no harm with you present."

"I understand your concern, Mr. Miller," John told the older man politely. "I will be pleased to see Alicia home after language classes."

He took his leave, having made a suitable impression on Alicia's parents.

During the first month of language class, Alicia and Sally allowed John to treat them to a cup of tea after class each night. As time wore on, however, they began to decline the invitation.

"I don't want you to think I didn't appreciate you taking Sally and I out for tea, John," Alicia explained one evening as they walked home from Sally's. "In truth, I very much enjoyed it. It was a pleasant way to end the day."

She sighed.

"It's just that Tuesdays and Thursdays are such long days for me. I'm up early for school, then I go to work, then back to school in the evening." She laughed. "By the time it's over, I'm almost too tired to enjoy a cup of tea."

They approached a street light and John slowed, studying her features.

"What do you do between work and language class, Alicia?" he asked.

"I go home," she told him. "Mama has supper ready when I get there. After supper I turn around and head back out for class."

He looked puzzled.

"Don't you work downtown?" he queried.

"Yes," she answered.

"Your work isn't too far from the university, if I recall correctly."

"That's right."

"Would you consider having dinner with me one evening before class?" When Alicia hesitated, John went on. "It would save you the long trip home."

"That's very thoughtful, John."

"It would also save me the agony of eating alone," he said in a teasing manner, then added more seriously, "One's own company can get tiresome after a time."

Alicia looked up at him.

"I will be happy to accept," she told him, "if only to spare you eating another meal alone."

The conversation continued in a light-hearted manner the rest of the way home. Before departing, John agreed to meet Alicia at her place of work the following Thursday.

When Thursday arrived, Alicia took extra care picking out her clothing. She assured herself that her diligence had nothing to do with her planned dinner with John, but was due to the fact that she needed an outfit that would still look fresh and unwrinkled after eight hours of wear.

The day dragged by slowly. Alicia had difficulty concentrating at school, and even more difficulty at work. Her thoughts frequently drifted to the evening ahead, and she was relieved when her hours at work were over.

Before leaving the building, she slipped into the ladies' room. After combing her hair and straightening her dress, she checked to be sure she was alone in the room. Eyeing her reflection in the mirror, she spoke aloud.

"This is not a date, Alicia Miller," she told herself sternly. "It is simply two friends having a meal together."

She tried hard to convince herself of that fact, but her emotions told her there was already more to the relationship than just friendship.

John was outside the door when she came out of the building, patiently waiting for her. He took her to a small restaurant not far from the university. The food was simple, but satisfying. As they talked over the meal, she learned that John had grown up in Chicago.

"I had no idea you'd come from so far away, John," Alicia exclaimed. "How did you hear about our school?"

"My father is a friend of one of the fellows who teaches at the school," John told her. "Both he and I felt it would be a good place for me to get the training I need for mission work."

Time passed quickly as they talked of their mutual desire to work in China. Before they knew it, it was time to leave for class.

"I enjoyed the evening very much, John," Alicia told him later, as they walked home after class. "Thank you for dinner."

"It was my pleasure," John answered.

They walked in silence the remainder of the way. When they reached the house, John bid her a quick goodbye, so quick that it left Alicia wondering if her friend had enjoyed the evening as much as she had.

She saw John the next morning at class, but other than a smile and a wave they had no contact. When the same thing happened the following Monday and again on Tuesday, Alicia began to think that John was avoiding her.

She sought Sally out after class. Knowing she had little time to talk, Alicia came right to the point.

"Do you think I could go home first tonight, Sally?"

The three of them were in the habit of leaving the university together, and going by the house where Sally was staying, before going on to Alicia's.

Sally frowned.

"It's rather out of the way, Alicia, but I suppose we could do it that way. Is there any particular reason?"

"I'd just like to get home earlier," Alicia told her. She was reluctant to tell her friend that she did not want to be alone with John.

Sally shrugged. "It's all right with me, if it's all right with John," she told Alicia.

"Thanks, Sally."

Alicia felt a sense of relief as they began the walk home after the evening class, knowing she would not be alone with John. It was obvious there was something about their situation that made him uncomfortable, and she had no desire to make things more difficult.

When they reached the corner where they usually turned, Alicia started on to her house, but John turned in the usual direction. Alicia's heart raced. It appeared he had not gotten the message from Sally. She moved close enough that she could nudge Sally, but her friend continued chattering as if nothing was amiss.

Alicia felt trapped. It was impossible to change direction without making a fuss, so she accompanied Sally home then turned reluctantly to finish the journey alone with John. For several blocks they walked in silence. They had almost reached Alicia's home when John spoke.

"I need to talk to you about the other night, Alicia," he said quietly.

Alicia tensed, wondering what was coming next. John cleared his throat.

"I enjoyed having dinner with you," he told her.

When Alicia did not reply, he stopped walking and turned to face her.

"Did you enjoy it, Alicia?"

"I did."

I enjoyed it a little too much, she thought. She'd felt the evening had moved them to a different level in their relationship – not dating exactly, but certainly more than just friends. She'd even dared to hope that the friendship might develop into love. It seemed fitting somehow; both of them studying for mission work in the same country. She'd thought that they had been brought together – two strangers with a common goal – and had envisioned them labouring side by side for their Lord in a foreign land.

But all that was before John had given her the cold shoulder at class for three days. Clearly she'd read more into the evening than she should have.

John cleared his throat again. It was obvious that he had something important to say, and that he was uncomfortable saying it.

"I enjoyed our dinner very much," he repeated, "although I'm sure my behaviour these last few days has done little to indicate that."

He began walking again.

"I must apologize, Alicia. It was not that I was uncomfortable with you, or that I had no wish to be with you. I would, in fact, like to have dinner with you again. I simply had some things that I had to work through before I felt free to ask you."

By the time John finished speaking they had reached Alicia's home. He walked her to the door. In the dimness of the porch light he turned to Alicia.

"Would you have dinner with me again, Alicia?"

Alicia hesitated only a moment. It was not in her nature to hold a grudge. John had apologized for his rudeness. He'd explained that he had things to work through before he could ask her to dine with him again. What those things were was none of her business.

She smiled.

"I would be happy to have dinner with you, John," she told him.

"Thursday night?" he asked.

"Thursday night would be fine."

Alicia watched John as he turned and walked away. Her heart was racing as she unlatched the door and entered the house.

***

Dating

Thursday evening dinners with John became a regular event, and soon became the highlight of Alicia's week. The rest of the week, although busy, seemed dull in comparison to the two hours she spent with John before language class on Thursdays.

They laughed as they talked together, getting to know each other and exchanging stories from their early years. Occasionally they would attempt to converse in Chinese, an event that always ended in laughter.

"I thought my Chinese was getting better," Alicia commented after one particularly frustrating exercise. She had been asking John to pass her the salt, but he had deliberately misinterpreted her request and had, instead, passed her everything else at the table.

"It is," John agreed, "but we both need to keep working on it. We need to master the language before we get to China."

Alicia's heart quickened. It was not the first time John had referred to China as if they would be working together in that country. She glanced at her watch, forcing herself to concentrate on the present rather than the future.

"We need to go," she told John. "Sally will be wondering where we are."

They rose and moved to the door. Alicia discreetly stepped aside while John paid the bill.

Outside the chill night air caused Alicia to pull her coat up around her neck. As they walked the short distance to their night class, she spoke.

"The only problem with having dinner with you, John Hammond," she told him in a teasing manner, "is that it usually makes me late for class."

She linked her arm in his.

"I don't like to be late for anything."

"I know you don't, Alicia," John told her. "That's one of the things I admire about you." He grinned. "It's a good thing Sally is usually on time and saves seats for us."

Alicia had worried that Sally would feel excluded when she began dining with John on Thursdays, but Sally had encouraged the relationship.

They arrived just as the class was about to begin. As they took their seats beside Sally, Alicia resolved to monitor her time more closely when she met John for dinner.

When the lesson that evening was over, the teacher challenged the class to form groups of two or three and commit to speaking only the Mandarin Chinese language when they were together.

"You will be amazed at how quickly your oral language skills will increase," he told them.

Alicia and John took the professor's advice seriously, and attempted to speak no English on the walk home. Sally tried to join in the conversation, but she found it difficult.

"I don't seem to be learning as fast as you two," she moaned.

"That's because you're not motivated enough," John informed her.

Sally paused in her step and stared at him.

"How can you say that, John?" she asked. "I haven't missed a single class and I do all my homework. How can you say I'm not motivated?"

"I didn't say you weren't motivated," John corrected gently. "I said you weren't motivated *enough*."

A lift of his hand silenced her retort.

"Let me explain," he begged. "You are a dedicated student, Sally. As you already pointed out, you attend class, and you work on your lessons outside of class.

"The difference between you and Alicia and I is that Alicia and I actually plan to go to China. We are motivated because we know we must learn the language in order to communicate when we get there.

"You are interested in learning the language, but you don't anticipate ever using what you learn on a daily basis."

Alicia listened to John's explanation with interest. It made sense. Sally had told them more than once that she was struggling to learn the Mandarin dialect, but Alicia had never looked at it the way John had. For Sally, language class was merely a subject of interest. For Alicia and John, it was the key to their future. One could not expect to be welcomed in a foreign country if one did not know the language.

Life settled into a busy but happy routine for Alicia. She enjoyed her work and her studies, but enjoyed her Thursday evening dinners with John even more. John became more time-conscious after Alicia's teasing remark, and they were not late for class again. Their language skills improved as they practised their chosen language whenever they were together.

On weeks when they were both free on a Saturday, John would sometimes take her to the market in Chinatown. Together they would stroll through the market and examine the goods for sale. Though their main reason for going was to work on their language skills, on occasion John would purchase a small gift for Alicia or treat her to a meal. She was not terribly fond of the food, but forced herself to eat it anyway, reminding herself that she might as well acquire a taste for it now as there would be little option when she went overseas.

Trips to the market always left Alicia feeling that she had visited China, and made her even more eager to complete her studies and go to that country. They were on their way home from one of their excursions to Chinatown, when John told her of a group he was interested in attending.

"It's called the China Inland Mission," John explained. "I think they meet once a month, but I'm not certain. In any event there is a meeting next week that I plan to attend. I wonder if you would be interested in accompanying me."

"I'd love to, John."

He smiled at her and she blushed, hoping her quick answer would be taken as enthusiasm for the event and not as a desire to spend more time with him.

"We'll plan to go together then," he told her.

Alicia felt as if she was floating when John dropped her off. She was excited about the meeting John had invited her to. *It's because I am interested in missions, and in the country of China,* Alicia told herself. *I'd want to go to this meeting even if John weren't going!*

The meeting the following week was held in a church hall, not far from their school. Alicia and John arrived early for the service and took a seat near the front. People kept coming in, and there were few seats left by the time the meeting started.

Alicia, who had been uncertain what to expect, found the service interesting and informative. When it was over, refreshments were served. She and John stayed for tea, and spent some time mingling with others.

They discussed the service on the way home.

"It's wonderful to find something that focuses on mission work in China," Alicia said enthusiastically. "All the other training is wonderful, but this is different. This is all about China. I want to go again."

"I agree," John told her. "It's important that we learn as much as we can about the geography of the country, the customs and the culture before we go there."

They parted, having agreed to add meetings held by the China Inland Mission to their scheduled evenings out.

Alicia had been attending the meetings on a regular basis with John for some time, when they arrived later than usual one evening, and found the room already full. As they stood at the back and surveyed the group, looking for a place to sit, Alicia noticed some of the girls from school and waved. They waved back, indicating that there was room for the couple to sit with them.

She turned to suggest it to John, but found that he was no longer beside her. Looking around, she was surprised to see that he had moved to a position several feet from her. She approached him, but when she mentioned there was room for them to sit with some of the other students, he shook his head.

"You go ahead and sit with the girls, Alicia," he encouraged her. "I'll find a seat with some of the fellows."

"There's room for both of us, John," she told him.

He shook his head again.

"No, you go, Alicia." He smiled. "Go ahead. I'll meet up with you again after the meeting."

He was gone before she could think of a response. She watched as he moved to an area where a number of young men were sitting and took a seat beside them.

Baffled by the incident, but having no desire to make a scene over it, Alicia moved quickly to join her school chums near the front of the room. She tried to concentrate on the session that followed, but found it difficult to do so. When the meeting was over, she met John, and was further disappointed when he ushered her out the door instead of staying for refreshments.

The walk home was a quiet one. John offered no explanation for his behaviour, and Alicia asked for none.

If I didn't know better, I'd think John didn't want to be seen with me, she thought. She shook her head. That idea was pure nonsense. Why, they'd been seen together all over the city!

All right, she corrected herself, *not all over the city, but we've certainly spent a lot of time together and gone a lot of places together, and he's never acted this way before.*

His *good night* when they parted was warm, causing Alicia to give herself a mental scolding. She was reading too much into the incident. Surely it would not happen again.

Nightly walks home after language class and Thursday evening dinners continued. Along with these activities, the trips to the Chinatown market and the monthly mission meetings, Mama and Daddy began inviting John for dinner weekly. He became a regular guest at the house – one who fitted into the family quite nicely.

Alicia was particularly pleased with how well her father and John got along. Her own time with John was cut short when he visited, as the two men sat discussing everything from the weather to theology.

One evening, a few months before Alicia was due to graduate, her parents asked if they might sit down with her and have a family discussion. Alicia agreed, and the following Sunday afternoon was chosen as the time for their conference.

When the noon meal was over and the dishes were cleared, Aunt Helen excused herself and went to her room, leaving Alicia alone with her parents. They took seats in the living room, with Mama and Daddy seated on the sofa and Alicia sitting in a chair across from them.

Alicia waited patiently, knowing it would be her father who would begin the conversation, and that he would speak when he was ready. At last he cleared his throat.

"Your graduation is approaching, Alicia."

"Yes," Alicia agreed. "I can hardly believe it. The time has passed so quickly."

"Your mother and I would like to know what your plans are after graduation," Daddy informed her.

Alicia looked from her father to her mother.

"I'm planning to go to China," she answered slowly. When neither of her parents responded, she added quietly, "I thought you knew that."

"And what are John's intentions?" Daddy asked.

"John is planning to go to China also," Alicia answered.

"Yes," her father told her. "I am aware of John's work intentions. What I am not aware of are his intentions toward you."

He looked at her.

"Has John spoken to you of marriage, Alicia?"

"No," she answered, "not directly."

"What do you mean by *not directly*, dear?"

The words, softly spoken, came from Mama. Alicia looked at her.

"John always talks as if we will be working together in China," she told her, "but he has never actually mentioned marriage."

"I see," Mama answered quietly. She looked troubled by her daughter's words.

"Yes," Daddy said. They looked at each other, then back at Alicia.

"Is this a problem?" Alicia asked. She looked at her father, waiting for a reply. Daddy was always more outspoken than Mama.

"I would not say that there is a problem, Alicia," her father told her, "but I will admit to having some concern over a young man who spends so much time with my daughter and has neither asked me for her hand in marriage nor spoken of the matter to her."

"I think John is just shy about the subject, Daddy," Alicia responded. "I feel certain that John and I have a future together. The fact that he has not yet asked me to marry him does not trouble me. John will propose when he is ready."

"I would prefer that he spoke of the matter to me first," her father reminded her.

"I'm sure he will, Daddy," Alicia assured him, then added, "when he is ready."

***

Graduation Heartbreak

"I'm so excited I could just burst," Alicia whispered to Sarah.

"Has John popped the question yet?" Sarah whispered back, observing the flush on her sister's face.

"No, but I feel certain that he will soon," Alicia answered dreamily. She glanced into the living room, where her boyfriend was seated. Beside him sat her father, while across from him sat his own parents. Mr. and Mrs. Hammond had arrived from the States the previous evening, with plans to attend their son's graduation ceremony.

When Mama had learned that John's parents were in the city, she'd organized an impromptu dinner party the evening before graduation. The entire family had been invited. Sarah, Jake, and William had dropped whatever plans they might have had to attend the dinner on short notice. It seemed everyone was eager to meet the couple they expected to be Alicia's in-laws someday.

"We'd best go in," Sarah told Alicia.

"I know," Alicia agreed, but she made no effort to move.

"Come on," Sarah said, encouraging her sister with a slight prod of her elbow.

"We'll go in a minute," Alicia answered softly. "I just need a little more time."

Though she could not have said why, she knew it was important that she preserve this moment; that she tuck it away in her mind like a photograph tucked into an album. Instinctively she knew that someday she would need to look back and reflect on it.

Dinner that evening was a noisy, happy affair. The dining room seemed crowded with such a large group gathered around the table. Daddy and Mama were in their respective positions as hosts at opposite ends of the table. Aunt Helen was seated on Mama's right, with William, Sarah and Jacob beside her. Alicia and John sat on the opposite side, next to John's parents.

"This is a wonderful meal, Mrs. Miller," John's mother offered, turning to face her hostess. "It was thoughtful of you to invite us."

Alicia's mother smiled.

"It is our pleasure," she assured her guests. "We are happy you could join us."

"Mrs. Miller's meals are always delicious," John informed his parents. "I've been fortunate to be able to partake of her cooking many times these past two years."

"We certainly appreciate the kindness you've shown to our son, Mr. and Mrs. Miller," Mr. Hammond told them. "John has written of you often. It has meant a lot to his mother and me to know that he had a couple like you in his life when he was so far from home."

Alicia felt John stiffen beside her. She glanced at him. She sensed that he was uncomfortable with his father's words, but could not understand why.

"Your son is welcome in our home anytime, Mr. Hammond." Alicia's father spoke from his place at the end of the table. "Alicia and John have become such close friends that we practically regard him as family already. It is almost as if he were our own son."

The comment, offered in all sincerity, caused John's father to chuckle.

"Our son has a way of fitting in wherever he goes," he said proudly.

His wife nodded.

"Simone's family said almost the same thing about John when they first met him," she offered.

Alicia felt shock go through her at Mrs. Hammond's words. She turned to John, her eyes seeking his, but he kept his gaze fixed firmly on the plate in front of him.

"Is Simone a friend from Chicago?" Daddy asked. Alicia wondered if she was the only one who noticed the chill that had crept into her father's tone. Mr. and Mrs. Hammond laughed.

"You might say that," John's father answered in a jolly manner. It was obvious he was unaware of the effect his words were having on the rest of the room.

"Simone is John's girlfriend," Mrs. Hammond explained. She looked at the group assembled and her voice dropped to a dramatic whisper.

"There's nothing official yet," she said, speaking as if to her closest friends, "but we anticipate a formal announcement will be made soon after our return to Chicago."

Alicia felt the world spinning around her and fought to hold on. Though she would have gladly welcomed the relief that unconsciousness would bring, she forced herself to hang on to reality. She finished the meal in silence, longing for the evening to end so she could excuse herself and go upstairs. When it was over at last, Alicia stood in the hallway watching as the Hammonds bid her parents goodbye.

"We'll see you at the graduation ceremonies tomorrow," Mr. Hammond said in parting.

"Yes," Mr. Miller responded. "We look forward to the evening very much."

A sob caught in Alicia's throat. She too had looked forward to this graduation with much anticipation. She had expected that the end of her formal education would coincide with her engagement to John. Nothing in her relationship with him had prepared her for the news his parents had shared tonight.

A hand touching her elbow caused Alicia to jump. She turned and saw her sister standing behind her.

"Are you all right, 'Licia?" Sarah whispered.

Alicia nodded, not trusting herself to speak.

"Do you want to talk about it?"

A quick shake of her head was all Alicia could manage before tears spilled from her eyes, causing her to retreat upstairs.

The mood was sombre the next evening as the family prepared for Alicia's graduation ceremonies. Together they made their way to the hall where the event was being held. Alicia was grateful that the ceremony was well attended; making it impossible for her family and John's to sit together.

She went through the motions of the evening, standing and sitting at the appropriate times, rising and walking across the platform when her name was called, and humbly accepting the certificate she had earned.

A sense of relief washed over her when the event ended, and she could go home. She was leaving the building with her parents when John approached.

"I'd like to walk you home, Alicia," he informed her.

She shook her head.

"No," she answered slowly. "I don't think that would be a good idea."

"There are things I need to say to you," John told her. "Things I need to explain."

The look in his eyes was so beseeching, and the expression on his face so sincere, that Alicia felt she had no choice but to allow his request. She turned to her father.

"John will see me home, Daddy."

Her father sent her a questioning look. He opened his mouth to speak, thought better of it, and closed it again. With a silent nod he turned, offered Mama his arm, and escorted her from the building.

Alicia and John left a moment later. They followed her parents, walking a discreet distance behind them. They had gone more than a block when John finally spoke.

"I owe you an apology, Alicia," he offered. "I never meant for this to happen. I fear you may have read more into our friendship than I intended."

When Alicia said nothing in reply, he continued.

"I was lonely when I came here. I was far from home, with no friends, and few people I knew. Then I met you. We had so much in common. We had the same beliefs and goals for our lives, and shared a common dream of living and working in China.

"You were so easy to be with. When I was alone with you, I forgot all about my life in Chicago. There was just you and me and our common desires."

"That's all there was for me too, John," Alicia told him quietly. "The difference is that for me, what we had was real. For you, it was just a game, a way to pass time till you went back to Chicago."

"Those are harsh words, Alicia," John told her, "and they are words that are untrue."

"Are they, John?"

"I never meant to hurt you," John protested, carefully avoiding her question. "And I never meant to mislead you."

Alicia said nothing in response. After all that had happened, what was there to say? There was no sense arguing. It would not change the situation.

They reached the walkway to the house. John reached out and opened the gate, but he made no attempt to go through it.

"Good night, Alicia."

"Goodbye, John."

"I hope we can still be friends." John's final words trailed behind Alicia as she walked up the path. She blinked. It was too late to be friends. As she opened the door, she blinked again. Upstairs, in the privacy of her room, Alicia allowed the tears to fall. She was not sure who she felt the sorriest for, or who she was crying for; herself, John, or Simone.

***

Summer of '48

Alicia felt sadness mixed with relief when she received word that John had returned to Chicago. She'd felt tense in the days that followed her graduation, knowing John was still in the city but no longer wishing to see her. Alicia worried that his parents would not understand why they hadn't seen the Miller family again before they left, yet was grateful to her own parents for keeping their distance. She had no desire to offend Mr. and Mrs. Hammond. It simply would have been too painful to spend an evening in their company again, knowing the future she'd dreamed of with John was over.

For a time following the break-up, Alicia wondered what direction her life would take now that John was no longer part of it. She still longed to go to China, but suddenly it seemed like a major thing to undertake on her own. She was musing about her future, trying to reconcile herself to the idea of serving in China without John, when Sally invited her to join a group of students going on a trip to Prince Edward Island.

"Why don't you come with us?" she asked Alicia.

"I'd like to," Alicia told her, "but I don't think I should. I ought to be working on getting things in place for going to China, not going off on a holiday."

"It's not exactly a holiday we're going on," Sally informed her. "It's a summer mission trip. We'll be seeing new places and doing interesting things, but the main reason we're organizing the trip is to give us experience speaking at meetings and running programs for children and adults."

She looked at Alicia.

"It would be good for you to get away," she told her gently. "You've had a rough time lately."

Alicia winced at her friend's reference to the break-up with John.

"I'm sorry," Sally apologized. "I didn't mean to bring up a painful subject. It's just that I'm worried about you. I think a change of scenery would be good for you. The trip would give you a chance to get away and think things through, and it would allow you to see how well suited you are to mission work at the same time."

"I'll think about it," Alicia promised.

"Don't take too long to decide," Sally told her. "We'll be leaving a week from Tuesday."

"What would you think of me spending the summer in Prince Edward Island?" Alicia asked her parents at supper that evening.

Mama looked up from the bread she was buttering.

"Did you say Prince Edward Island, dear?"

Alicia nodded, her eyes bright with excitement at the thought. She had been thinking of the trip ever since Sally left, and had decided it might be just what she needed to help her get over John.

"One of the boys that was in my class at bible school is from P.E.I.," she explained. "Sally told me today that he is arranging for a group of young people to go down and do mission work for the summer. I think I'd like to go."

"It does sound like a wonderful opportunity," her mother agreed. "Would you travel by train?"

"No. Arnold has a car and plans to drive," Alicia told her. She laughed. "I asked Sally if she was sure there'd be room for me, and she said Arnold will pack as many people into the car as want to go."

"I'm not certain I like the idea of a group of young people travelling so far by automobile," Alicia's father commented.

"Arnold's a good driver, Daddy," Alicia assured him. "I don't think the car will be really packed either. I think there'd only be five or six all together, including me if I go." She went on to describe the plans Sally had shared for the summer work.

When she had finished Mama looked at Daddy.

"I think it would be good for Alicia to go, don't you, dear?" she asked.

"Yes," he answered quietly. "I do. I've no doubt it would be a good experience."

"I'll speak to them at work tomorrow," Alicia told her parents, "and see if I can arrange for extra time off."

To Alicia's surprise and delight, her boss was willing to accommodate her request.

"I can give you a month's leave," he told her, "but I can only pay you for the week of holidays that you are entitled to."

Alicia thanked him for granting her the time off, then returned to her work station. She spent the remainder of the day working to ensure that everything was caught up before she left, and that she was leaving no unfinished business. Satisfied that everything was in order, she said goodbye to her co-workers and left at the end of the day. She left the office with a light-hearted feeling that she had not experienced since her break-up with John.

The days that remained before her departure were filled with activity. There were shopping excursions with Mama, trips to the park with Sarah and William, and packing.

If I have this much trouble packing for a month, Alicia thought, *what am I going to do when I leave for China? I'll have to pack everything I'll need for four years then!*

The thought sobered her. She returned to her packing with renewed zeal, determined to finish quickly so she could spend her final evening at home with her family. At last the task of sorting was completed. She stood back and observed the neatly stacked piles of things she hoped to take.

"Oh dear," she moaned aloud, "where will I put it all?"

There was far more than she could fit into one or two bags. She was about to start sorting through everything again, when a knock sounded at the door and Mama entered.

"I've come to see if you need help packing, dear," she told Alicia. She looked around the room. "It appears my offer to assist has come too late."

"Actually, you may be just in time to help, Mama." Alicia sighed. "I thought I was doing a wonderful job organizing everything. I set out clothes for all types of weather, and took extra as I don't know what laundry facilities will be available for us there. Besides, I figured we may be too busy with our activities to have much time to wash clothes.

"Now that I have it all laid out, I realize my plan was foolish. There is simply no way I can take all this!" She waved at the stacks of clothing that filled the room. "I think I need to start all over again, and take only what I am sure I will use."

Alicia started to sort through one of the piles, but her mother stopped her.

"It is always better to take more than you need, Alicia. It's better to have too much than too little."

"I know, Mama, but I can't fit all this into one or two suitcases."

"No," her mother agreed, "you can't."

"There won't be room for any people in Arnold's car if we all pack this much."

They both laughed at Alicia's comment.

"Your father has a solution," Mama told her. "He has ordered a travel trunk for you from Simpsons'. It will be delivered this afternoon.

"You can pack what you will need for the journey in a small suitcase. The rest can go in the trunk, which your father will send down by train."

"But, Mama," Alicia protested. "The cost of a trunk..."

Her mother smiled.

"You will need it when you go overseas," she reminded her. "We are simply purchasing it a little earlier than we had planned."

The trip to P.E.I. turned out to be more of an adventure than Alicia had anticipated. Six young people piled into Arnold's car on Monday morning. Determined to get an early start, they left the city before daylight. The sun rose as they travelled eastward. It filled the sky with brilliant hues of red and orange as it made its ascent, but Alicia and Arnold were the only ones who witnessed the scene. The other four passengers fell asleep by the time they reached the city limits.

Because of her location in the city, Alicia had been the last one in the group to be picked up. As a result, the better seats had all been taken, and she had been forced to squeeze into the middle position in the front seat.

Never having travelled any distance by automobile, Alicia observed Arnold as he manoeuvred the large vehicle down the highway. It seemed to her that his hands and feet were never still. She watched in fascination as he expertly shifted gears with his hand and manipulated the clutch with his foot. She was not aware that Arnold had noticed her interest until he spoke.

"Do you drive, Alicia?" he asked. The question took her by surprise.

"Oh no!" she answered. "My family doesn't even have a car."

"That explains why you are watching my moves so closely." Arnold chuckled softly. "I was concerned that you thought I was doing something wrong."

Alicia blushed.

"I'd like to learn to drive someday," she said, making an attempt to cover her embarrassment.

"I'd be happy to teach you," Arnold told her.

"I'd like that."

They drove in silence for a time, enjoying the scenery, then Alicia spoke again.

"I've been thinking about your offer, Arnold," she told him. "I appreciate that you would be willing to teach me to drive, but I'm not sure there'd be any point in it. No one in my family owns a car, so it really doesn't make sense for me to learn to drive one. I'd have no opportunity to practice."

"There'll be plenty of time for you to practice over the next month," Arnold assured her. "It's good to know how to operate an automobile, even if you don't have one yourself. It might be useful sometime in the future.

"Learning to drive is like learning to ride a bicycle. Once you learn how you never forget."

"One takes a lot of tumbles before they are able to ride a bicycle," Alicia reminded him. "What if I do something wrong and damage your car?"

"I'm not worried about that," Arnold told her confidently, "and you shouldn't be either."

Their conversation was interrupted by the sound of someone stirring behind them. A moment later a male voice called out from the back seat.

"Are we there yet?"

Arnold laughed.

"Good morning, Sam," he answered. "No, we are not there yet."

Awakened by the noise around her, Sally spoke up.

"How much longer till we get to P.E.I.?" she asked sleepily.

She joined in the laughter when she realized Sam had asked a similar question just moments before.

"We've a long way to go yet," Arnold informed them. "Don't worry – I promise we'll arrive in time for the service on Sunday."

He flashed them a smile, causing Alicia to wonder if he was serious or not.

"How long will it take to get there, Arnold?" she asked quietly.

"It will be a few days," he told her.

"A few days!" she exclaimed. She hoped her small suitcase held enough to last that long. Why hadn't she thought to ask Sally how long this trip would take before she packed? All she'd thought about was the length of time she would be gone from home, not how long it might take to get to and from the island. For the first time she regretted sending most of her belongings by train.

"We could get there quicker if we wanted to," Arnold told her, "but we wouldn't get to see nearly as much. Who knows, this may be the only chance some of the group will ever have to travel to Canada's east coast. I want to show them as much as I can along the way."

Arnold had planned the trip well, Alicia decided as they neared their destination at the end of the week. They'd seen many new things along the way. Already she had so much to write home about that she was afraid it would take more than one letter to tell it all.

They'd stopped at a home in Quebec the first night. There had been much to see as they travelled on through that province and into the Maritimes. They'd travelled along the St. Lawrence River as far as Quebec City. There they had crossed the mighty river via the Quebec Bridge, considered by many to be the eighth wonder of the world when it was opened to the public thirty years earlier. Alicia had enjoyed crossing the massive structure. The bridge, according to Arnold, had originally been designed for use as a railway bridge, but today accommodated both automobiles and trains.

From Quebec they'd travelled to New Brunswick. There they'd visited Grand Falls, and been impressed by its natural beauty. While not as majestic as Ontario's Niagara Falls, the group still found the site impressive. Later, Arnold took them to the Bay of Fundy, where they experienced the thrill of walking on the ocean floor at low tide.

"You wouldn't want to be here when the tide comes back in," Arnold told them. "This area has the highest tides in the world!"

They'd gone on to Nova Scotia, where they'd stayed overnight with friends of Arnold's in Truro. From Truro they'd gone to Halifax. In that city they'd been privileged to have a tour of the Zeeland, a boat from the Netherlands that was anchored in the Halifax harbour.

Now they were on the ferry crossing over to Prince Edward Island. Alicia was not familiar enough with the geography of the area to know how many of the places they'd stopped at would have been on their route anyway, and how many were extras thrown in by Arnold to show off his part of Canada.

"We're on the home stretch now," Arnold informed them as he drove off the ferry. A bright smile lit his face. "There's no place quite like home, and I can't think of anywhere I'd rather call home than Prince Edward Island!"

"Are we close to your folks' place?" Sally asked.

"We've a ways to go yet," Arnold answered, "but it won't take long now."

There was no mistaking the pleasure he felt at being back on the island.

***

Prince Edward Island

The first week in P.E.I. was filled with so many activities that Alicia felt as if she were caught up in a whirlwind. Each morning her group ran a vacation bible school for children from the surrounding area. In the afternoons there were meetings for the women, and in the evenings they held services that were attended by all ages.

The spare moments at the end of the day were filled with preparation for the next day's meetings. Crafts for the children had to be planned ahead, and the pieces for them organized so the activity could be completed in the allotted time. Lessons had to be studied and, in Alicia's case, music had to be practised.

They had been loaned a small portable organ that could be moved from place to place for the meetings. Alicia was the only one skilled at playing such an instrument, so it fell to her to provide the musical accompaniment for the singing at all three daily meetings.

The first opportunity to rest came on the Saturday following their arrival on the island. Cheers sounded when Arnold announced on Friday night that they would have the next day free.

"In that case, I do believe I'll spend the entire day sleeping," Sally responded. Her statement was emphasized by a dainty yawn.

"I'd like to go fishing," Sam declared. "Are there any good streams nearby?"

As the good-natured banter continued, Alicia mentally formed her own plans for the following day.

The first thing I must do is my washing, she decided. *Then I will sit down and write letters to Mama and Daddy, to Sarah and Jake, and to Aunt Helen. If I have time, I might even write a short letter to William.*

Satisfied that she had her day planned appropriately, she turned her attention back to her friends.

"We'll have tomorrow free," Arnold repeated. "Each of us can spend the day as we please. There'll be no meetings or formal activities."

He paused.

"On Sunday we'll attend the morning service here, then we'll head on up island for next week's meetings. It would be a good idea if you could have everything packed tomorrow night.

"Take only what you will need for the week. The rest of your belongings can stay here. We'll drive back here after the evening meeting next Friday."

Alicia rose early Saturday morning, determined not to waste her day of leisure sleeping. She crept from the room and made her way downstairs to the kitchen. She'd carried her laundry down the night before, fearing the noise she would make gathering it in the morning might waken her roommates.

While the other girls slept, Alicia worked. By the time they came downstairs mid-morning Alicia had her dresses all hung out on the clothesline. Personal items were strung on makeshift clotheslines indoors. They would take longer to dry inside, but modesty dictated that such items not be displayed outdoors for the world to see. She was grateful the girls had been given a separate house to use while they were on the island. Laundry would have been difficult in shared facilities.

With the laundry taken care of, Alicia sat down with pen and paper at the kitchen table. She had just begun her first letter when a knock sounded at the door. She opened it, and was surprised to find Arnold standing on the other side.

"Are you busy, Alicia?" he asked, after they had exchanged greetings.

"You've come at a good time, Arnold," Alicia told him. "I've just finished my washing."

She steered him to a seat on the front porch. It would not do to invite him into the house when her undergarments were spread around the kitchen.

"Did you have other plans for today?" Arnold asked when they were seated.

"I have letters to write," Alicia answered, "but they can be done later." She sighed. "The truth is there's so much to write about that I hardly know where to start."

Arnold laughed.

"It's been a busy week," he agreed.

"It's not just this week," Alicia reminded him. "I haven't had time to write a real letter since I got here. All I did when we got here was send a note off stating that we had arrived safely. I promised that I would send details of the trip later, but I haven't had opportunity. I have almost two weeks news to share!"

"Would you like to include your first driving lesson in the news you send home?" Arnold asked in a casual manner.

"I can't think of anything more exciting to write home about," Alicia responded, a huge smile lighting her face as she spoke.

"Then there's no time like the present," Arnold informed her.

The remaining weeks on the island passed in much the same way as the first one. Each Sunday they travelled to a different location for the week long meetings, always returning to their home base on Friday evenings.

Wherever they went, Arnold found opportunity to give Alicia driving lessons. Alicia admired the patience Arnold had with her. He seemed instinctively to understand how nervous she was, and was careful to end each outing with words of praise and encouragement.

"You've learned well, Alicia," Arnold told her, as they came to the end of their fourth week on the island. "I don't think you'll have any difficulty passing the test for your full license."

"Thank you, Arnold." Alicia beamed at the praise. "You've been a good teacher."

Arnold's words echoed in Alicia's mind that evening as she packed her bags. She wondered if she would have a chance to drive again after she returned to Ontario. She couldn't help feeling sad that her time on the island was over. It was difficult to leave now, when the rest of the group were staying on. But she had been granted only a month's leave, and that month was almost over. Her boss had been generous in allowing the time off. It would be unfair to ask for an extension.

She finished her packing, turned out the light and crawled into bed. Arnold would be there early in the morning to take her to the train station.

Alicia fought to hold back tears as she exchanged hugs and kisses with her friends and members of the community the morning of her departure. She was surprised at the number of people that assembled to see her off.

When the men had wrestled her trunk into the back of the car and secured it, Arnold turned to her. He held out his hand, displaying the keys.

"Would you care to drive, Alicia?"

She smiled as she reached for the keys. It was just like Arnold to do something like this to make her forget her sorrow at leaving. Alicia settled into the driver's seat, with Arnold positioned beside her on the passenger side. In an effort to impress those watching, she pressed her foot to the floor. The vehicle coughed and sputtered in protest, threatening to stall, then grudgingly lurched forward. A trail of black smoke followed them as Alicia drove away.

Embarrassed by the incident, Alicia lifted her foot from the gas pedal and determined to proceed cautiously for the remainder of the way. She drove so cautiously, in fact, that Arnold commented on it.

"If you don't speed up a little," he told her gently, "you may not arrive at the station before the train departs."

They reached an open stretch of highway, and Alicia lowered her foot, accelerating. Feeling confident once more, she brought the automobile up to the speed limit. They came to the bottom of a hill and Alicia accelerated again, as Arnold had taught her, endeavouring to maintain her speed while climbing. She neglected to ease up on the gas when she reached the crest of the hill, and they flew down the other side. When she continued travelling well above the posted speed limit, Arnold spoke again.

"You can slow down now, Alicia," he said. "I think we've made up for the time we lost back there."

He laughed.

"The only reason we might not make it in time now would be if the police stopped you for going too fast."

The words were no sooner out of Arnold's mouth than they rounded a bend and saw a police car ahead. Alicia eased up once more on the gas pedal, allowing the car to slow considerably. She hoped to drive on by unnoticed, but the red lights on the top of the cruiser began flashing as she approached.

"He must have seen you speeding back there."

Arnold's teasing words did little to calm Alicia.

"What should I do, Arnold?" she asked, attempting to keep the fear out of her voice.

"Just slow down and pull off to the side of the road," Arnold told her calmly. "We'll find out what this is about in a moment."

Alicia did as he'd instructed.

"Do you really think he knew I'd been speeding?" she asked, fear gripping her heart at the thought. It would not bode well for a driver with a mere learner's permit to be caught going over the speed limit.

"It's not likely," Arnold told her. "It's far more probable that the officer is just doing a routine check."

Before she had opportunity to ask Arnold what a routine check might be, the policeman was standing beside her door. She rolled down the window and greeted him.

"Would you mind stepping out of the car, Miss?" the man asked.

Trying not to tremble, Alicia stepped from the vehicle. Arnold was by her side in an instant.

"Is there a problem, officer?" he asked politely.

"I'll need to see the young lady's license," the man responded. Nervously, Alicia pulled the learner's permit from her purse.

The officer examined it, then turned his attention to inspecting the vehicle. He spoke little as he walked around the car, other than to ask them to demonstrate the lighting system and the signals. Arnold carried on a one-way conversation all the while, telling the officer that he was a native of Prince Edward Island, that he and other students from the bible college in Toronto were involved in work there for the summer, and informing the gentleman that they were eager to get Alicia to the train station before her train departed.

The officer said nothing as he listened patiently to Arnold's monologue. When the young man finished at last, he surveyed Alicia's license once more.

"What is your name, Miss?" he asked.

"My name?" Alicia was so frightened she could barely remember. "My name is Alicia Miller."

"I'm not sure how they do things in Ontario, Miss Miller," the officer told her, "but in this province it is a common practice for one to sign their license in order for it to be considered valid. You might consider doing that."

His words were softened by the smile and wink that followed as he handed her permit back. When Alicia began searching her purse for a pen, the man spoke again.

"You can wait till you get on the train, Miss Miller," he told her. "I wouldn't want you to be late on my account."

He reminded them that they should drive safely, then bid them farewell and drove off. Concerned that now they truly would be late for the train, Alicia begged Arnold to take the wheel.

"Even if I could get us there in time, I'm too nervous to drive now," she told him.

When they arrived at the station a short time later, the train was already loading. The conductor approached the vehicle as Alicia struggled to help Arnold unload her trunk. He examined her ticket, then urged her toward the waiting locomotive.

"You go ahead and board, lady," he told her. "I'll see to it that the train doesn't leave without your trunk."

Content that her luggage would be well cared for, Alicia bid a hasty goodbye to Arnold. Before boarding the train, she opened her purse and withdrew the few dollars she had left. She pressed them into Arnold's hand.

"You and the others will need this more than I do."

His attempt to protest fell on a deaf ear.

"I'm going home," she reminded him. "I'll have no more expense till I get there. You and the rest of the group will need this."

Alicia turned and raced up the steps to the train before Arnold had time to reply. She felt a sense of satisfaction as the whistle blew and the train pulled out of the station. She was going home.

It's strange, she thought, *last night I was mourning the fact that I had to go home, today I am rejoicing in it.*

She could hardly wait to see Mama and Daddy, Aunt Helen, Sarah, Jake and, most particularly, William. She wondered how much he had changed in the month she had been gone.

As the train's wheels rolled over the tracks and the hours and the miles passed by without nourishment, Alicia's stomach began to rumble. She was more than a little hungry by the time she reached Montreal.

I'm only a few hours from home, she consoled herself. *I'm sure I'm more than half way now.*

When the conductor came by with the news that there would be a four hour layover in the city of Montreal, Alicia felt like crying. She had been certain she could last without nourishment till she reached Toronto, but she had not reckoned on the long delay in Montreal.

Forced to disembark during the wait, Alicia spent her time wandering back and forth. The scent of food wafting from a nearby café tormented her. She moved as far from the odour as she could, trying to ignore the empty feeling coming from within.

She found a seat in a quiet corner, and settled down to wait. Her eye was drawn to a sign on a nearby booth. The words *Travellers Aid* were prominently displayed on the sign. She had heard of the organization. In fact, Mama had reminded her before she left that this group existed to assist her should she run into difficulty at any stage of her trip.

I'm not exactly in difficulty, she reminded herself. *After all, it's not as though I am stranded or anything. It is simply my own foolishness that has me in the predicament I am in.*

For the first time she regretted giving her last bit of cash to Arnold. There was no sense moaning over it now, however. Crying over spilled milk never changed anything. It had seemed like the right thing to do at the time.

She looked at the sign again, wondering if the lady at the booth spoke English. At last, fearing she would faint if she did not get some sustenance before she reached Toronto, she stood.

Timidly she approached the booth. She glanced around, blushing at the thought that it might appear to others that she was begging.

To her relief, she found that the woman behind the counter was fluent in both English and French. The kind woman listened to her story, then opened a drawer and withdrew a two dollar bill.

"This should buy you a bite to eat, Mademoiselle," she said as she offered the money to Alicia.

Alicia hesitated. It didn't seem right to just take the money. Still, she was hungry and the woman was offering assistance.

As if understanding her dilemma, the woman reached for an envelope.

"Our address is on here, Mademoiselle," she informed Alicia. "You can use this envelope to repay us when you get home."

Reassured that she was being offered a loan and not charity, Alicia took the money and the envelope. After expressing her gratitude she went and purchased a meal. She put the change from her dinner in the envelope and carefully tucked it away in her purse. Repaying her debt would be the first thing on her agenda when she reached Toronto.

***

Preparing for China

For a time following her break-up with John, Alicia wondered what direction her life would take without him, but the month spent in ministry on Prince Edward Island helped convince her that she should still go to China. She would just have to go alone. She had, after all, set her heart on going overseas long before John Hammond came into her life. There was no reason their break-up should affect her plans.

With renewed determination Alicia set up an appointment to meet with the mission board and discuss her future. She entered the meeting feeling confident and well prepared. Her sense of composure dwindled as she faced the all male committee and answered their endless questions.

For more than an hour they grilled her, asking why she had chosen China as her destination, what her qualifications were, and whether she was in contact with anyone in that country. She answered their questions openly and honestly, telling them of the work she had done to prepare for the journey.

The men listened with interest as she related in detail the events of the past three years; her morning classes studying the scriptures, her evening classes learning the Mandarin dialect, and her recent mission work in Prince Edward Island.

"I feel I have been called to go to China," she told them in conclusion, "and I feel I am prepared. I am ready, willing and able to leave as soon as I am approved for service and the mission board sees fit to send me."

An elderly gentleman seated at the end of the table peered at her over his glasses.

"Have you plans to marry, Miss Miller?" he asked.

Alicia flinched at the question. For a moment she wondered if the men knew about her friendship with John. She had deliberately omitted mentioning it when she'd told them of her preparation for service. She lifted her chin.

"I have no plans to marry, sir," she answered firmly.

Her words caused a stir on the other side of the table. Eyebrows raised, glances were exchanged and even a whisper or two was heard.

"I see," the man answered. He frowned.

"This is not a good time for a single woman to be travelling to China, Miss Miller," one of the other men told her. "The political situation there has become rather unstable, you know."

Alicia felt defeated. Was she to be refused the opportunity to go to China after all her hard work? Were her years of preparation for nothing?

She breathed a silent prayer, then addressed the men in a calm voice.

"I understand that situations may arise in a foreign country that would be more difficult for a woman than for a man," she told them. "I am prepared for that. The Lord has not seen fit to give me a man to serve beside me in China, but in spite of that he has called me to serve him there. I hope you will not deny me the privilege of following that call."

She sat back and waited, knowing there was nothing more she could say to influence the men.

"Would you mind waiting outside while we discuss your situation, Miss Miller?"

The question came from a middle-aged man seated at the center of the table. Alicia agreed and the man rose and escorted her to a seat in the next room. He re-entered the room they had been in and closed the door behind him.

The deliberations did not take long. Moments later the door opened, and the man came toward her with a smile on his face.

"Have you any medical training, Miss Miller?" he asked.

"No," Alicia answered, wishing she could tell him otherwise.

"Would you be willing to take a nursing course?"

Alicia hesitated.

"I would," she told him, "if it would help me get to China."

They both laughed.

"There is a need for medical missionaries," the man informed her. "The mission board might be able to find a place for you in China if you had some medical training."

He looked at her sympathetically.

"We realize that will mean waiting another year, but we believe it would be beneficial in the long run. Perhaps by that time..." His voice trailed off.

"By that time?" Alicia asked.

He shook his head. Having reconsidered his former statement, he said instead, "If you are agreeable to our terms, we will recommend your acceptance to the fall training program."

"I've never considered medical training," Alicia told him honestly, "but I am willing to."

"You'll find it useful no matter where you serve," the man told her. "In fact, we often recommend that missionaries take a basic medical course. One never knows how far they will be from the nearest doctor when they go overseas."

It seems nothing is turning out quite the way I'd thought it would, Alicia told herself as she walked home from the meeting. *And yet, in spite of it all, I have a sense of peace.*

She wondered what Mama and Daddy would say when she informed them she was going to take medical training.

When the fall nursing course began, Alicia found herself returning to school once again.

Here I am almost twenty-five years old, and I'm still going to school, she thought as she donned her crisp, white nursing uniform for the first time. *Some days I wonder if I will ever finish!*

Consoling herself with the thought that by this time the following year she would be in China, Alicia plunged whole-heartedly into her studies. She found the medical training challenging. It was unlike anything she had ever done before, or had ever expected to do.

Determined to do well on the course, she studied diligently, reaping the rewards for her hard work each time she handed in a written assignment.

Everything went well until her practical study began. Teamed with another nurse, Alicia fumbled her way through the assignments she was given. She bathed patients, gave back rubs, and even managed not to let nausea overwhelm her when she was forced to empty bedpans.

She became comfortable in the role of nursing as the days passed. She had reached the point where she felt confident in her skills when the head nurse asked for her assistance one day in the care of an elderly gentleman with gangrene.

Alicia followed the matron into the room, and obediently set out everything that would be needed to change the man's dressing. All went well, until the moment the nurse removed the bandage and the rotted flesh was exposed.

The odour coming from the wound was offensive enough, but the moment Alicia looked at the infected foot she lost control. No amount of training or will power could keep her on her feet. With a whisper of a sigh she went down, leaving the nurse in charge with two patients on her hands.

When Alicia came to, she was lying on a lounge in the nurses' quarters. She had no idea how she had gotten from the patient's room to this location, and was too embarrassed to ask.

The matron requested her assistance with the same patient a week later, but changed her mind at the last minute. Fearing a repeat of the earlier episode, she chose instead to place Alicia on cases that required medical knowledge, but were not quite so repugnant.

Alicia was nearing the end of her training when she was informed that she was needed to assist on the night shift. Her work thus far had all been day work. She felt some concern when another nurse told her there was little to do on the night shift, and wondered how she would ever manage to stay awake if that were the case.

It took only one shift working nights for Alicia to learn that there was more to do on the night watch than she had been led to believe. In addition to the regular rounds to check on patients, there were other duties to perform, including paperwork to complete and instruments to get ready for the next day's work. She found it a slower pace than the day shift, but had no difficulty keeping busy.

Occasionally she was called upon to calm a restless patient. At times a patient would wake, troubled by their pain. The nurse in charge would administer a sedative, and Alicia would sit with the patient, talking to them in a soothing voice until at last the pain eased and they fell into slumber once again.

She was returning to the desk after such an incident, when she turned a corner and came face to face with an elderly male patient.

"I need my clothes, nurse," he told her as she rounded the corner.

"It's time you were in bed, Mr. Jones," Alicia answered. She took his arm, attempting to lead him back to his room.

"I must have my clothes," he repeated. "It's time I got ready for work."

"We'll look for your clothes in the morning," Alicia told him. "Right now it's time to sleep."

"No," he insisted, standing firm and refusing to be moved. "I need to go to work now!"

Alicia felt a sense of relief as she saw the duty nurse hurrying down the hall toward them.

"Mr. Jones would like his clothes," she told the older woman. "I've suggested that he go back to bed, and we will look for his clothes in the morning."

The other nurse nodded.

"The young lady is right, Mr. Jones," she told him. "It's time for bed."

"I must have my clothes, so I can go to work," he stated once again. "I cannot show up in my pyjamas."

"Of course you can't," the nurse agreed, attempting to soothe him. "After you have a good sleep, we'll look for your clothes. Come to bed, now," she coaxed. "You can think about work in the morning."

"No," he insisted. "By morning it will be too late. I must go to work now."

Realizing her attempts to appease the man were having little effect, the nurse changed her tactic.

"It's the middle of the night, Mr. Jones," she informed him. "People don't work at night."

Clear blue eyes looked from the nurse in charge to Alicia and back again. He observed each one in detail, from their sturdy duty shoes and white stockings to their crisp uniforms and their snow white caps – only one of which boasted a black band across it. After carefully assessing their attire, the elderly man looked directly into the older woman's eyes.

"You said people don't work at night?" he asked quietly.

"That's right, Mr. Jones," the woman affirmed.

"Then may I ask what the two of you are doing?" Shaking his head, the man shuffled back to his room.

June arrived and with it came another graduation ceremony. Alicia's family attended, clapping with the rest of the crowd as the certificates were handed out. Dutifully, Alicia posed for photos – alone, with friends and family, and in a group for the class photograph.

She moved through the motions of the day, enjoying the events that were scheduled, but all the while thinking that at last her formal training was over. She had a meeting scheduled with the mission board the following week. At last she was ready to go to China.

A sense of excitement filled Alicia as she prepared for her meeting the Monday after graduation. She dressed carefully. The dress she wore was not chosen to impress members of the board, but to remind Alicia of her own femininity. Most of the past year had been spent wearing a uniform, and it felt good to dress up again.

Alicia felt a thrill as she walked into the room where the men waited. She smiled as she presented them with her certificate.

"I have completed all the required training," she told them. "I am ready to go to China."

Six sober faces stared at her from the other side of the table. Not a word was spoken as they passed the certificate from one to the other. When it reached the last person in the group, one of the men spoke.

"I'm afraid it is not as simple as that," he informed Alicia. He cleared his throat. "I regret to tell you, Miss Miller, that the door to China is closed – perhaps permanently.

"Not only is the Communist Regime no longer allowing new missionaries to enter that country, it is becoming increasingly evident that it may soon be necessary for those already there to leave."

Alicia listened to the words in stunned silence. She had been so busy studying this past year that she'd had no time to keep up on world events. How could she not have been aware of the situation in China?

"Are you telling me there's no possibility at all of going to China?" she finally asked.

"Not at present," the man replied. Sorrow filled his face as he added, "and perhaps never."

Alicia held out her hand for her certificate. Somehow she found the strength to thank the men for their time before she stumbled from the room.

What do I do now? Alicia asked herself as she walked home. *I've spent three years training for something that now I am told might never happen. What will I do now?*

***

Closed Door, Open Window

Word that Alicia would not be going to China spread quickly through her circle of friends and co-workers. Bombarded with questions about her future, her answer was always the same.

"I don't know what the future holds," she would say with a smile each time she was asked what her plans were, "but I know who holds the future."

She gave her standard answer to Mr. Kimble, an older gentleman from her church, one Sunday when he inquired about her plans. He studied her intently for a moment, then said, "Well, Alicia, maybe the Lord wants you to serve him right here in our own country."

The elderly man's words replayed themselves in Alicia's mind often in the days that followed. She thought of the summer she'd spent doing mission work in Prince Edward Island. Was it possible God had closed the door to China that she might see a window of opportunity in her own land?

She returned home from work later that week to find a letter from Sally waiting for her. Following graduation from bible college, Sally had returned to her home town and married her childhood sweetheart. Recently the couple had moved to northern Alberta.

Alicia read her friend's letter telling of the work she and Howard were doing in Alberta. She thought again of Mr. Kimble's words. It seemed Sally had found a place of ministry right here in Canada.

A few weeks later Alicia and her mother attended a missionary conference hosted by their church. As they entered the room, Alicia found herself reflecting on the tales Sally had told of the work she and Howard were doing. Sally's latest letter had ended with the suggestion that Alicia consider joining them in the west.

I don't know why I'm thinking about this now, Alicia berated herself. *I'm here today to hear about mission work in foreign lands, not about work in a small town in a remote part of northern Alberta!* She settled into a seat beside her mother and forced herself to concentrate on the words coming from the front. This was neither the place nor the time to be thinking of Alberta.

The first speaker at the conference was good, but Alicia found her mind wandering during the woman's talk. It was all things she had heard before – stories of people half a world away who were starving both physically and spiritually.

I planned to go to some of those people, Alicia thought with a tinge of bitterness. *I trained for years, only to have the door closed just as I was about to walk through it.*

The second speaker was introduced and Alicia found herself drawn immediately to the woman. She was a tiny wisp of a lady, barely tall enough to be seen over the podium. Her white hair was pulled back neatly into a bun, with loose strands at the front held in place by bobby pins on either side of her head.

"Good evening."

The woman's voice was soft, even with the assistance of a microphone. A hush settled over the room. It was evident to all that the speaker would not be heard unless the room was still.

"I'd like to thank each one of you for coming tonight," the woman began. She smiled warmly. "It always surprises me that so many people come out to hear what I have to say. My message is simple."

She went on to tell of her work in the Belgian Congo and of the great need in that part of the world. She spoke with such fervour and intensity that by the time she finished Alicia was wondering if she should consider volunteering as a missionary to the Belgian Congo now that China was no longer an option.

The speaker had returned to her seat on the platform when suddenly she rose, asking if she might share a further thought. Making her way back to the podium, she stood erect with both hands clasping it.

"I have spoken of my work in the Belgian Congo," she told those assembled. "But there is another work I have not spoken of, and which I feel a great burden to share."

"I have recently had opportunity to visit the western provinces of this nation." She paused. "It may come as a surprise to you when I say that I consider that part of our country as needy as the Belgian Congo or any other foreign country I have laboured in."

Her eyes searched the audience.

"There is an urgent need for workers in our own country, particularly in the northern regions of the western provinces." With that simple statement, the woman returned to her seat, leaving Alicia with the feeling that the missionary's final words had been meant just for her.

Letters telling of the work Sally and Howard were doing and the adventures they were having continued to arrive on a regular basis from the northwest. Reading them, Alicia became convinced that she was meant, for a time at least, to serve in northern Alberta. When a letter arrived informing her that Sally and Howard would be visiting Ontario, Alicia was delighted. At last she would have opportunity to speak with her friend in person.

As the date of the visit neared, Alicia learned that Howard and Sally's time in Ontario would be filled with travelling from town to town for speaking engagements. They would be in Toronto for only one day, and Howard would be speaking at two different churches on that day. It seemed that she would have little time alone with her friend.

I guess I'll just have to be content to visit with Sally at church, Alicia thought.

She arrived early at the building on the day of Howard and Sally's visit, eager to have as much time as possible with her friend. To her disappointment, she found that other people had come early with the same idea. Many in the congregation remembered Sally from her bible school days, and were interested in hearing of the work she and her husband were doing. Seeing the group crowding around Sally and Howard, Alicia took a seat, consoling herself with the thought that she would talk to Sally after the service.

The hymns sung that morning were old and well known. It was obvious to Alicia that they had been carefully chosen, as each one spoke of missions and the call to service. Following the singing, the guest speaker was introduced. Alicia listened carefully as Howard spoke of the work he and Sally were doing in northern Alberta.

"It is hard to believe that in this day and age, there are towns in the north without even one evangelical church," he told them. "Works have been started by groups in many of the northern towns, but have been abandoned. It is not always lack of interest that causes them to fail. Sometimes it is lack of workers. It is not an easy task to convince one to leave family and friends behind and live in a remote area, far from the luxuries we have grown accustomed to in this modern day. Truly it is as our Lord said – *The fields are white unto harvest, but the workers are few.*"

Howard went on to show coloured slides of the area they laboured in, and of the work he and Sally were doing. When the service ended, Alicia made her way to where Sally and Howard stood greeting people. She stood to one side, waiting patiently till everyone else had gone before approaching her friends.

After exchanging a hug with Sally, Alicia told Howard how much she had appreciated his talk, and how she had enjoyed the pictures he had shown.

"Was Howard's talk good enough to convince you to join us in our work?" Sally asked Alicia in a teasing manner.

"There truly is a need for workers in our area," Howard told Alicia.

"I have been considering it," Alicia answered.

"It would be wonderful to have you living nearby," Sally encouraged.

Their conversation moved to other topics, but before they left Howard brought the subject up again.

"You know you would be welcome to come to Alberta, Alicia," he told her, "whether it is to help in the ministries there, or simply to visit."

"Thank you, Howard. I appreciate that," Alicia responded. Sally had issued a similar invitation, but it was nice to hear it from her husband as well.

"I will think about it, and let you know," she assured them as they prepared to depart.

Convinced now that she should go west, Alicia broached the subject of mission work in Alberta that night with her parents. Ever supportive, they encouraged her, telling her that if she believed God was calling her to go to Alberta then she should go.

A week later she was able to arrange a meeting with the leaders of her church to discuss the idea with them. Like the mission board she had met with two years earlier, these men had concerns about a young, single woman travelling to a remote area to minister. In spite of their concerns, they agreed to support her in the endeavour and a letter of recommendation was drawn up for her.

Correspondence began between Ontario and Alberta, setting plans in place for Alicia to join Sally and Howard in their labours. Her resignation from her office job was accepted, along with the assurance that should she ever wish to return, a position would be made available for her.

A week before she was to leave, a farewell was held for Alicia at the church. To her surprise and delight, she was presented with a gift of cash to help her with her expenses. As she thanked those present for their kindness, it occurred to her that after her many years of preparation she was finally going out in mission work. She would not be working in the field she had originally envisioned, but it was mission work nonetheless.

***

Westward Bound

As Alicia stood on the platform at Union Station waiting for the late night train, she felt the same sense of excitement she had experienced as a child each time she had ridden the street car. She looked at the group that had assembled to see her off.

There were seventeen in all. Six were family – Daddy and Mama, Aunt Helen, Aunt Elizabeth and Uncle Andrew, and Sarah. Jake had said his goodbyes earlier, volunteering to stay home with William so Sarah could be present. The rest of the group was composed of friends, folks from Alicia's church, and fellow workers from her office.

She marvelled that so many people cared enough to come to the station at this late hour to witness her departure. Her father had spoken with one of the officials at Union Station in advance, and made special arrangements for the group to accompany Alicia onto the platform to wait.

A whistle sounded in the distance, signalling the approach of the train and Alicia began making her round to say goodbye. She noticed her father slip away and smiled, knowing he had gone to supervise the loading of her trunks. He returned in time for the boarding call and picked up Alicia's travelling case. Using the excuse that it was too heavy for her to handle on her own, Daddy accompanied her onto the train and escorted Alicia to her compartment. He made a quick visual assessment to be certain her accommodations were satisfactory, then moved past her and opened the window. Turning, he gave Alicia a quick peck on the cheek, then made his way back to the group waiting on the platform.

Alicia moved to the open window. She knelt on the seat in front of it, and leaned forward. Allowing her head and upper part of her body to hang outside the window, she waved at her friends and shouted goodbye. Her friends and family moved to the edge of the platform, so close that she could almost touch them. The whistle sounded again, the final warning before the train wheels started to turn and the vehicle began its long journey westward.

As if the whistle had been their cue, the group assembled opened their mouths, but instead of the goodbyes Alicia had anticipated they burst into song.

God will take care of you
Through every day, o'er all the way
He will take care of you
God will take care of you

The sweet strains of the old hymn filled Alicia's ears as the train slowly chugged its way out of the station.

The trip from Toronto to Edmonton lasted four days, making Alicia grateful that her father had insisted she purchase accommodation in a compartment rather than a berth. She mingled with other passengers during the day, but enjoyed the privilege of being able to escape to the solitude of her private quarters whenever she felt the need. She further enjoyed the luxury of not waiting for a conductor to make up her bed each night, as the compartment was equipped for both sitting and sleeping.

Meals were taken in the dining room, although she had the option of being served in her room if she desired. Overall, she found the accommodations quite luxurious. They were more than she needed, and likely more than she would get if she ever travelled again, but her aunt and her parents had desired that she have such comfort, and had paid the difference to upgrade her ticket.

The train arrived in Edmonton at last and Alicia disembarked. She was met at the station by friends of Sally's, who insisted she stay with them for a few days before travelling to the northern regions of the province. As she drifted off to sleep the first night in Alberta, Alicia could still hear the hum of the train wheels rolling over the track and feel the motion of it.

The days in Edmonton were filled with sight-seeing, mixed with trips to the department stores downtown. Though there were things she knew she would need to set up housekeeping, Alicia was reluctant to purchase anything. She was already travelling with two trunks and a suitcase filled with possessions she'd brought from home. She had no wish to add more to her supplies until she saw what her accommodations would be.

In addition, she thought soberly, there was a need to think carefully before spending the bit of money that she had, as there was no way of knowing when her father would see fit to replenish it.

She walked through the stores with her friends, stopping now and then to comment on something she saw, but purchasing nothing, in spite of their encouragement.

"You'll not find a selection like this further north," one of the girls informed her.

"Anything you are able to buy up there will cost more too," the other girl added.

Alicia smiled.

"I've brought quite a bit from home," she reminded them.

"Do you have bedding?" the older girl asked, stopping at a display of Hudson's Bay blankets. "You'll need lots to keep you warm up in the north country."

"I have bedding," Alicia answered. She stopped to run her hands over the soft woollen blanket. It was blue – her favourite colour. For a moment she was tempted to purchase it.

"No," she said aloud, uncertain whether the words were for her own benefit or for that of her friends. "I already have bedding." She did not reveal the fact that her entire selection of bedding consisted of two used sheets from home and one blanket.

They moved on through the store, her friends stopping every few feet to suggest something else she might need.

"This lamp is lovely," one of the girls commented when they came to the lighting section.

"It is," Alicia agreed.

"Do you have a lamp?"

"No," Alicia answered, "but I'm certain that if I need one it will be provided."

"What about pots and pans?" the girls asked when they reached the kitchenware. "Did you bring anything to cook with?"

Alicia suppressed a sigh. She had never known anyone so eager to spend someone else's money as these two were!

"I'll wait till I see how much space I have before I worry about pots and pans," she told them. "I really don't expect I'll be doing much cooking anyway. After all, there'll only be me to cook for." She laughed. No words were spoken in response, but the look her friends exchanged caused Alicia to wonder just what the two of them were thinking.

By the time they left the store, Alicia was exhausted. She had never done so much looking in her life. It was a new experience, and one she was not altogether certain she enjoyed. She much preferred her mama's way of shopping; taking a carefully planned list of items to purchase and looking at little other than those things.

Alicia spent the morning of her last day in Edmonton packing. When her friends announced at the noon meal that they had an afternoon of baking planned, she groaned inwardly. Summoning her courage, Alicia asked if she might be excused from the activity, as she still had numerous letters she'd hoped to write before leaving Edmonton. Her friends readily agreed, assuring her that they could do without her help and encouraging Alicia to take as long as she needed for her writing.

As she sat down and began her letters, Alicia was not certain whether she should be relieved or disappointed that her presence was not needed in the kitchen.

The afternoon hours passed quickly as Alicia wrote. Knowing letters to family would likely be shared, she endeavoured to fill the pages of each letter with different events and happenings. When the last envelope had been addressed and sealed, Alicia analyzed her afternoon's work. Six portraits of King George stared back at her from the three cent stamps in the right hand corner of each envelope. The address where she was staying in Edmonton was penned neatly in the opposite corner. Satisfied that her work was complete, she bundled the letters together for mailing.

A gnawing sense of hunger hit Alicia as she finished, and she glanced at the clock. She started. Six o'clock? Surely she was mistaken. She moved across the room and picked up the timepiece from the bedside table. The long hand pointed boldly to the twelve, while the short hand lay directly below it, aiming at the six.

She held it to her ear, listening. Perhaps she had forgotten to wind the clock last night and it had stopped in the early morning hours.

A steady ticking sound in her ear assured her that the clock had been wound, and that her letter writing had taken longer than she had anticipated. She worried that her hosts would think her rude, sequestering herself away on her last day with them and now, she blushed in embarrassment, making a late appearance at the supper table.

A knock sounded at the door and a head peeked in.

"Am I interrupting, dear?"

"Not at all, Mrs. Smith," Alicia answered. "I have just finished my letters." She indicated the bundle on the stand beside her bed. "I'm afraid that I lost track of time while I was writing them. I do apologize. I hope you haven't kept supper waiting."

"Actually, I've brought supper to you," Mrs. Smith informed her. The door opened wider to allow the woman to enter, revealing the contents on the tray she was carrying. A square china plate was heaped with sandwiches neatly cut in four. Steam poured from the tea in the matching cup and saucer beside the plate.

"With my daughters in the kitchen all afternoon, I didn't have an opportunity to prepare a proper meal," Mrs. Smith apologized as she set the tray down.

"This looks delightful," Alicia told her warmly. "Thank you!"

The plump woman seated herself in the chair Alicia had vacated at the desk, and encouraged her to eat. A steady stream of chatter accompanied Alicia as she partook of the dainty sandwiches.

"You picked a good time to go north, dear," Mrs. Smith told Alicia. "You'll be blessed with a few months of decent weather before winter sets in. 'Course, winter in the north country comes about the same time as fall does back east."

Alicia smiled as the woman laughed heartily at her own humour.

I must have been hungrier than I realized, Alicia thought as she finished the last sandwich. She looked at the plate, wishing there was one more. For a second she was tempted to polish off the crumbs on the plate. Instead, she picked up her cup of tea and sipped it slowly.

She had barely swallowed the last sip and replaced the cup in the saucer when Mrs. Smith rose.

"I'll take this back down to the kitchen," she told Alicia as she picked up the tray. She turned when she reached the door, as if she had forgotten to relay the message she'd been sent with.

"Did I tell you the girls are having some friends in this evening?"

Alicia shook her head.

"No," Mrs. Smith went on. "I didn't think I'd mentioned it. Some of the ladies from church are coming over. The girls told them about you, and they are interested in meeting you."

She glanced at her watch.

"They'll be arriving any time. You'd best comb your hair and get your good dress on now."

When the door closed behind the woman, Alicia paused to reflect on the message. She wondered why her friends had not mentioned the visit to her. She opened the door, thinking to ask one of them, but the echo of voices blending below prompted her to heed Mrs. Smith's advice instead.

When she descended the stairs fifteen minutes later, Alicia found the living room crowded to overflowing. A quick glance told her there must be close to twenty people packed into the small space.

Her friends squealed with delight when they saw her, and eagerly escorted her around the room introducing her to those gathered. When the formal introductions were complete, they showed Alicia to a seat that had been reserved in her honour near the front of the room.

Understanding that the event was a surprise and that Alicia had not been given time to prepare a talk for it, the ladies asked questions about her planned work in the north.

"Why did you choose Northern Alberta?" one woman asked.

Alicia laughed. "I didn't exactly choose to go there," she said. She went on to tell them of her plans to go to China, and her years of preparation for it.

"When the door to China closed, I didn't know what I was going to do," she told them, "until someone suggested that I could be a missionary without going overseas. I'd spent a summer doing mission work in Prince Edward Island, and knew there was a need right here in our own country. When I learned that churches in the north were closing for lack of workers, I decided to come and help out."

"You keep talking about the north," one girl commented. "I thought Edmonton was pretty far north. How much further north do you plan to go?"

A gasp was heard when Alicia told them the name of the town she would be living in.

"But that's hours from here!" the girl stated. She stared at Alicia, then added boldly, "You'll never find a man up there!"

"I'm not looking for a man," Alicia told her. She thought for a moment before adding, "but if I were, I don't really think it would matter where I was living. If the good Lord has a man for me, he'll bring him into my life whether I'm living in the most northern part of Alberta or in the heart of Toronto."

The girl laughed. "I guess that's one way to look at it."

She stood in front of Alicia, chatting amiably for several minutes. When at last she stepped aside, Alicia was surprised to see that a box full of wrapped gifts had been placed on the floor behind the girl. A plain white envelope bearing Alicia's name sat on top of the gifts.

"The ladies took a collection, Alicia," Mrs. Smith announced. "We know you'll be setting up house for the first time. We thought these items might prove useful."

At their insistence, Alicia reached forward and removed the envelope from the top of the pile. Opening it, she found a card bearing the signatures and personal good wishes of more than two dozen ladies. She turned her attention to the wrapped packages. Her eyes misted as she opened item after item of practical things for her new home. Many of the gifts were items she had admired on the shopping trips with her friends. Alicia smiled, suddenly understanding why they had been so insistent that she go shopping with them.

She reached into the box and removed the last package. A gasp escaped her throat as she tore the wrapping from it. Nestled inside was the blue blanket she had admired at the Hudson's Bay Store. She caressed the soft fibre before placing it on the dining room table with the other gifts. Everything she would need to set up housekeeping had been included, from bedding to cookware and dishes. Alicia's gaze moved from the gifts to the group assembled. Most of these ladies were complete strangers. She marvelled that they would hold such an event in her honour.

Alicia stood, and the conversation that had been humming around her ceased.

"I'm sure there are words appropriate for an occasion such as this," Alicia began hesitantly, "but I fear I cannot think of any. The kindness you have shown me is overwhelming, and I thank you from the bottom of my heart."

Alicia sat down to the sound of polite applause. The speech did not fully express her gratitude, but she could not have said more without breaking into tears.

When the evening was over and the last guest had gone home, Alicia thanked her friends again for the kindness they'd shown her during her stay. She climbed the stairs to her bedroom, and looked at the stack of letters she'd written earlier in the day. She smiled. She had worried there would be nothing to write home about after she left Edmonton. The events of this evening alone were enough to fill a good letter home.

Lying in bed, waiting for sleep to overcome her, she began composing her next letter home.

***

Sally's Secret

The train ride north seemed longer to Alicia than the trip from Toronto to Edmonton had been. She tried to sleep, but each time she dozed off the lurch of the train coming to a stop awakened her. Alicia wondered why they stopped so frequently. There were no towns or villages. She saw nothing that was large enough to even be called a settlement. From what she'd seen, it looked like there was nothing but bush north of Edmonton. It was hard to imagine Sally and Howard living in such a remote area.

By the time the conductor informed her they were nearing her destination, Alicia was more than ready to get off. She thanked the man for alerting her, then brushed her skirt and straightened her hat. Satisfied that she had done all she could to make herself presentable, Alicia gathered her personal possessions. She had no intention of wasting time when the train arrived at the station.

Gazing out the window, she was able to make out two lone figures in the distance. She smiled. It appeared that Sally and Howard were at the station awaiting her arrival. She rose, and holding tightly to her belongings, made her way down the aisle to the door. In her eagerness to see her friends, she forgot to brace herself, and would have fallen forward when the train lurched to a stop if the strong arm of the conductor hadn't reached out to stop her.

"Steady there, missy," the official exclaimed. "Your friends won't mind waiting another minute or two. It wouldn't do to have you fall and get hurt this close to your destination, now would it?"

He chuckled and Alicia blushed. Murmuring her apologies, she stepped back and waited patiently while the man opened the door. She watched as he hopped from the train and placed a stool on the ground. When he offered his arm, she accepted and allowed him to help her step down. She had barely set her foot on the platform and let go of the man's arm when Sally ran toward her and gathered her in a warm embrace.

"Alicia," she cried. "I'm so very glad to see you!" Sally stepped back, and turned toward her husband.

"You remember Howard?"

"I do," Alicia smiled. "It's good to see you again, Howard."

"I'm happy you're here, Alicia," Howard told her. He winked. "Sally has been preparing for your arrival for weeks, and has talked of little else ever since she got the letter saying you were coming."

Sally laughed.

"It hasn't been quite that bad," she protested, "but I admit I have been excited."

She squeezed Alicia's arm. "I really am glad you're here, Alicia."

"So am I," Alicia told her.

The girls began chatting about Alicia's trip, and about the week she'd spent in Edmonton. They might have gone on talking indefinitely if Howard had not intervened. He cleared his throat, then waited for their attention. When at last they stopped speaking and turned to face him, he smiled.

"There'll be lots of time to catch up on each other's news," he reminded them gently. "Right now I think it would be a good idea if we went home. I'm sure you must be hungry after your long train ride, Alicia."

"I'm sorry, Alicia," Sally burst in. "I was so excited to see you again that I didn't even think. Of course you must be hungry. We'll have a bite to eat as soon as we get home."

Sally linked one arm in Alicia's and the other with her husband and began leading the way to their vehicle, chattering as she went.

"But my luggage..."

"Wait..."

It took more than one protest and a good tug on Sally's arm before Alicia got her friend's attention. Even then Sally wasn't really listening.

"Your luggage?" she asked, proving that she had heard what Alicia said even though she had not acknowledged it.

Alicia nodded.

"I'm sorry," Sally said. "How thoughtless of me."

She dropped her friend's arm and held out her hand for one of the bags Alicia was carrying.

Alicia laughed.

"No," she protested. "I don't mean this luggage. I mean my trunks."

Her words brought a blank stare from both Sally and Howard.

"Your trunks?" they asked in unison.

Alicia nodded.

"Yes," she told them. "I have two travel trunks."

She turned and pointed to the large rectangular objects that had been unloaded at the end of the platform.

"Those belong to me."

"Oh," Sally commented. "I see."

"Hmm..." Howard added thoughtfully. He eyed the luggage.

"Surely you knew I would have more than just this?" Alicia asked, holding up her suitcase.

"Yes," Sally answered. She glanced at Howard, her eyes beseeching him to explain.

"It's just that we didn't expect your trunks to be unloaded here," Howard told her.

Alicia suppressed a sigh, wondering just where in Alberta her friends had expected her trunks to be unloaded if not here.

"I'm sorry, Alicia," Howard went on. He ran his fingers through his thick, dark hair. "It looks like we didn't communicate very clearly with you. We should have had your trunks unloaded at the next station."

Alicia looked around in confusion.

"We live near here," Sally explained, "but we've found a place for you in the next town. It's fifteen miles from here."

Alicia watched Howard grimace as he attempted to lift one of the trunks. Unable to budge it, he shook his head and moved on to the second one. It was not light either, but Howard was able to move it more easily than the first one. He turned to face Alicia.

"I think I can manage the blue one," he told her, "but I'll need to get help lifting the brown one." He grinned. "What did you pack in it – bricks for the new church building?"

Alicia shook her head. Missing Howard's attempt at humour, she explained.

"The brown one is filled with books and personal items," she told him. "The blue one has my clothes."

Too late she realized the wisdom that lay in her father's suggestion that she put a layer of heavy items in the bottom of each trunk and place the clothes on top.

Howard turned back to the trunk. With minimal effort he moved the blue one to the edge of the platform, and from there manoeuvred it on to his truck. That accomplished, he turned his attention to the second trunk. He tugged and pulled, pushed and prodded, but was able to move it only a few inches. He straightened and rubbed his back.

"I'll take you ladies home," he told them. "Then I'll find someone to come back and help me load the second trunk."

Howard opened the door and Alicia followed Sally into the cab of the truck. After seeing that the ladies were settled, Howard scooted around to the driver's side. Positioning himself behind the wheel, he turned to Alicia.

"Welcome to the northland," he told her with a smile. He eased up on the clutch and the vehicle slid forward, bouncing over the rutted roads. Alicia braced her feet against the floor, looking around for something to hold onto as she struggled to remain in an upright position.

"I must warn you," Howard told her, "that sixteen miles can seem more like sixty on roads like these."

They'd gone only a short distance when Howard turned off the main road. A moment later he pulled up in front of a small trailer.

"This is where we live," Sally told Alicia. She squeezed her arm. "Come on! I can't wait to show you our home."

The tour of Sally and Howard's home did not take long. The ten foot wide by sixteen foot long trailer was a compact unit, efficiently laid out with a bedroom and bath at one end and a kitchen and living quarters at the other.

The space was small but had a welcoming feel, thanks to Sally's homemaking skills. Floral curtains hung from the two small windows, while cushions and a throw adorned the couch. There was little room to hang anything on the walls, but carefully chosen family portraits had been placed on a shelf Howard had fastened to the wall above the couch. A calendar, sent from Ontario if one could judge by the advertising it boasted, was displayed in the kitchen.

"If you ladies don't mind," Howard told them, "I'll excuse myself and leave you two to visit. I have a little matter of an overweight trunk to attend to," he told them with a grin.

Sally's protests that the trunk could wait till after lunch were cut short.

"I've a feeling the two of you have matters that are best discussed without a man present," he commented, giving Sally's arm an affectionate squeeze. The words brought a tinge of colour to Sally's face, but she offered no further objections.

"What do you think, Alicia?" Sally asked when they were alone. A wave of her hand indicated that she was referring to the trailer.

"I know it's small," she went on, before Alicia had a chance to answer, "but it's our home, and I love it!"

"It's like living in a doll house," Alicia exclaimed, surveying the small abode, "but it's lovely, Sally."

Sally smiled at her friend's words.

"We're happy here."

She looked around.

"Of course, it will be a little crowded when the baby comes, but we'll manage."

Alicia stared.

"Baby? Did you say baby?" she asked excitedly. "Sally, are you expecting?"

Sally nodded, a look of pure joy on her face.

"So that's what Howard meant when he spoke of matters best discussed without a man present," Alicia commented, hugging her friend. "Oh, Sally, I'm so happy for you. Congratulations!"

***

Life in the North West

Alicia settled into life in Alberta easily. As the first month drew to a close, she paused to assess her situation. She was amazed at how comfortable she felt in the small northern community after living in a city all her life.

The accommodations Howard and Sally had obtained for her at the local doctor's were not fancy, but they were certainly adequate. Her first weeks had been spent sleeping on a Murphy bed in the basement apartment that was home to Dr. Carleton Caswell and his family, while a room was prepared for her upstairs.

The doctor had arrived in the area some years earlier and had – with forethought to the potential for growth in the town – built a large, square two-storey structure with a full basement. He had divided the basement into two apartments. One of the apartments housed the local dentist and his family, while the doctor's family inhabited the second unit.

The main floor of the building had been constructed as a clinic with offices for both the doctor and the dentist. There were several rooms on the upper floor, one of which was now home to Alicia. Her neighbours included a group of men who worked on the oil rigs and a lawyer who rented space which served as both his office and living quarters

Alicia had felt slight discomfort at learning that she was to be the only female on the floor, but Dr. Caswell's wife Emily had assured her she was welcome to come back to the basement apartment and visit anytime she felt the need for female companionship.

Thus far she had done little more than speak in passing to her fellow lodgers. She'd found the lawyer to be a quiet, soft-spoken man who seemed quite content to spend his time in his quarters. The workers, on the other hand, came and went frequently, and seemed oblivious to the noise they made. The echo of the men's voices and the thumping of their feet ascending and descending the stairs at all hours troubled Alicia at first, but she soon became used to it.

They've as much right to be here as I do, she reminded herself. *Besides, it is likely that my accordion practice for Sunday services disturbs them as much or more than their noise bothers me.*

She giggled at the thought.

Alicia straightened and looked at the calendar, then moved to her dresser and pulled a small envelope from the middle drawer. It was time to pay her monthly rent.

Carefully she counted out the twenty-five dollars she had agreed to pay the doctor and his wife each month. Setting it aside, Alicia turned her attention back to the contents of the envelope.

A frown creased her forehead as she counted the remaining bills. She hoped her father would send additional revenue soon. The stash of cash that had seemed so large to her when she'd left Ontario was dwindling fast.

I'll tell him my need, she decided, *and trust him to provide as he sees fit.*

She placed the envelope back in its hiding place, then made her way to the doctor's basement apartment and knocked timidly. Though she had lived with the Caswells for two weeks and had been invited back when she'd moved upstairs, she still felt awkward approaching them.

There was no answer, and she was about to turn away when she heard voices inside the apartment. Summoning her courage, she knocked more loudly.

The door was promptly opened by the doctor's son, Sam. A smile lit his face when he saw Alicia.

"Licia!" he exclaimed. "You comed back."

"You came back," Emily corrected the lad as she entered the room.

"No I didn't," Sam stated firmly. "I was already here. It was 'Licia who comed back."

He wrapped his chubby arms around her legs and held on tightly.

"I missed you," he declared, angling his head backward so he could look at her as he spoke.

Alicia looked into the boy's bright blue eyes and her heart melted. Sam reminded her of her nephew William when he was younger. She felt a brief longing for home as she stroked the boy's hair.

"I missed you too, Sam," she told him sincerely. There was no point reminding the lad that he saw her every week at Sunday services. At Sam's age it was a long time from one Sunday to the next.

"I'm glad you've come to visit, Alicia," Emily told her warmly. "Sam has been asking for you almost every day. Do come in."

She stepped back to make room for Alicia to enter. Alicia blushed.

"I really just came down to pay my rent, Emily," she explained, feeling embarrassed.

Emily smiled. "I'd be happy to take your rent, Alicia," she told her, "but I'd be even happier if you'd take time for a cup of tea with me." She moved to loosen Sam's grasp on Alicia.

"Sam isn't the only one who's missed your company," she added.

Feeling chastised, Alicia accepted Emily's offer. She was soon seated at the kitchen table enjoying a hot cup of tea served with fresh bread and saskatoon berry jelly. For a time Sam sat on Alicia's knee, reluctant to let her go. An hour passed as the women shared their common interests.

"I hope you'll come again, Alicia," Emily told her when she was ready to depart. "You know our door is always open to you."

Alicia smiled. "I appreciate that, Emily, really I do. And I'm sorry if I seemed standoffish earlier. I admit I'm still trying to get used to the way things are done here.

"Back home one would never think of visiting without being invited, or at least calling first. Here it seems that no one makes appointments."

Emily laughed.

"Appointments are only for doctors and dentists," she told Alicia, "and even that doesn't always work. Friends and family just drop by unannounced, and know they will always be welcomed."

Alicia was quiet, reflecting on Emily's words.

"I'm not sure I could ever just show up at someone's house without an invitation," she said, blushing again, "unless it was to pay my rent."

Both women laughed.

"Up here," Emily informed her, "we offer an open invitation. When we tell someone they are welcome anytime we mean exactly that. There is no time or date attached to the invite, and it never expires."

"I'll remember that," Alicia answered. "Thank you, Emily."

Alicia considered Emily's words as she made her way back to her room.

Would I be offended if someone just showed up at my door uninvited? she wondered.

Of course not, she decided. *There are lots of times when I am alone that I would welcome company.*

She smiled. It appeared Emily felt the same way.

***

Growing Pains

Alicia looked at the group assembled in the doctor's home. There were eighteen of them – twelve adults and six children. Their group had grown in the months that she'd been in Alberta. The first Sunday there had been only six in attendance at the church service; Alicia, Sally, Howard, and the Caswell family – Carleton, Emily and their son Sam.

The Sunday morning meetings were still sparsely attended, but the afternoon Sunday School for the children was growing. Last week there had been more than a dozen children. If the growth continued, Alicia would need to recruit Emily and Sally to help teach.

The room quieted as Howard stood. He cleared his throat.

"I'd like to thank everyone for coming tonight," he told those gathered. "As you know, we have important matters to discuss."

He paused.

"That little word 'discuss' is significant. It is important that each one of us is given opportunity to express our thoughts and feelings on the matters before us. Each of you has something worth sharing regarding the path our future should take.

"Before we begin our discussion, I'd like to ask the doctor to lead us in a word of prayer."

Dr. Caswell stood. A reverent silence filled the room as heads were bowed and hearts were quieted before God.

"Heavenly Father," Carleton's booming voice sounded loud in the small room. "We are gathered here today to seek your direction on the path our assembly should take. Should we continue to meet here in our home as we have been doing, or is it time for us to erect a church building that would stand as a witness to the work you are doing in this town?

"Guide our thoughts, Lord. Let our discussion be pleasing to you, and let us be in unison regarding the future of our assembly."

The *amen* that followed the prayer was echoed by each one present in the room.

"Thank you, Doctor."

Alicia suppressed a smile. Doctor Carleton Caswell was one of the most unpretentious men she'd ever met. He was forever telling people to call him by his first name, yet there were those, like Howard, who could not bring themselves to do so. To them he would always be Doctor Caswell.

"The doctor has already stated the matter before us in his prayer," Howard continued, "and it seems simple enough. Yet it is something that cannot be easily, or hastily, decided.

"Doctor and Mrs. Caswell have been kind enough to allow us to meet in their home for some time now. I've no doubt they would continue to welcome us, should we decide to keep on meeting this way."

He smiled as the couple nodded their agreement.

"What we need to consider, however, is that our numbers are growing, and there is a limit to how large our assembly can grow if we continue to meet in a home."

"But have we grown enough to warrant building a church?" a man at the end of the room asked.

"That is the question we need to decide tonight," Howard replied. He waited, but no one spoke. Finally an elderly lady raised her hand. Howard turned to her.

"What are your thoughts, Mrs. Beecham?"

"I'd like to see a church built," the older woman answered softly, "but only if it will last. I've lived here long enough to see two denominations come and start work, only to have them leave when numbers dwindled. How can I be sure this group won't do the same thing?"

"I think that's one of the reasons we need a building," another woman replied.

"We need a meeting house, sure enough," her husband agreed. He turned to Carleton and Emily. "I mean you no disrespect, Doc. It's right kind of you and your wife to host these meetings. But building a meeting house of our own would show folks in this town that we plan to stay. They wouldn't think we were just another group that would move on when things got tough."

Murmurs of agreement followed the man's speech.

"I agree with Jack." The words came from a man Alicia knew only as Fred. He was new to the group, having attended only a few Sundays. "We need a church."

"We need someplace people will recognize as a house of worship," one of the ladies said. "A building that stands as a tribute to our faith, where all are welcome."

"I don't know how long youse have been meeting," another person put in, "but I just found out about it a few weeks ago. It's hard to recognize a church group when there's no church!"

Laughter followed the statement. Alicia looked at Sally, eyebrows raised questioningly.

"How long have you been meeting, Sally?" she whispered.

"Almost two years now," Sally whispered back.

"It sounds like we do need a building to meet in," Carleton said. He looked around. "But our group is still small. Can we afford to build?"

"We could all help with the labour," Fred offered.

"We've a number of skilled workers among us," Howard agreed. The fact that he was proficient himself in the area of construction was not mentioned. "Our greatest expense would be purchasing land and building materials."

Howard turned to Carleton.

"You've had some experience in that department, Doctor. What costs do you think might be involved?"

"I was fortunate when I built," the doctor told the group. "The land cost me very little. The town sold it to me at a reasonable price because I was building a medical clinic. We may be able to make a similar arrangement if we were building a church."

Carleton's words caused a stir of excitement.

"My construction costs were much more than the land was," he continued, naming an amount.

264

The sum Carleton mentioned was large enough to make Alicia's mind whirl, and to provoke great discussion among the men that were present.

"But you didn't do any of the work yourself when you built, did you, Doc?"

"How much of that figure was labour and how much was materials?"

"This is a mighty big building, Carleton. We wouldn't need anything this big for a meeting house."

Alicia sat figuring while the men talked. Based on the price Carleton had mentioned, she started calculating what it might actually cost to build a church.

She started by cutting the figure the doctor had given in half. The man who'd said the church needed to be only half as large as the medical center was right. Assuming that half the amount that was left was labour and half materials, the number could be further reduced.

Satisfied that she could now make a reasonable estimate of the cost, she divided the amount Carleton had told them by four. She had just finished her calculations, when Fred spoke again.

"This isn't the best time of year to be thinking about building," he reminded those assembled, "with winter coming on and all."

"Fred's right."

"Maybe in the spring."

"Guess our numbers will have to stay as they are for now. There's not much room left for growth here."

Alicia let the talk flow around her. She was still thinking of the costs involved in building. The amount of cash they would need was large. There was no way their small assembly could be expected to come up with such an amount. Even if other churches helped – she was sure there were people at her home church in Toronto that would be willing to contribute – it still seemed like a big undertaking.

Was building or staying where they were the only options they had? Even if they had the money, Fred was right. They couldn't build in winter.

There must be some other way, she thought. *If only...*

"Perhaps there is a way of moving to a larger location without building."

The words were out of Alicia's mouth before she realized she was going to say them. Her face reddened as everyone turned to look at her.

"What are you thinking, Alicia?" Emily asked.

Alicia shook her head, embarrassed. She'd had no intention of speaking out at the meeting.

"I'd appreciate it if you'd share your thoughts with us, Alicia," Howard encouraged her.

"I was just thinking about the cost of building," Alicia ventured, "and wondering if there might be some other option."

"There is," Carleton assured her. "You know you are welcome to continue meeting here."

"I know," Alicia told him, "but the others are right. We need more space."

She looked around the crowded room.

"What will we do if our numbers double or triple again as they have these last months?"

"That's why we're looking at building," one of the others answered.

"But until we can build, maybe it would be possible to rent space somewhere."

Silence greeted Alicia's question. It was obvious no one had considered the possibility until now.

"It would give us the extra room we need, let people in the community know we are here, and allow us to plan for the building of a church in a year or so."

"That's a wonderful idea, Alicia," Sally told her, "but where could we rent? There aren't any vacant buildings in town that I know of."

"No," Carleton said, coming on board with Alicia's idea. "There are no vacant buildings, but there are buildings that are not used on Sunday. Isn't that right, Alicia?"

She nodded, her eyes bright.

"We could make a list of such places and see if any of them would be willing to let us use their facilities."

"What do the rest of you think of this idea?" Howard asked.

Heads nodded and whispers of agreement were heard.

"It sounds good to me," Fred told them.

"I still like the idea of having our own meeting place," Jack responded, "but this would give us the space we need till we're able to proceed with building."

"We could look into purchasing land and draw up plans for a worship center," Howard reminded them, "but we wouldn't have to rush into anything. That is, if that's the direction we've agreed we want to go."

"I think," Mrs. Beecham said, "that this town needs to know we're here to stay. Spreading the word that we're looking for a place to meet would be a good start."

By the time the meeting ended, Howard and Carleton had been appointed to seek out a place where the assembly could meet. In reality though, as Emily pointed out, each member of their group could help by spreading word that they were looking for a place to use on Sundays.

The meeting came to a close, but as the group departed, there was a new sense of optimism about the future of their mission in the town.

***

Waiting on Father

"I wish we didn't have to go, Alicia."

Sally's concern was evident in the tone of her voice as well as in her words.

"But, Sally, you've been looking forward to this visit for months," Alicia protested.

"I know, but it doesn't seem right to leave you alone on your first Christmas away from home." Sally looked at the little one nestled in her arms. "If it weren't for Caroline, I'd cancel the trip."

"Nonsense, Sally. There's no reason for you to change your plans. I'll be just fine."

"You're sure I can't persuade you to come with us?" Sally asked. "You know you'd be welcome."

Alicia shook her head.

"No."

Sally looked at her doubtfully, but Alicia's firm response kept her from questioning her friend any further.

I don't relish the thought of spending Christmas by myself, Alicia thought as she walked to the post office, *but I could hardly admit to Sally that I couldn't accept her offer because of lack of funds.*

She sighed. She relied on her father completely for her financial support, and was grateful for everything he supplied. Yet there were times, though she would never have told him so, when she wished he would not wait till the last minute before meeting her needs. How much simpler life had been when she'd had a regular paycheque to budget from.

She entered the post office, exchanged cheerful greetings with the postmaster and took the packet of letters he had for her. A glance at the return addresses revealed that three of the envelopes were from Ontario and one was from her friends in Edmonton. She smiled as she tucked the letters in her purse. She would wait till she was alone in her room to open them.

At home, Alicia took the letters out and opened them. She read the one from Edmonton first. It was short and to the point, bearing an invitation for her to return to Edmonton to spend Christmas with the Smith family.

Setting the letter aside, she turned her attention to the envelopes from home. Two bore early Christmas greetings from friends while the third contained a newsy letter from her mother. She read it carefully, savouring every word before refolding the paper. A tear dropped from her eye as she placed the letter back in the envelope. How she would love to be home for Christmas!

It was not the thought of gifts under the tree or a big meal on Christmas day that made her wish for home. It was more the longing to awake in her childhood home on Christmas morning, and to have the pleasure of her family's company on that day.

She turned back to the letter from Edmonton with a thoughtful look. A trip home this Christmas was out of the question, as was the trip to Sally's relatives, but maybe – just maybe – she could afford to go to Edmonton.

She pulled the envelope that held her cash out of the dresser drawer and checked the contents. Tucking the envelope into her purse, she donned her coat and rubbers and headed back outside.

Her route this time took her to the train station. Once inside she approached the agent, asking what a return fare to Edmonton would cost. Hearing the rate, she nodded and asked to reserve a seat on the train to that city for the twenty-third of December.

"Would you care to pay for your ticket now, Miss?" the agent asked.

"I didn't realize I had an option," Alicia told him.

"Oh yes, Miss," the agent responded. "We can reserve a seat for you now in case it gets busy. It sometimes does this time of year," he winked, "and you can pay for it when you pick it up."

"In that case," Alicia told him, "I'd prefer to pay when I get the ticket."

The agent nodded.

"I'll just need your name," he told her.

"Alicia Miller."

The man wrote her name down, then handed her a slip of paper.

"This confirms you are booked for the twenty-third, Miss Miller," he told her, "and that you will be paying for your ticket at that time."

"Thank you, sir."

Alicia took the piece of paper and tucked it in her wallet. As she walked home, she wondered if she had acted foolishly in booking transportation to Edmonton. Later, as she sat down to compose a letter to her friends in Edmonton, she decided it had been the right thing to do. It would be good to have a little holiday. Besides, she still had four weeks before she needed to pay for her ticket. Surely her father would replenish her coffers by that time.

Alicia made frequent trips to the post office in the weeks that remained before Christmas. Her step was always light and her heart hopeful as she started on her trek, but her feet dragged and her heart felt heavy as she came home empty handed each day.

On the twenty-second of December she entered the building for the last time before her proposed trip. She waited till late in the day before venturing out, wanting to be certain that all the incoming mail had been sorted before her arrival. Surely her father would send something today. If he did not, she would have no choice but to cancel her trip.

I won't allow myself to think like that, she told herself as she waited in line. *If I am supposed to go to Edmonton the money will be provided. If it is not here today, I will know I am meant to stay here for Christmas.*

They were brave words, and she wondered how she would feel if there was nothing waiting for her.

I guess I'll know soon enough, she thought as the lady in front of her moved away from the counter.

"Good day, Miss Miller," the woman behind the counter greeted her warmly. "You're later than usual today."

"Good day, Nancy," Alicia replied. "I am a little later today."

"You must have been waiting to be sure we got everything sorted," Nancy joked.

Alicia smiled.

"Anything for me today?" she asked, attempting to keep her tone of voice casual.

The clerk shook her head. "Nothing today. Sorry, Miss Miller."

"You're certain?" Alicia asked, trying to keep her disappointment from showing.

"I'm certain," Nancy told her. She leaned on the counter. "You've been coming in on mail day every week, Miss Miller. I figure you must be looking for something awful important. You waiting for something special?"

"Yes," Alicia answered quietly. She turned her head, fighting to keep tears from flooding her eyes.

"Are you all right, Miss Miller?"

The clerk was around the counter in an instant. Alicia nodded.

"Yes," she answered, forcing a smile. "I'm fine."

The plump woman patted the younger girl's shoulder affectionately.

"I don't know what you're waiting for honey, or who it's from, but it sure must be important. You come and check again next week. Maybe it will be here then."

Alicia nodded.

Next week will be too late, she thought as she made her way home. Back in her room, she pulled out her money and counted it again. She looked at it, and a thought occurred to her.

There would be enough money for the trip if she didn't pay her rent till she got back. She eyed the twenty-five dollars she'd set aside for the Caswells. It was enough to pay for the trip to Edmonton and to buy Christmas gifts for everyone there, with some left over! If she waited till she got back to pay the rent...

Alicia picked the money up and looked at it, contemplating. She felt certain that by the time she returned, her father would have sent funds.

She shook her head.

No, she decided resolutely. She would not test his goodness that way. He would provide when he saw fit. She would use this money for the rent as she had planned. Her holiday would have to wait.

Alicia reached for her coat. The rent was not due for another week, but there was no sense waiting. She would pay it now. She pulled her galoshes on over her shoes. After she had paid the rent, she would head down to the train station and cancel her reservation. From there she would proceed to the telegraph office, where she would send word to Edmonton that her plans had changed.

Satisfied that she had made the right decision, Alicia walked down the two flights of stairs to the Caswell's basement apartment and rapped on the door.

Emily looked surprised when she opened the door and saw Alicia, fully clad in her winter outerwear, standing outside. She recovered quickly and greeted her with a warm smile.

"Alicia. Won't you come in?"

Emily stepped back to allow entry, but Alicia stayed rooted outside the door.

"I haven't time for a visit, Emily," Alicia told her. "I have some errands that must be done immediately."

"Of course," Emily replied. "I understand. It is a busy time of year for all of us, and you must be even busier than most preparing for your trip south."

Alicia winced at the reference to the plans she'd made for Christmas, but said nothing. She turned her attention instead to her handbag, fumbling with the clasp in an attempt to open it.

"I've come to pay my rent," she explained, when she was able to open her purse and retrieve the envelope. She offered it to Emily, but her friend made no attempt to take the money. Alicia's gaze travelled from Emily's unmoving hands to her face.

"Your rent?" Emily asked in a strange voice.

"Yes," Alicia replied. "I know it's early, but I thought it wise to bring it down now."

She did not mention that if she did not hand the money over now, she might spend her rent money on other things.

"Has Carleton not spoken with you, Alicia?" Emily asked.

"About the rent?"

Emily nodded.

"No," Alicia answered. "Carleton has said nothing to me about it."

Why would Carleton want to speak with her? Her mind reeled with the possibilities. Was the price of her room to increase? She had heard of such things – landlords who increased the rent annually at the first of each year – but she had never concerned herself with such matters before.

Even worse than a rent increase, she thought, *is the possibility that my room is needed for someone else.* Whatever would she do if she had to move?

"I'm sorry, Alicia. I just assumed Carleton had spoken with you. I should have checked to be sure he had." Emily hesitated. "I know he wanted to tell you this himself, but he's been so busy. And now you're here."

Alicia waited, but Emily seemed at a loss for words.

"Perhaps I should just leave this with you for now," Alicia ventured, holding the envelope out once more, "and speak with Carleton at his earliest convenience."

"I can't take it, Alicia." Emily burst into laughter. "I know Carleton wanted to tell you this himself, but under the circumstances you're going to have to hear it from me.

"Carleton and I have decided not to accept rent from you for the month of January. It's not a Christmas gift really – it's more just something we feel we are supposed to do. You've poured your heart and soul into the work here and never once asked for anything in return.

"Carleton and I had been wondering what we could do to show you our appreciation. After thinking and praying about it, we both believed this was the thing to do.

"Merry Christmas, Alicia. Thank you for everything you do." Emily's words were followed by a heartfelt embrace.

"Merry Christmas, Emily and thank you to both of you. This is an answer to prayer."

A smile lit Alicia's face as she climbed the stairs to her upper room.

Looks like I'll be going to Edmonton after all, she thought. The first lines to the hymn by William Cowper came to mind. They stated that "God works in mysterious ways, His wonders to perform."

He certainly does, she decided. Here she had been making daily trips to the post office looking for assistance to come from someone at home, when all the time her heavenly father had planned to meet her needs in another way.

***

Whispers of Spring

Alicia found her first winter in the north long and hard. There were days when she watched the snow swirling around and despaired of spring ever returning.

Someone warned me that winter in this part of the country arrives in October and can last till May.

She shuddered at the thought. She hoped this winter would be an exception. It was not the snow that bothered her, though there was certainly enough of that. It was the bone chilling cold that took her breath away the moment she stepped outside that troubled her the most. She had never experienced such cold temperatures, and expected it would take more than one such winter before she grew accustomed to it.

Her Christmas holiday in Edmonton had been a pleasant break. She had spent a week with her friends, and returned feeling refreshed and eager to get back to her work again.

I'm not sure most people would consider what I do work, Alicia reminded herself. She had no set hours and no days off, nor was there a weekly paycheque to take home as evidence of the value placed on her time. Still, it was the ministry to which she had been called, and one which she enjoyed.

She chuckled, recalling the question that had been put to her in Edmonton.

"How long do you plan to stay up there in no man's land?" one of her friends had asked in a teasing manner.

"I'll stay till my work there is finished," Alicia had answered, "and only God knows when that will be."

"Have you found a man yet?"

The question had come from the same girl who'd stated months earlier that there were no available men in the northern regions of the province.

"None that interest me," Alicia had answered sweetly. She'd expected the comment to spark further discussion, and it certainly had.

It's not that I haven't met any available men here, Alicia thought as she dressed for the Sunday morning meeting. *If truth be told, there are more men than women up here! It's just that I haven't found anyone with the same call to ministry that I have.*

"John Hammond had that same call, and look where that got you!"

The thought hit Alicia with such force that she pricked her finger with the hat pin she'd been inserting. An involuntary yelp escaped from her mouth.

It serves me right for thinking of John Hammond, she rebuked herself as she nursed her wounded finger. *I can be grateful it was my finger I poked and not the back of my head.*

She placed her hat on her head again and secured it firmly with the pin. Satisfied that she was properly attired, she pulled on her coat and headed off to Sunday service.

Their congregation had grown since they'd acquired the use of a hall for their weekly meeting. Alicia arrived early, as usual, and busied herself setting up chairs for the meeting. By the time the others came in, she was at the piano practising the songs they planned to sing. Her gift of being able to play without music came in handy, as it allowed her to meet the eyes of people as they entered and greet them with a smile.

She'd developed the habit soon after they began meeting at the hall, when she'd requested that the piano be turned so she was facing the congregation instead of sitting with her back to them.

The service that morning was well attended, in spite of the cold. When it was over they gathered, as was their custom during the winter months, for a meal before the children's afternoon Sunday School class.

"I think we should continue meeting for lunch even after winter ends," Alicia commented to Sally as they partook of the food.

"Howard and I would like that," Sally agreed.

"Of course, we may never have to worry about spring," Alicia joked, "as it appears that winter will be with us forever."

Sally shook her head.

"Spring is coming, Alicia," she promised.

Alicia looked at her doubtfully.

"I've lived here long enough to recognize the signs," Sally insisted. "There are whispers of spring in the air."

Whispers of spring. Alicia repeated Sally's words to herself as she walked home after Sunday School. The words had a poetic sound. She said them aloud.

"Whispers of spring."

I hope Sally is right, she thought, *although I would prefer that spring announce her presence in a loud manner rather than a whisper!*

***

Building Begins

Spring, when it finally arrived, came quickly. Alicia was bemoaning the fact that this was the longest winter *ever,* when she woke one morning to the view of mud-ridden streets. Where yesterday there had been banks of snow, today there was dark brown mud.

So this, Alicia thought as she waded through the thick substance, *is how spring arrives in Alberta. So much for Sally's whispers!*

With the advent of spring came renewed interest among the congregation in building their own house of worship. Meeting in the hall for weekly services had allowed them the space they needed to grow, but was limiting as it was only available one day a week.

"We need a place where we can hold mid-week meetings," someone commented after one of the Sunday services.

"Someplace that's open seven days a week," another voice echoed. "A place where a soul can go anytime they feel the need."

And so plans were drawn up and a committee was formed to oversee construction of the new church. Land was obtained at a reasonable cost, and it was agreed that the work would be done by the congregation themselves rather than contracted out.

"I know the men will be the ones doing the actual building," Alicia commented to Sally as the two discussed the project, "but it is still nice to feel that we are part of the work."

"Who said that women can't help build?" Sally challenged.

"No one actually said it," Alicia responded, "but I think we all know it."

Sally shook her head.

"I think we should all help," she stated emphatically. "With the men working at their regular jobs, they'll be hard pressed to find time to do the building. They'll work at it when they can, but it will get done quicker if we all pitch in."

Alicia stared at her friend.

"I've never built anything in my life, Sally. I wouldn't know where to begin. I certainly wouldn't expect to be entrusted with the responsibilities of constructing a church."

Sally laughed. "You'll soon learn which end of the hammer to hit the nails with. I know there's lots of stuff we can't do – although it pains me to admit it. Some of the work is just too heavy or too dangerous for us to undertake. But I helped Howard build our trailer. I've become quite adept at holding a board in place or pounding a few nails, and I intend to help build this church!"

"What does Howard think of that idea?" Alicia asked.

"Howard admits, albeit reluctantly, that they'll need all the help they can get," Sally told her. "The time we have for construction is short here in the north. You know how early winter arrives."

"I remember all too well," Alicia answered with a laugh. She paused, calculating the time left before the first snowfall might arrive.

"Have we bitten off more than we can chew, Sally?"

"I don't think so," Sally answered calmly. "We're all used to hard work and we're clearly dedicated to the project. I think with everyone working together, we'll be worshipping in the new building by Thanksgiving, especially if they let the women help with the construction."

They both laughed.

Whether it was that conversation or another that set the date for their first service Alicia was never sure, but somewhere along the way it was agreed that they would hold a dedication service in the new building on Thanksgiving Sunday.

The work on the building progressed well in the early stages. The foundation had been laid and construction begun when they ran into their first obstacle. Prior to starting the work, there had been discussion over whether to build the structure with bricks or with wood. Howard, having previous experience in the construction business, had felt strongly that it would be wiser to build with brick.

"It costs more initially," he'd told them, "but it pays off in the long run."

Costs had been calculated for building both ways, and in the end it had been decided to follow Howard's advice. It had seemed a wise choice until they ran into difficulty when supplies were not available. Waiting for more bricks to arrive caused a delay of several weeks. It was a delay which they could ill afford, as Howard pointed out "when the days are long and the sun is shining."

The bricks arrived at last and construction resumed. The men had scarcely found time to add another layer to the wall when the rain set in. At first they continued their labours, determined to make up for the time they had already lost. When the rain continued into the third day however, work was halted and a meeting was called to discuss the situation.

"I don't mind working in the rain," Fred assured those assembled. "I ain't so sweet that I'll melt."

Smiles greeted his words, but no one commented on them.

"I feel the same way," another man added, "although I'm certain Howard had a good reason for putting the project on hold."

"I did," Howard agreed, seizing the opportunity to speak. "I appreciate your willingness to continue working, gentlemen, and I'm not opposed to working outside in such weather myself," he glanced out the window, "although I admit that I prefer warm, sunny days to cold, wet ones for outdoor work."

Chuckles were heard throughout the room.

"The problem is," he went on, "that the bricks also prefer warm, sunny days."

Eyebrows lifted at the comment.

"The mortar won't set in this weather," he explained. "We need a few days of dry weather before we can proceed."

"Are we going to finish on schedule?" one of the men asked.

Howard smiled. "I admit that is a concern."

"I am hopeful the building will be completed before fall, but a lot will depend on the weather."

"I guess we need to be praying for good weather," someone offered.

"Wouldn't hurt to pray for a few more workers either," a voice from the back of the room offered.

Alicia glanced at Sally, wondering if she would make mention of the fact that the women's offer to assist had been turned down.

"You are both right." Howard answered so quickly that Alicia felt certain he was also afraid Sally would speak up. "Warm, dry weather and an extra pair of hands would both be an answer to prayer."

Few words were spoken as the meeting ended and the congregation went their separate ways.

***

A Stranger in Town

The summer rains ended at last and work resumed on the building of the church. Progress was, as Howard said, like a tortoise; slow but steady. Having chosen to do the labour themselves, the hours the men could devote to the project were few. Howard maintained that the building would be finished on schedule, but secretly Alicia wondered if it would be.

I just don't see how we can finish on time, Alicia thought as she made her way to one of the mid-week meetings they'd recently started. Curiosity as to how the work was progressing gripped her and she glanced at her watch.

Seeing that she had plenty of time before the meeting began, she changed direction, intending to stroll past the construction site on her way. It was quiet when she arrived. She walked tentatively around the building, careful not to disrupt anything.

The foundation had long since been laid, and the outer walls were almost finished. Before long the roof would go on. Even then there would still be much work to be done inside before the building would be ready for use. Howard had insisted that the shell of the building be constructed first.

"The inside work can be done in any weather," he'd reminded them, "but the outer work can't."

The evening breeze reminded Alicia that fall was not far away.

It's too bad we don't have that extra set of hands Howard keeps talking about, Alicia thought as she surveyed the project. *Why, the job could be finished ahead of schedule if there was another man as knowledgeable as Howard who could devote a few weeks to the work here. What we could do with a full time worker!*

She shook her head. There were no such workers to be found – at least none that were willing to work, as their own people were working, without being compensated for their time.

She sighed. It was not that there was a shortage of labourers for the project. Every able-bodied man in the congregation was helping out. They were so dedicated to the work that there'd been serious opposition when the mid-week meeting first began. The men had challenged that there were not enough hours to complete the building already, without cutting another day from the work.

In the end, however, it had been decided that if Mr. and Mrs. Jenkins were willing to open their home for a mid-week meeting, it should be well attended. The labourers had agreed to lay aside their tools on Wednesday evenings, just as they did on Sundays.

Thoughts of the meeting brought Alicia back to reality. An involuntary gasp escaped as she looked at her watch and saw the time.

Oh dear, I will be late now, she thought as she hurried through the streets. She had dallied far too long at the construction site.

Alicia entered the Jenkins home just as the meeting began. With a nod and a smile of apology, she slipped into a vacant seat by the door.

She opened her bible and followed along as Howard read a passage from the scriptures, then listened carefully as he expounded on it. When it was time for prayer, she closed her eyes and bowed her head along with the rest. A number of people prayed, each easily identifiable to Alicia just by their voice.

There was a lull, and she expected Howard to offer a closing prayer. Instead she heard a deep male voice that she did not recognize. Unable to resist, she opened her eyes and looked in the direction from which the words came.

The man speaking was a stranger in their midst, but it was clear that he felt comfortable in the setting. In simple terms he lifted the small congregation in prayer to God, speaking as if he were sharing their needs with his best friend. When the man finished, Howard closed the meeting.

Walking home in the still night air, Alicia's thoughts turned to the stranger. She wondered where the man was from and where he was going. Was he staying in their town, or was he simply passing through? Was there a chance she might see him again?

Weeks passed. By the time September arrived construction on the outer part of the church had been completed, but the work inside had barely begun.

Alicia was not sure whether she should be frustrated or relieved that Sally's prediction of women being involved in the building process had not come true. From her own experience, or lack thereof, she was not certain if the women helping would have moved the project along more quickly, or if it would have caused delay.

Caught up in her ministry of visitation, leading meetings for the ladies and running a Sunday School, Alicia forgot all about the stranger who had attended an evening meeting at the Jenkins' house. She was surprised, therefore, to see the man walk into church one Sunday morning in the fall, accompanied by Mr. and Mrs. Jenkins.

Alicia was seated at the piano, coaxing well known melodies of ancient hymns from the keyboard, when the trio entered. Her eyes were drawn at once to the guest.

The man was tall and lean, towering a good six inches above Mr. Jenkins and his wife. His height was accentuated by the pinstripes in the dark brown suit that clothed him. When he glanced her way, Alicia nodded and smiled. The man smiled back, white teeth gleaming in a darkly tanned face.

Alicia felt the stranger's gaze on her several times during the service. He smiled each time her eyes met his, and she found herself smiling back.

When the service was over and the others left, Alicia stayed at the hall, munching on the bag lunch she'd brought with her as she studied the lesson she would be sharing with the children that afternoon.

The food was better when we all stayed for lunch after the service, Alicia thought as she finished her sandwich. She didn't mind being alone though. In fact, she welcomed the solitude and the time it gave her to prepare.

She was in the midst of her lesson when a knock sounded at the door. A glance at the clock told her it was too early to be one of the children.

She rose to answer it, but the door opened before she reached it. The man who had attended the service with the Jenkins entered.

"Pardon me, Miss," he greeted her, bowing slightly, "but I believe I may have left my hat here this morning."

Alicia glanced around the open room.

"Yes, there it is. Right where I left it." The man chuckled. He moved across the room to retrieve the misplaced item so quickly that Alicia wondered if he'd left it behind on purpose.

"I'm very sorry to bother you, Miss," he told her, as he turned back toward the door.

"It was no bother at all, Sir." Alicia blushed. The words sounded stiff, even to her own ears.

"I'll be on my way, then."

"Very well."

Oh dear, Alicia rebuked herself. *That wasn't the right thing to say at all!*

She looked to the door, where the man stood unmoving. Taking a deep breath, she forced herself to think before speaking.

"It was nice having you in the service this morning, Mister ..."

"Edwards," he offered. "Basil Edwards."

"I do hope you'll come again anytime you're in the area, Mr. Edwards."

He nodded.

"I plan to, Miss..." he hesitated.

"Miller," Alicia put in. "Miss Alicia Miller."

She blushed again, hoping he would not think that she had emphasized the *Miss.*

He nodded.

"I will see you again, Miss Miller."

The door closed behind him, leaving Alicia with burning cheeks and little time to compose herself before the children arrived.

***

Mr. Edwards

"You know that extra pair of hands Howard keeps saying he needs?" Sally asked Alicia when they met for lunch in the middle of the week.

Alicia nodded; her mouth too full to reply.

"We have them!" Sally informed her. "At least, I think we do. Howard's over at the Jenkins right now talking to Mr. Edwards."

"Is Mr. Edwards planning on staying in town?" Alicia asked, being careful not to sound too interested.

"We don't know yet," Sally replied. "But we certainly hope so."

Their talk moved on to other things, and before they knew it Howard arrived to take Sally home. She phoned Alicia the next day, asking if she were free to come for dinner that evening. Alicia agreed, and a time was set for Howard to pick her up.

Alicia's thoughts turned to the dinner invitation several times during the day as she went about her tasks. It was not like Sally to invite her so soon after they'd had lunch together. She wondered if the invitation meant that Sally had news she would rather share in person, and if so, what that news might be.

Alicia arrived home an hour before Howard was to pick her up, allowing herself ample time to bathe and dress. Clad in only her slip and undergarments, she stood in front of the closet debating what to wear.

I certainly don't need anything fancy, she told herself as her hands moved over her dresses. *After all, it's just dinner with Sally and Howard. Since I am dining out, however, instead of eating alone in my room, it is only fitting that I be suitably attired.*

She giggled as she removed one of her better dresses from the hanger. It was frivolous, she knew, to dress this way for a simple meal with close friends, but tonight it felt right.

She slipped into the dress; then moved to assess herself in the mirror. Adjusting the belt around her slender waist, she nodded approval. Alicia picked up her hair brush, running it through her curly locks until they shone.

A glance at the clock told her that Howard would be waiting. She picked up her handbag and headed for the stairs.

To Alicia's surprise, she found that she was not the only guest Sally and Howard had invited that evening. Seated across from her at the table in their tiny kitchen was Mr. Basil Edwards.

Over dinner Alicia learned that the man was originally from Ontario and had grown up on a farm an hour north of Toronto. After working in remote communities in The Territories and Alaska for a time, he'd decided to return to Ontario and spend the winter with family there.

"How did you come to be in this part of the country, Miss Miller?" Basil asked.

"Call me Alicia, please," she responded. Her face reddened as she recalled their conversation the previous Sunday.

"Alicia was on her way to China, but never made it," Howard told Basil with a laugh. "It's quite a story if she's willing to share it."

Basil looked at her.

"China, eh?"

Alicia nodded. "I'd planned to work there as a medical missionary."

"How interesting," Basil replied. He smiled and she noticed that one corner of his mouth lifted more than the other. "I had planned to spend my life in South America doing mission work."

Alicia felt her heart stir at the words. Was it possible she'd finally found someone with the same call that she had? She dismissed the idea and forced herself to concentrate on the conversation flowing around her.

The evening passed quickly and ended far too soon. When it was over and she was alone in her room, Alicia lay back on her bed, trying to recapture the mood that had prevailed throughout the evening.

She smiled. She had no recollection of what Sally had served for dinner, or for dessert. She couldn't remember whether or not she'd helped Sally wash up the dishes.

The only thing she could remember clearly, and could see each time she closed her eyes, was the darkly tanned face and lopsided smile of Mr. Basil Edwards.

***

Basil's Intentions

Mr. Edwards was present again at the morning meeting the Sunday following the dinner at Sally and Howard's. Alicia took Sally aside after church.

"Does this mean he's staying here instead of going back to Ontario?" she whispered.

"Would it matter to you if he was?" Sally whispered back, watching her friend's face closely. Alicia blushed, and Sally smiled.

"Let's just say that Basil has delayed his trip home for now," Sally said mysteriously, causing Alicia to wonder what Sally knew that she didn't.

On Monday, Alicia had occasion to walk by the site of the new church. Seeing Basil's truck outside, she thought about going in, but decided against it. Her path on Tuesday would not normally have taken her by the church, but her curiosity caused her to detour.

Basil's truck was outside again, as was Howard's. Throwing caution to the wind, Alicia entered the building. She found the two men hard at work on the interior.

I thought this man was a farmer turned missionary, Alicia thought as she stood silently observing him work, *but from the appearance of things, he's a skilled builder.*

She watched unnoticed for a time, then turned and left the building. When Sally came into town the next day for a doctor's appointment, Alicia met up with her.

"I saw Howard and Basil yesterday," she told Sally.

"I know," Sally replied. "Howard told me."

Alicia stared.

"I didn't think they'd noticed me," she stammered. "They were both so hard at work that I left without speaking to them. Now they will think me rude."

"Not at all," Sally assured her. "Howard is used to having people drop by to check on the progress of things. Some speak.

289

Some, like you, leave quietly, desiring not to disturb the men when they are working."

"Basil looked like he was pretty comfortable in the role of church builder," Alicia commented, changing the subject somewhat.

Sally nodded.

"It seems that Basil is a man of many talents, and a single man at that." She emphasized the word *single*.

"I wonder why a man his age would still be single," Alicia mused.

"Because he's married to his work, like someone else I know," Sally answered. "And just like that other party, his work is sharing God's love with those in need no matter where he is – China, South America or Canada."

She paused to let her words take effect.

"You're one of the reasons Basil's still in town, Alicia," Sally confided.

"Me?"

"You." Sally leaned closer. "Basil was on his way back east when he decided to make a detour to our part of the country and visit the Jenkins. It seems he was hoping that by doing so he might chance to meet up again with a certain young lady he'd seen when he passed through town the last time."

Alicia listened to Sally in disbelief.

"Are you sure he meant me, Sally?" she asked.

"I have it from a very reliable source," Sally assured her. "It seems he's been thinking of you ever since he saw you at the Jenkins."

"But we didn't even meet that evening," Alicia told her. "I arrived late and left early. He couldn't possibly have noticed me."

"Basil not only noticed you, Alicia Miller, but he has been unable to forget you. He changed his route home so he could see you again."

"But he's shown no interest in me," Alicia protested.

"Perhaps you just haven't noticed his interest," Sally suggested.

"Perhaps," Alicia answered quietly. She recalled the conversation she'd had with Basil his first Sunday in town when he'd come to the hall to retrieve his hat. Later, when they met again at Sally and Howard's, Basil had shown considerable interest in the work she was doing. She'd found him interesting to talk to and had enjoyed listening to him as well. Even so, she'd seen nothing in his behaviour to indicate that he was looking for anything more than friendship.

She looked at Sally.

"What you've said may be true, Sally," she said slowly. She paused, choosing her words carefully in case they should be repeated. "But if Mr. Basil Edwards is truly interested in me, he will have to express that interest himself."

Though he had not been privy to the conversation, Basil did express his interest the next time he saw Alicia. She was leaving the mid-week meeting when he approached.

"I wonder if I might drive you home, Alicia?" he asked.

"Thank you, Basil. I'd appreciate that," she replied. It was a lovely evening and she would have enjoyed the walk, but she had no desire to frighten the man away now that he had finally spoken.

Basil led the way to his truck and opened the passenger door for her. He offered his arm to assist her in climbing into the cab. Moving to the driver's side, he settled himself behind the wheel and turned the key. The engine came to life with a roar.

"I apologize," Basil told Alicia with a smile. "She's a little noisy, but she's reliable."

He put the truck into gear and eased into the street. There was little traffic at any time in their small town, but this evening the streets were deserted.

There was no conversation between them as Basil drove the few blocks to the medical center. He cleared his throat twice, as if he intended to speak, but not a word was uttered. Alicia, at a loss for words herself now that she was alone with the man, sat awkwardly.

She felt a sense of relief when they pulled up in front of the building she now called home.

Alicia reached for the door handle, but Basil hopped from the truck and opened the door for her.

"Thank you for the ride, Basil," Alicia told him, finding her tongue at last. "It was kind of you."

"I'll see you to the door if I may, Alicia," Basil responded, and she nodded in agreement. Together they walked the few steps to the building.

"Thank you again, Basil. I'll see you on Sunday," Alicia told him as she opened the door.

"Yes, on Sunday," he replied.

"Good night, Basil."

"Good night, Alicia."

She entered the building and was about to close the door when Basil spoke again.

"Alicia?"

"Yes?"

There was another awkward clearing of his throat.

"I've a meeting to attend on Friday evening. I wondered if you might like to accompany me."

She smiled. "I'd be happy to, Basil."

"The meeting is at seven, but I'd like to get there ahead of time. Is six o'clock too early for you?" he asked.

"Six o'clock is perfect for me," she told him.

"Till Friday then."

"Till Friday."

***

"I Will"

The weeks that followed Alicia's first evening out with Basil passed in a whirl. When Sally teased her that it was love that was making the time fly by so quickly, Alicia blushed, but she did not deny the charge.

Each day she went about her regular activities, while Basil continued working on the building of the church. With the full-time efforts of the two men, along with assistance from others as they were able, the work was coming along nicely. It was expected that the building would be ready for use by Thanksgiving Sunday.

In the evenings, when their work was done, Alicia and Basil spent time together. Whether it was walks through the town, visits with friends, or long drives in the country, each evening they spent together brought them closer as a couple.

Alicia learned of Basil's life as a child on the farm, his call to the ministry as a young man and his preparation for mission work. She laughed with him as he told of his early life and the pranks he and his brother had played on each other. She wept for him as he shared with her the loss of his mother that had occurred at a time when he was thousands of miles from home.

She in turn gave him news of her own family. She told of growing up in the city and introduced him, through her stories, to each member of her family – Mama and Daddy, Sarah, Jake and William, Aunt Helen and the rest of her extended family.

In an intimate moment, Alicia revealed that there had been a previous love in her life. She cried as she talked of the feelings she'd had for John, and of the pain she'd gone through when she realized he'd never felt the same way. Basil had talked of a young woman he'd been sweet on in his early years, but whose parents had disapproved of their plans for marriage.

"I could never marry a woman without her father's permission," he'd told Alicia, causing her to smile. It was a sweet and rather old-fashioned sentiment, but one which she admired. It pleased her to think that if the relationship developed, Basil would speak to her father before proposing to her.

She wrote often to her family, but was unaware how many times she was mentioning Basil until a letter arrived from Sarah. It was blunt and to the point.

So when's the wedding? Sarah's letter asked. *You haven't said a word about a wedding in your letters home, but I'm expecting there will be one. You've been writing more about Basil than you have about the building of the church or your work there, so he really must be special to you.*

Sarah's words brought Alicia up short. *Have I really been writing about Basil that much,* she wondered. She wished she'd kept copies of the letters she wrote home so she could check. She hoped she wasn't misleading her family with the references she made to her new friend.

Alicia and Basil were enjoying a rare evening with Sally and Howard a short time later, when Howard mentioned that they were thinking of selling their trailer.

"I'm thinking it's time to move into a house," he remarked casually. "We need something with a little more space."

Alicia glanced at Sally. There was a red tinge to her cheeks. Their eyes met. A slight nod from Sally confirmed that the thoughts she'd had about her friend were true. Sally was expecting again. She smiled. Congratulations would come later, when they were alone. It would not be proper to say any more now when they were in mixed company.

"We've been looking at a place in town, near to the church," Howard continued. "We think we've found what we want. Now we just have to find a buyer for the trailer."

"I may be able to help you in that department."

Basil's words came as a surprise to Alicia.

"I'm not certain yet what my own plans are," Basil told Howard, "but I expect to know soon. If things work out as I'm hoping they will, I might be looking for something like this."

Alicia frowned. Basil had said nothing of his intentions to her, but she still expected him to head for Ontario when the church building was finished. Was it possible he was planning to stay?

She got into his vehicle, determined to ask Basil about it on the way home, but he spoke before she had opportunity.

"I wonder if I might have your parents' address, Alicia?" he asked. "I've been thinking I'd like to write to them."

Alicia was grateful that the cover of darkness hid her red face. Did this mean what she thought it might?

"Certainly, Basil," she answered as calmly as she was able. "I'll write it out for you and give it to you next time I see you."

"Would you be able to give it to me tonight?" he asked. "I don't mind waiting if I need to while you get it."

"Of course," she replied, as they pulled up in front of her building. "I'll just run upstairs and write it down for you."

Her heart pounded as she raced up the stairs. Was it possible Basil was writing to ask for permission to marry her? She wrote the address down hastily, and returned to where Basil stood patiently waiting.

"Thank you, Alicia." He took the paper from her. "I shall send a letter off tomorrow."

He looked troubled.

"I know I should speak with your parents about this before I speak to you, Alicia," he told her, "but because time is a factor here, I will bring up the matter with you first."

There was a long wait, during which Alicia felt like her heart would burst. When Basil finally spoke, his words were slow and deliberate.

"I'll only be staying here till Thanksgiving, Alicia," he told her, and her heart sunk.

"You're going east then?" she managed to ask.

"Yes," he answered. "I'd planned all along to winter in Ontario. I came this direction to see the Jenkins before I left; among other reasons. My family is expecting me and I've delayed far too long. I need to leave right after the dedication service for the new church."

"I see," Alicia said quietly. "Will you be coming back?"

"I shall return to the west in the spring," he answered firmly. "Where I will settle depends on the answer I get to certain questions, including the one I plan to ask your father."

"And that question is?" Alicia prompted.

"I should like you to marry me, Alicia," Basil told her. "I know it's been only a short time since we met, but I've come to love you and would like to spend the rest of my life with you. If your father agrees, will you marry me, Alicia?"

"I will."

The words spoken, Basil leaned down and Alicia received her first kiss.

As the train moved eastward the day after Thanksgiving, Alicia thought back over the events that had led her to this day. She recalled her plans to live and work in China and the disappointment she'd felt when that door closed and her years of preparation for the work seemed to have been in vain. She thought of her friendship with John Hammond and remembered her emotions when she'd realized she had read more into their relationship than he had.

She looked at the man beside her. The feelings she had felt for John were nothing in comparison to the love she had for Basil. Grandma was right, she thought with a smile. When God closes a door he opens a window.

***

2010

A knock sounded at the door and a woman in uniform entered. Lost in her memories, Alicia was unaware that she was not alone until a hand touched her arm. She jumped, and her eyes flew open. For a moment she stared in confusion, trying without success to make out the woman's features in the darkened room.

"It's just me, Alicia."

The woman's voice was kind and her tone was soft, like Mama's. Alicia blinked, forcing her mind back to the present. She smiled.

"For a moment I thought you were my mother," she told the nurse.

The girl laughed.

"No, dear, I'm not your mother." She patted Alicia's arm.

"I was lost in my memories," Alicia said, seeking to explain her confusion.

"You were dreaming; were you?" the nurse asked.

Alicia wished the woman would sit down and talk to her, instead of bustling about the room.

"No," she answered firmly, "I was not dreaming. I was remembering."

"I see," the nurse replied, opening the curtains as she spoke. "That's nice, dear. I hope they were happy dreams."

Alicia sighed.

Why is it, she wondered, *that when one is old no one really listens to what one has to say?*

"Were they happy dreams, Alicia?" the nurse asked. She spoke loudly, as if it were Alicia and not herself who was having difficulty following the conversation.

"Yes," Alicia answered meekly. "They were happy."

She sighed again. Her frustration was not so much with the young nurse, as with herself.

Why is it, she wondered, *that my memory works so well when I am alone, but not when I am with others?*

297

How I wish I could record everything, she thought, *all the memories, all the hopes and dreams, all the triumphs and the tragedies that have been packed into the eight decades of my life.*

My children think they know it all, but there is so much they don't know. Have I ever told them how I met their father?

She frowned, trying to remember if she had. She was afraid to ask them, afraid of the response she would get if she was repeating herself.

"You've told me that a dozen times, Mom," was a line she heard frequently from her daughters.

If only they could understand that her mind still worked well, but her memory didn't.

It was only at times like this, when there was no one to tell her story to, that she seemed able to remember clearly the events of her younger life. She smiled as she thought of the events she had recalled that afternoon.

These are the things I would tell them if I could, she thought. *These are the memories I would preserve for my children and grandchildren.*

***